CRÉ-WITCH CHRONICLES

BORN IN WATER

SARAH HEGGER

COPYRIGHT

❀ Created with Vellum

DEDICATION

*To anyone who could do with a touch of magic in their reality. I'm
looking at you, Iola.
Also a big thank you to Anna Sharpe for her eagle eye.*

PREFACE

"The immense diversity and pluriformity of this creation more perfectly represents God than any one creature alone or by itself."

St. Thomas Aquinas (1225-1274)

CHAPTER ONE

CRÉ-WITCH CHRONICLES

A beautiful English summer's day greeted Alexander and his morning coffee—as good a day as any to fulfill his fate. In movies days that defined a hero's fate demonstrated a preponderance of stormy weather, at least a dark cloud or two. Perhaps today's sunny outlook was more in the nature of a commentary on his eligibility for heroism.

He walked through the glass doors between his drawing room and the garden and took a deep breath of the flower-scented air. Green swathes of lawn mowed into stripes ended at a rough-hewn fence. Beyond that, stretched acres and acres of pasture he rented to the farmer next door. Birds sang, bees buzzed and cattle lowed, all beneath a gentle sherbet-yellow sun.

Not a day to suggest dark thoughts or even grimmer senses of foreboding, but there you had it. His premonition had ripped him awake at four-thirty, and he'd not gone back to sleep. The details remained confoundedly vague, but he'd seen her clear as day: a curvy redhead with big green eyes. The scent of honey and sage had chased him awake. Unable to go back to sleep, he'd gotten up, worked out in his home gym and tried to escape the dark augury buggering up his morning.

Portents, auguries, evil and darkness brought his thoughts to their inevitable end: Mother.

Car tires crunched on the shell driveway on the far side of the manor. He'd bet his balls one of Mother's minions had come calling.

Some people had wonderful mothers. The sort you sent Mother's Day cards to and bouquets of flowers for her birthday, the ones written about in those sappy greeting card messages.

Still others had more blurry relationships with their mothers. There was love and some respect, but most of it muddied by messy resentments and failed expectations.

His door knocker broke the manor's bucolic peace.

In Alexander's experience, motherhood was a spectrum. Wasn't everything in this latest decade? Most mothers fell somewhere between next best thing to an angel and hell-spawned crazy lady who should have been neutered at birth.

The knocker went again, louder and longer announcing his unwanted visitor's determination to perform its duty.

Alexander's mother was off the spectrum at the deep, deep end of the hell-spawned pool. Or more succinctly put, an evil megalomaniacal bitch.

Footsteps crunched on gravel as his visitor hurried around the side of the house. The footsteps stopped and then rushed forward.

"My lord." His mother's minion oozed closer with an ingratiating smile. It was wasted on him, but Alexander gave him a nod. Encouraged, the minion said, "Our lady would like to see you."

Our lady, like she was some beneficent earth saint spreading love and blessings in her wake.

That one almost had him snort laughing, but Minion was still groveling and hovering. Alexander didn't blame him. He wouldn't go back to her without an answer either. "Where is she?"

"At the statue." Minion scraped the ground with his forehead. Unfortunate deluded prick that he was.

Alexander took another sip of his coffee. It had taken hundreds of years, well at least since the seventeenth century, to perfect his blend. Not the sort you could pick up at Starbucks. There was a lot to be said for the expediency and efficiency of this century, but the downside was that people had forgotten how to savor things.

Coffee, like a beautiful woman or a great single malt, should never be rushed. Shoving it in a paper cup and jostling it in your car cupholders was negating a sensory banquet. First there was the aroma. His blend was mostly floral with the barest hint of nut and spice. It finished on a lingering—

"My lord?"

Malt. It finished on a trace of malt. "What?"

"Your lady mother awaits."

Clearly, Minion was not an appreciator of luxuriating in the finer things. One should relish the exquisite, particularly when one hovered on the precipice of never being able to do so again. "What's your name?"

"Clyde...my lord."

"Clyde, do you have to keep my lording me?"

Clyde gaped at him, extra flesh on his rosy cheeks quivering. "Well, it's your title and more importantly...you're her son. Aren't you?"

"So she says." Alexander had been forced to surrender his dearest hope that the stork had dropped him at the wrong house many decades ago.

"Well then." Clyde's cheek flesh firmed into a grin. "You are the son of our dearest lady, the heir, so to speak."

Alexander could never resist messing with a minion. "Does she know you're expecting her demise?"

"What?" Clyde paled. "Never. She is immortal."

Or as close to it as any being could get. "Then why would she need an heir?"

Clyde was flummoxed, and he frowned as he tried to reconnect the scattered dots of his beloved mythology. Inspiration struck with a fervent gleam in Clyde's heavily lashed brown eyes. "But you are the son of death, are you not? He who shall bear the fruit, which will shape all magic to come."

Ah yes, that smashing prophesy, his *raison d'etre* if Mother was to be believed. *The son of death shall bear the torch that lights the path. And the daughter of life shall bring forth water nascent and call it onto the path of light. Then they will bear fruit. And this fruit will be the magick. The greatest of magick and the final magick.* As close a translation as they could manage from the original druidic poem.

"Bear the fruit." Alexander took another sip of his coffee. Jawing with Clyde had brought it perilously close to the cooler side of warm. The flavor hinged on the right temperature. "Would I bear the fruit or is that the daughter of life's gig? I rather saw myself as the fruit fertilizer, as it were. He who shall implant the fruit, more than she who will bear it."

Clyde swallowed. "Eh?"

"Never mind." His coffee was ruined, so he set the cup on the walnut side table inside the French doors. A lovely little piece he'd picked up in Spain, baroque but minus the overdone swirling crap the Italians had insisted on. "Lead me to the bearer of the impregnator of the fruit."

"Eh?"

"My mother, Clyde, where is she?" Then he remembered and motioned Clyde to silence. Clyde had already told him she was at the statue, but he might have guessed as much. The old finger and thumb's obsession with the statue had reached new levels of fanatical.

Stalwart soul that he was, Clyde led the way to his car. "I'll drive you."

"And behold. The son of death shall come riding in a silver Prius."

"Eh?" Clyde bleeped the locks and opened the passenger door for him. Then he got in and gave a nervous titter. "Oh, funny. Very clever. Like the bible. Only a Prius not an ass."

Clyde had given it more thought than he had. Alexander folded his tall frame into the seat.

On such a lovely morning he would have preferred to walk but that would have landed Clyde in more hurt than anyone deserved. Mother liked her orders obeyed to the multitudinous, and often capricious, letter.

Stopping before entering the lane, Clyde looked left and right and left again. He eased forward, eyes intent on the lane, a concentration flush on his cheeks. Poor bugger was nervous as hell.

"So, Clyde?" He leaned back in his seat and stretched his legs out in front of him. The inside of the Prius was surprisingly roomy. "How long have you been a follower?"

"Five months." Clyde glowed with fervor. "I was most gratified to be called on for this special task."

Clyde would probably live to rue that gratification because Mother had several nasty special tasks for her minions, and she didn't hesitate to select a volunteer. "Do you live in Greater Littleton?"

Most of the earlier minions had come from the village of Greater Littleton. It was to be expected, given that the village nestled at the foot of Baile Castle. A ripple of unease snaked down his spine.

His dream had featured Baile. Alexander had only been inside the castle once but the details of it were imprinted on his mind. That entire hideous fucking day was imprinted on his mind. He hadn't known it at the time, but that day had marked the beginning, the beginning of an ending that was about to play itself out.

Clyde beetled them around a bend in the lane and Baile wove into view. Clear against the blue sky, she stood on a rocky promontory that poked into the sea. Sunlight sparkled off the sea and etched the bold, strong lines of Baile's many turrets and ramparts. The finest example of a medieval castle in England, possibly the entire world, and the fevered obsession of Mother's every waking moment.

Mother wanted into Baile. More specifically into the network of caverns running through the cliff Baile perched on. Even from this distance, Baile's muted power played like a cat having its fur stroked the wrong way over Alexander's nerve endings.

That power came straight from Goddess herself and was the only thing that could stop Mother now. On his darker days, Alexander doubted it would be enough. But somehow it had to be.

When they reached the green, Clyde parked and pointed. Reverence bathed his features as he stared at Rhiannon. "There she is."

"Thanks for the lift." Alexander climbed from the Prius. He checked his mental barriers were all in place and reinforced weakening areas. He could afford no mistakes with Rhiannon. She'd eat him alive, regurgitate him and start the torture again.

Rhiannon stood with her back to them, head raised as she stared at the statue.

Even had Clyde not pointed her out, Alexander could find her if he were blindfolded and disoriented. The nauseating stench of blood magic swirled around her constantly. The link she'd forged between them on his birth was always there too, like a barely discernible murmur.

Her onyx hair absorbed the light around it. Even dressed as she was in jeans, a blouse and high-heeled sandals, Rhiannon stood out. Without understanding why, a group of school kids paused their laughing chatter and gave her a wide berth on their way across the green to school.

Smart kids. He wished their parents could be as smart.

"I can feel him," Rhiannon said by way of greeting. If the statue had been flesh, it would have been melting off Roderick's bones with the intensity of her scowl. "He stirs, which means Baile stirs."

He stopped beside her. He and Roderick had hated each other for most of their long, long lives. "I thought I sensed him."

"He seeks to wake."

Alexander waited for the rest.

She turned to him. Like her hair, her dark eyes sucked the light in. "He cannot wake. But if he does, you know what I expect of you."

"Of course." He shrugged. "I will kill him."

One of the two reasons she'd spawned him. Once his usefulness was exhausted, she would get rid of him. He held too much power, and she tolerated no challengers to her supremacy.

"He stirs because of her." She dug her long red nails into his forearm. "You feel her?"

"Yes." Rhiannon spoke not of Maeve, tenderly cradled in Roderick's stone arms, but of the other reason he'd been created, the primary reason. "She's on her way."

"You know what you must do?" She turned the full force of her intense stare on him. A plan hatched so many hundreds of years ago would make a maniac of anyone. Add the promise of total world domination to the potion and you had one extremely motivated black witch on your hands.

"I know." He held her stare. "Let me do what I am created to do."

Indecision played across her face. She didn't like leaving anything to chance. "Don't fail me, or I will intercede."

"I understand."

She glared at him. "Do you?"

"Yes. I won't fail."

He'd better not fail, or Roderick, Maeve, the little water witch on her way to fulfill her destiny, he, and the remaining cré-witches were all dead. And the rest of humanity would pay the price for eternity.

No pressure.

CHAPTER TWO

Standing on the sidewalk outside the pub as she waited for the tour guide, Bronwyn didn't like throwing shade, but so far the Brits had been a huge disappointment. It could be because her ancestry test had come back 100 percent British & Irish that she'd come to England with the vague notion she'd feel something in common with her people.

Five days into her dream trip to England, the one she'd promised Deidre she'd take, and Bronwyn's *people* had lost her luggage, and then behaved as if the whole thing was her fault for presuming to bring her tainted American luggage into the sanctity of Heathrow Airport. It had taken the airline two days to locate her luggage, and then they told her it would take another two days to get it to her. Two days to drive a suitcase from Heathrow across London to Canary Wharf.

Bronwyn didn't think England was big enough for any drive anywhere to take two days, but the airline woman had moaned on and on about a shortage of drivers until Bronwyn had relented. Her luggage had caught up with her late last night, freeing Bronwyn to trace her roots to their origin, a small town called Greater Littleton on the Devonshire coast.

Bronwyn was celebrating her release from the jeans she'd been wearing for four days with her second most comfortable pair and a pale pink cashmere sweater she'd bought for this trip.

The desk clerk at the Hag's Head in Greater Littleton had sighed and eye rolled her way through checking Bronwyn in. The wooden sign hanging outside had a cutout of a witch, wart on her chin and pointy hat, above the name. It was cute. The Hag's Head instead of the normal Nag's Head, thus capitalizing on the swirling stories of the supernatural surrounding this tiny coastal village. Her ancestral home might not be the most hospitable place, but it was delivering on the old-world charm.

"Good morning, everyone." Her tour guide chirped from the front of a small group. Bronwyn had joined the tour group on more sighed directions from the Hag's Head's desk clerk. Bright eyed, hair in a jaunty ponytail, their middle-aged guide caught them all in the arc of her traveling smile beam. "My name is Hermione." She twinkled at them. "Yes, like Harry Potter, and yes I am local to Greater Littleton."

An appreciative murmur rose from Bronwyn's fellow tourists.

"Now!" Hermione bounced on her toes. "This is the village, the green and the castle tour." She paused and let that sink in. "If you're signing on for just the castle tour, please wait here until we swing past and fetch you. Harvey." She indicated a desiccated older man with wiry eyebrows dressed in a mismatched assortment of uniform parts that looked to be pulled together from differing shades of blue uniforms. "Harvey is another local, and he's our bus driver for the day."

"Hi, Harvey," Bronwyn parroted with her group.

Harvey waved.

"Now." Hermione clapped her hands. "We will all meet for lunch at the Copper Cauldron before proceeding to the castle, and Harvey will meet us there with the bus." A ring of steel coated Hermione's voice, and Bronwyn wouldn't want to be

Harvey if he failed to bring the bus around at the designated time.

As he limped away, Bronwyn wanted to catch him and give him a jar of Deidre's liniment for his sore knee joint.

"You may have noticed a theme to a lot of the business and names around our lovely village." Hermione arched her brows expectantly. "Anybody?"

"Witches." A woman in her thirties spoke from the front of the group. "There's the Hag's Head, and the Copper Cauldron." Straight out of New Jersey if her accent was anything to go by, she went on. "Sorcery Lane." She jabbed her finger at the road name two feet away from them on the corner. "Toil & Trouble Hardware. The Speckled Grimoire Book Shop. Wands—"

"Yes, indeed." Hermione smiled at her new favorite pupil. "Our little slice of England is known for having the most supernatural occurrences anywhere in the United Kingdom."

"Even more than Stonehenge?" Jersey frowned like she had insider information that jibed with Hermione's spiel.

Hermione gave her the condescending look of someone who'd answered that question plenty. "To the best of my knowledge, there have been no verified incidents of the supernatural in Stonehenge."

Jersey scowled. "But—"

"Now." Hermione twirled her hand in the air. "The village dates back to the early twelfth century."

"When's that?" The man with Jersey whispered loud enough for the group. "Is that like the twelve hundreds or the eleven hundreds?"

Hermione sailed on. "The first recorded settlement here was 1127, and that was the gifting of the land to Roderick of Elwick."

"Who?" Jersey's husband frowned.

"Roderick of Elwick." Bronwyn took pity on him. "He came here in 1127."

He whistled. "Now that's what I call a family tree."

So did Bronwyn and her heart rate increased. This was why she was here, to unravel the mystery of her family. To discover where she came from. Why her family mostly only ever bore girls and why they all died young. Her maternal grandmother, Deidre, had lived longer than most, but even she'd died at only fifty-nine. Her car had skidded on black ice and slid her head-on into a semi.

I'm here, Dee, I'm finally here.

The memory of Deidre's answering smile warmed her from the inside. Maybe because it had been only the two of them for so long, but Bronwyn had been particularly close to Deidre.

Finally, here in Greater Littleton she might find the answers for both of them.

"Roderick was quite the local celebrity in his time." Hermione tittered. "They had a number of names for him: Roderick the Fair, Roderick the Bold, Roderick the Ready." She leaned in, eyes sparkling with mischief. "They say he had several mistresses who lived at Baile with him."

Jersey snorted. "Talk about your playa."

"Indeed. If you would follow me?" Hermione led them across the road and onto the village green. She stopped by a statute in the middle. With her best Vanna White hands, Hermione announced, "The statue is called *The Lovers*, and nobody knows who carved it or how it came to decorate our beautiful green." She leaned closer. "Our village is famous for it."

Cell phones sprouted out of hands as the group took pictures.

Bronwyn's nape prickled. She stared at the statue. The longer she stared at it, the more she got the sense of it being familiar. Yet she was willing to swear she'd never seen it before.

The statue was of a large man in what was remarkably detailed carving of chainmail—the stonemason's talent was undeniable it was so lifelike—sheltering a slim woman in his arms. He was cradling her, but Bronwyn didn't necessarily see how they could be mistaken for lovers.

"Who are they?" Jersey stared up at the statue.

The male carving drew Bronwyn's gaze back. He was handsome in a rugged way, big and brawny, but he exuded protectiveness.

"Another mystery. Like we don't know who carved it or who put it here, we're also not quite sure who they are." Hermione grinned at them. "Rumor has it that the male figure is actually Sir Roderick himself."

Deidre had called it their knowing, and it struck Bronwyn now, a warm trickle of certainty deep within her. That was Sir Roderick in the statue.

A German couple asked a few more questions about Sir Roderick, but Bronwyn tuned them out.

Maeve. The name flitted into her head and stuck. Like she knew the man in the statue was Sir Roderick, she now knew the name of the woman. Except, having no way to explain how she knew, or at least no explanation that wouldn't leave her looking like a lunatic, she wouldn't be sharing with the group.

"Some say it was magic." Hermione giggled as she responded to a question about what had happened to Sir Roderick. "That he disappeared one night, never to be seen again."

Bronwyn's flesh crawled, and she shuddered hard enough for the German woman in her Man U sweatshirt to glance at her.

Never ignore your instincts. Deidre's voice sounded like it came from right beside her. Something she'd said to Bronwyn a thousand times while she was growing up. *Your instincts will guide you right. We have the gift in our family.*

The gift. Two words that meant so much and so little to the Beaty women. It meant their strange way of knowing stuff, especially when it came to the health of others. It also meant the curious ways their hands would heat when they touched someone ill or injured.

Honey and sage surrounded her in a subtle fragrance bubble. The scent was connected somehow to her gift, but nobody had ever been able to tell her why. At least nobody in Bronwyn or Deidre's lifetime.

"What's that smell?" Jersey looked around her. "Like lilies or something."

At first Bronwyn thought it might be her, and then she moved closer to the statue and picked up what Jersey smelled. It was lily and…oranges?

"You smell it?" Hermione beamed at Jersey. "Some do, and some don't." She leaned in. "Around here, we say those with the magic can smell it."

Man U sniffed. "I don't smell anything."

"I've heard people say oranges, some say lemons, others talk about lilies and some even say lavender." Hermione winked at Man U. "But I must not have the magic, because I don't smell it either."

A trick of the light, for sure, but Sir Roderick seemed to be staring right at her. The statue looked so lifelike, and Bronwyn couldn't drag her eyes away. Nobody else was as fascinated by the statue as she. The rest of her group were all listening to Hermione tell them about how Roderick had been gifted this land by King Stephen.

"Are we going to see the castle soon?" Jersey's companion lost patience with Hermione's description of the role the village green played in medieval life. "I came to see the castle."

The rest of the group nodded in agreement. Baile Castle was quite something, perched above the town like a huge, stone bird.

Seeing it in real life made her gasp. She knew that castle and knew it well. She'd been seeing the same castle in her dreams since she was a little girl. Later, she'd looked it up and found pictures of it, but the real thing had them all beat.

"Privately owned? Jesus." Jersey's husband grunted and stared up at the castle. "I wouldn't want to pay the heating bill on that."

"I have to go there." Bronwyn didn't realize she'd spoken aloud until all gazes snapped her way.

Hermione looked sour. "We will go there once we've had lunch in the Copper Cauldron."

Bronwyn didn't want lunch in the Copper Cauldron, and she didn't want to wait. She needed to get into that castle. It was like a physical ache in her chest, as if an invisible rope threaded through her middle was tugging her in that direction.

"It's quite something isn't it?" A man spoke from beside her.

Bronwyn turned.

Tall and broad-shouldered, a man stood next to her. Her brain slowed, and she stared. Something stirred inside her but danced beyond her comprehension. It was something more than the insane beauty of his face. Realizing she had to say something, do something, react in a manner suggesting she might be alive, she said, "Yes."

Sun played light and dark tricks around his head and got absorbed in the glossy darkness of his hair. He was so familiar, yet she couldn't place him. "Have we met?"

"I don't think so." His smile made her breathless. It crinkled the skin at the corners of his sin-dark eyes and carved attractive furrows on either side of his mouth. He was talking, and she needed to pay attention. "I'm guessing you're a visitor to our village."

"Yes." The sculpted lines of his face made her itch to trace them with her fingers. His dark eyes were set beneath strong, arching brows. "Are you sure we've never met?"

"I would have remembered." He had the most beautiful

mouth, full bottom lip, perfectly bowed top lip. His lips quirked, as if he were holding in laughter.

Heat flooded Bronwyn's face. She was behaving like a superfan in the presence of their idol. Still, she could swear she knew him. Or maybe that was stratospherically wishful thinking.

"I need to..." She jabbed her thumb at her group as they moved past the statue toward the Copper Cauldron. "I need to go."

She didn't want to go. She wanted to stay with him.

"What a tremendous pity." He clipped his consonants and shaped his vowels, elevating English to a delightful auditory experience. It made her want to beg him to read anything—a shopping list, or better yet, a bedtime story.

"I need to go." Heat flooded her cheeks. By her count she'd told him that three times. He must think her elevator didn't make it all the way to the penthouse.

"Yes, you do." He leaned closer, his breath warm on her neck and ear. "You wouldn't want to miss Trudy's two-day-old sandwiches."

"Two days old?" Bronwyn wanted to purr and press her face to his. Her fingers twitched, and she shoved her hands in her back pockets before they grabbed the front of his pressed pale blue button-down and yanked him closer.

He smelled like linen and soap, and heat radiated from him. "Avoid the egg mayonnaise."

"Okay." Her mouth dried, but perspiration broke out over the rest of her. Unadulterated lust rampaged through her. A tiny part of her brain sat back and gaped at the rest of her. She barely managed to string a sentence together. "I might skip the sandwich altogether and go for a salad."

He winced. "I really wouldn't recommend that."

"You really must hate Trudy."

"No." He laughed, deep, smooth and rich. "But I have a vested interest in your continued good health."

Her heart tripped over its next beat. Was he flirting with her? On Deidre's soul, please let him be flirting with her.

His dark eyes met hers. Heat flared in their onyx depths. Everything around them melted away, like the two of them were trapped in a warm, golden bubble. It was like falling into another human being and Bronwyn went willingly.

"Yoohoo!" Hermione's voice doused her in reality, and Bronwyn disengaged her gaze from his.

He glanced over her shoulder and raised an eyebrow. "I think one of us is in trouble."

Almost stumbling over her feet to reach them, Hermione hurried across the green.

"Uh-oh. I'm guessing me." Hermione must have really wanted her to eat with the group.

Bronwyn's brain came back online. What the hell was she doing going nuclear meltdown over a complete stranger? Her gut twisted in denial. He didn't feel like a stranger, and her reaction felt right, inevitable.

He smiled at her, and her doubts wavered. "I wouldn't count on it."

She couldn't remember what they'd been talking about moments ago.

"Lord Donn, how lovely to see you?" Hermione wriggled in her excitement. "We did not expect you in the village today."

"Why would you?" He raised a dark brow with brutal precision.

Wait? What? She was talking to a *bona fide* English lord. Man, when blessings were handed out, her guy had been standing right at the front of the queue.

Hermione flushed. "Well, we wouldn't, would we? But we're glad to see you anyway."

"Alexander." He held his hand out to Bronwyn. He wore a signet ring on his right hand.

She took his hand, his grip warm and calloused. Sparks shot up her arm and her pulse raced. She never wanted to let him go. "And Lord Donn, apparently."

"Yes, but I won't tell if you don't." His dark eyes dragged her back beneath his spell.

"Bronwyn," she said. If he walked away now, she might never see him again, and everything in her fought that idea. "Bronwyn Beaty. I'm American."

"And I am enchanted." His lips pressed hot against the back of her hand. "See you shortly, little witch."

CHAPTER THREE

CRÉ-WITCH CHRONICLES

Chills broke over Bronwyn's skin as Baile Castle drew nearer. Perhaps it was the lingering sense of her encounter with Alexander making her jumpy. Her reaction to him had been weird and intense. The more time that ticked past between meeting him and now, the more ridiculous she felt about it. Probably some crazy knee jerk thing she had for men with English accents and ancestral titles. She needed to cut back on those historical romances.

Harvey kept them on the one and only road that wound out of Greater Littleton and up toward the castle. As far as she could see, that was the only place the road went. The castle soared against the summer sky, even larger than it appeared in her dreams.

On one side, the castle faced the village, behind it rose a mountain, and on the front end lay the sea. The cliff on which it perched had a staircase coming down from the castle to a large cave opening. There didn't seem to be any other way to get there, which would really suck if you were scared of heights.

"Baile, a word meaning home, is a classic example of a motte and bailey castle." Hermione had the bus microphone and an endless supply of facts. "If you look to your right you will see the raised portion of earth, or motte, on which the castle was constructed." They all dutifully looked right. "Surrounding it, is the enclosed area called the bailey. In Baile's case, the bailey is on three sides, with the cliff edge being guarded by a stone wall."

Jersey's husband pressed his face against the window glass. "Are those stairs going down?"

"Indeed." Hermione's smile sent him to the top of the class. "And another unique feature about Baile. Beneath the castle are a large series of caverns. In the central cavern, there is a stream, which is believed to supply the water needs of the castle."

Knowing trickled through her, and she said, "No."

All eyes snapped her way and Hermione's eyebrow went up. "Is there something you would like to ask?"

"Er...no." Heat climbed her cheeks. She had no explanation for how she knew that pool was not about water for the castle. A soft melodic chime sounded in her mind. The knowing strengthened until she was almost shivering.

"Then I'll continue." Hermione gave her a quelling look. "Now where was I?"

"The stream?" Jersey pressed against the glass right next to her husband. "Can you swim in it?"

Hermione chuckled. "I'm not sure, but the ladies who own the castle might take issue with that."

"How does that work anyway?" Jersey's husband turned his attention back to Hermione. "How can people own a castle? Aren't all castles in England the queen's?"

"Goodness me, no." Hermione tittered. "The queen, of course, owns her own castles, but Baile is owned by the Cray family. They are a direct line all the way back to Sir Roderick."

"He was married?" The German lady in the Man U sweatshirt got in before Jersey or husband could ask another question. "But you said he had a castle full of mistresses."

"Indeed, I did." Blushing the same brick red as her tour guide waistcoat, Hermione cleared her throat. "Sir Roderick never married. Instead he had an interesting arrangement with several women who lived in the castle."

People sat up straighter in the bus.

"Like shacked up with them?" Jersey and husband exchanged glances.

"Er...quite." Hermione pursed her lips. "What must be remembered about the medieval period is that people were more earthy than they were in later periods. They had a rather more pragmatic view of certain base needs."

"Go Hot Rod!" Jersey's husband guffawed.

A few people tittered politely with him.

"Right." Hermione went on. "Like our village, the castle has several fascinating legends about it. There is another intriguing legend around Sir Roderick. He appears constantly in several texts dating from the twelfth century up until the mid-sixteen hundreds. If those texts are to be believed, then Sir Roderick lived to the ripe old age of five hundred, give or take a few birthdays." She smiled, back on comfortable ground. "Of course, it's impossible that all these mentions refer to the same Sir Roderick. More likely to have been descendants who carried the same name."

"I read there are witches in that castle." A small Asian woman spoke so quietly Bronwyn nearly didn't hear her.

Hermione perked right up. "Indeed! I'm so glad you mentioned that. The witch legends surrounding our village do, in fact, originate from the castle. Back in the day, it is said it was the home of a large coven."

"How large?" Jersey's husband was a details man.

"We're not entirely sure. Old texts being unreliable sources of information, and the castle has been in the same family all this time," Hermione said. "They are a mostly private family and keep to themselves."

Harvey drove them onto a stone walled bridge toward the castle entrance. On either side of the bridge, the land dropped away into a steep gorge.

"What happened to the witches?" Bronwyn needed to know. The knowing prickled that the answer to her question was one she desperately needed.

Hermione's smile died. "That is a sad and grisly story, I'm afraid, and best we tell it now before we enter the castle. I always feel it insensitive to mention it when the Cray ladies are around." She took a deep breath and sighed it out. "Like your Salem." She looked pointedly at Jersey and husband. "We had our own witch hunts here in England. A rather unpleasant individual called Mathew Hopkins appointed himself the Witchfinder General. We know from several accounts of the witch hunts of 1645 that he developed quite the obsession with Baile and her alleged witches."

Harvey drove slowly over the cobbled floor of the bailey and toward a massive arched wooden door. Bands of steel reinforced the door, and it looked like it would take an army to break them.

"What happened?" An unbearable sadness swept through Bronwyn and she wanted to weep. Her emotions were all over the place. It must have been that she was finally there, fulfilling a dying wish of Deidre's.

I wish you could see this, Dee.

Dee's head would have been on a swivel trying to take it all in. She would have peppered Hermione with question after question.

"Hopkins and his fanatical group broke into the castle and killed all the occupants." Hermione stared up at the rising stone wall in front of the bus. "To our shame as a village, some of our ancestors took part in the murder of around ninety innocent women."

"So they weren't witches?" Jersey whispered her question.

"No. They were midwives and herbal healers at worst." Hermione cleared her throat and hauled her happy face back on. "There is, of course, no such thing as witches."

"You seem awful sure of that." Jersey gave Hermione the side eye and nodded to her husband. "I always say nothing is impossible. Have you watched that show *Supernatural Hunters?*"

Hermione stood and jerked her waistcoat into place. "I've not had the pleasure." She clapped her hands. "Now, a couple of rules before we enter the castle proper. As we have said, the castle is still privately owned, and the owners use it as their primary residence. They allow tours on Tuesdays and Thursdays only and only one tour a day. Everyone is to stick with the tour and remain in only those parts designated as public." She looked at Jersey's husband. "We would not want to have this wonderful opportunity to visit their home ruined."

"Will we get to see the caves?" Jersey's husband filed out of the bus behind his wife.

Hermione grimaced. "Unfortunately not. Our insurance does not cover a nasty fall from the cliff."

He straightened his shoulders. "I wouldn't fall."

"I'm sure you wouldn't," Hermione said with the sort of endless patience that had covered this conversation thousands of times. "But the caverns are also off limits to the tour."

"What the hell is the use of that?" He grumbled to his wife but loud enough for everyone to hear. "You pay good money for a tour, you should get to see everything."

Bronwyn stepped off the bus. Her feet settled like they were on familiar ground, like they knew the feel of the cobbles against them. She couldn't drag her stare away from the castle. It was beautiful, for sure, like something out of a fantasy film or a fairytale, but it was more than that. She knew this castle and—weirdly—this castle knew her.

What if not all the witches had died that night with Mathew Hopkins? It was not implausible that one witch had escaped that night. Maybe she'd been away from the castle and heard about the killing. From there, it wasn't a far jump to conclude that her or one of her children might have made their way to the new world.

"Hello," she whispered.

Sister.

Water witch.

Healer

Even softer whispers, no more than a sigh or a breath of wind surrounded her. It should have freaked her out, but it comforted her. The rest of the group was carrying on as normal. Not one of them had heard what she had.

Her ancestry test had brought her here, and there had to be a reason. "Are the family here?"

"I can't be sure." Hermione gave her a sympathetic smile. "But don't concern yourself about them. They make themselves scarce on tour days."

She pushed open the doors, and they all followed her into the castle. Easily the size of a football field, with vaulted ceilings rising high above them, a hall spread out before them.

"This is the great hall." Hermione's kitten heels clacked against the stone floor. "Please note the banners hanging on both sides of the hall."

The rest of her group noted the banners, but Bronwyn couldn't stop staring at the stained-glass window at the far end of the hall. Three women were depicted beside a pool and beneath the shade of a tree. The image was wrong in a way she couldn't put her finger on. All the women stood equidistant from each other, except for a space to the right of the last woman. It was almost like there should have been someone there.

A nasty cold crept up her spine and made her shiver. Her stomach lurched, and she felt nauseous.

"As you may well know, Baile is considered an architectural masterpiece. Please note the ceiling. Until recently, when the Cray family allowed tours inside the castle, it was thought that Durham Cathedral was the first example of a building with a stone vaulted ceiling on a large scale." Hermione pointed to the vaulting. "Although Baile and Durham were built around the same time, we here in Greater Littleton like to believe we have the first example of a stone vaulted ceiling of this scale. " She tittered and wrinkled her nose at the group.

Jersey stopped in the center of the great hall at a table with benches. "The furniture doesn't look that old."

"Which is another unique feature of Baile." Hermione grinned. "Possibly because of such limited access to her, but Baile looks no older than if she'd been built yesterday. You will note no decaying of woodwork or staining on the stones. None of the wear and tear one would expect of such an ancient building." She leaned closer to them and whispered. "It's a truly special place."

They followed her deeper into the great hall. To their left, a wooden staircase rose to a central landing and then rose again to the left and right of the landing to the gallery above. A red rope cordoned off the stairs and Hermione swept them past. "We will continue to the library. Baile has one of the largest collections of rare books in England. The library is one of my favorite places."

Bronwyn studied the hall banners as they went beneath them. Symbols decorated them, and she would love to have spent more time examining the symbols.

A woman ran down the left arm of the staircase. "It's you!"

"Oh my." Hermione giggled. "We are lucky today. Good afternoon, Miss Cray."

Long red hair swept straight down the woman's back. She was slim and tall, her skin a white so pure it glowed. She wore a maxi dress that skimmed her hips, and beneath the hem, her feet were bare. She hopped over the red rope and trotted straight for the group. "I knew it would be today."

For a second, Bronwyn thought the woman was talking to her.

"I told Niamh I had a special feeling about today." She stopped in front of Bronwyn and smiled down at her. "And I was right. Here you are."

"What?" Bronwyn looked at the woman. She didn't know her, but somehow, she did as well. The knowing started beneath her skin and spread rapidly.

The woman shoved out her hand. "I'm Mags." She rolled her eyes. "Actually, my full name is Magdalene, but everyone calls me Mags."

Bronwyn didn't think she'd seen this woman in her dreams even, so she couldn't know her. Still, she took her offered hand. "Bronwyn."

Mags had a smile that transformed her face from interesting to beautiful. "Welcome, Bronwyn. We've been waiting an age for you."

"What?" Bronwyn was sure she was gaping.

"Well then." Hermione popped up beside them. "You did not say you knew Miss Cray."

Mags grinned at her and giggled. "She doesn't, but she will."

"Okay." Bronwyn didn't know what else to say.

"Come to tea." Mags took her hands and squeezed them. "Come to tea, and I can tell you everything you're here to discover."

Not knowing how to respond, all Bronwyn managed was a strangled. "Okay."

"Right then. On with the tour." Hermione gave Bronwyn a thin smile. "Unless there is someone else you would rather speak to before I continue?"

"Er...no." Still looking at Mags, she followed Hermione back to the tour group.

Mags mimed drinking from a tea cup and saucer. "Tea," she called. "And the answers to all your questions."

IT FLOATED THROUGH THE NOTHING, weightless and directionless. It had no beginning and no end. It had no purpose. It just was. Formless, incorporeal, weightless.

Then it became aware, aware of being.

A being. Awareness swirled around it once having been a being. Cognizance burgeoned of having once had substance and now existing merely as spirit, a soul still drifting, still insubstantial.

The substance had been female. A woman. Like a distant echo, her gender wafted past and around her. There but finding no purchase and no structure.

Something. Something she needed to remember hovered on the very edge of her awareness. Then vanished. Bubbles of knowledge floated up through the endless dark but disappeared again before they could converge into thought.

She floated. Nothing more.

Infinite nothing. Endless nothing.

A concept dripped into the void. A thing she should know, but the void devoured it before she could be sure.

Still her memory of the thing that had been persisted and would not leave her. Her memory of it built it back up again, strong enough to stand against the rapacious void. Now that it stood firm, it tormented her with her not knowing.

She grew to hate the thing, the thing she should know and did not, because the thing opened a door in her consciousness.

Through the door crept knowledge, and that knowledge grew a name.

Time. The knowledge was called time, and its awareness bloomed like a blood stain through her expanding mind.

Time had passed. More time than she could imagine. More time than she could lose.

CHAPTER FOUR

CRÉ-WITCH CHRONICLES

Bronwyn worked her way through the iffy dinner at the Hag's Head. On her plate was what the menu claimed to be Welsh Rarebit, but it more strongly resembled soggy grilled cheese, go large or go home on the Velveeta.

Today had been weird. Nope, today had been fucking weird, and this from a weird member of Sawtooth, Maine's weirdest family. Mags had her beat on the weird-o-meter.

Yet, she'd instinctively liked Mags, been drawn to her. Only once they'd left Baile, had she pieced things together. It was the DNA. It had to be. Other than both being redheads, she and Mags didn't look alike. Mags dwarfed her and was willowy to Bronwyn's curves, but other evidence was mounting, and it couldn't all be coincidence. Her DNA test bringing her to Greater Littleton, the knowing that had been nagging at her almost constantly, the undeniable sense of kinship, it was all pointing to her having found her roots.

In addition, she couldn't ignore the castle itself, a castle she'd seen in her dreams since way back. She'd bet the farm on nobody else in today's tour group having dreamed of Baile since they were little. That might account for why Baile had felt so like home, but she believed it was more than that. Baile was somehow part of her family story, and in the morning, she was going to investigate further.

Her nape prickled and heat washed over her skin. *Little witch.*

She turned toward the knowing.

Standing in the dining room doorway, Alexander was watching her. He smiled and shoved both hands in his pockets. Wearing gray dress pants and a white button-down, he threaded through the tables toward her.

Her pulse drummed beneath her skin. Heat spread through her middle, and her limbs grew pliant.

"Good evening." Alexander motioned the other chair. "May I?"

"Er...yes." Her mouth was so dry she had to peel her tongue from the roof of it. "Hi."

"Hello." He smiled.

Bronwyn stared.

An answering heat darkened his eyes, and the dining room faded away. Like they were the center of their own private universe, they sat and stared at each other.

"My lord." A waiter bowed so low he almost bumped his forehead on the table. "May I serve you?"

Alexander dragged his gaze to the man. "Red wine, please. From my cellar."

The waiter scuttled off.

Bronwyn had heard the class system was alive and well in England, but that waiter was taking it to extremes. With Alexander not staring at her, she managed to dredge herself together and indicated her nearly full glass. "I'm still working on that."

"The house red." Alexander shook his head and grasped the glass. "I wouldn't wish that on my worst enemy."

He held her wineglass out and another waiter appeared at his elbow and took it away.

"They know you here." She indicated the disappearing waiter.

Leaning back in his chair, he draped one arm over the back. "Yes, they do." He studied her face as if he wanted to draw it in his mind. "Did you tour Baile?"

"Yes." His dark eyes drew her in and locked her attention on him. She nearly asked him again if they knew each other, but that would be too dumb for words. "It's beautiful."

"Is that all?" He seemed to be waiting for her to say more.

She didn't know this man. She really didn't, despite their insane connection, so she shrugged. "What else?"

"What else indeed." He leaned forward and peered at her dinner. "Dear God, do they actually feed that to people?"

"Um...yes."

The first waiter was back with a dusty bottle of wine and two glasses. He showed Alexander the bottle with a flourish. "My lord?"

"That's fine." Alexander didn't take his gaze from her. "Forgive me, I'm staring."

"I know."

"I can't seem to help myself." He motioned her plate. "Would you remove that, please?"

The waiter leaped to obey and scuttled away with her dinner before she could stop him.

"Hey!" It might not have been great, but it had been her dinner, and she was hungry.

He leaned forward and the potency of him trapped her in her seat. "Let me take you to dinner."

"What?" He didn't look like he was joking. "Why?"

"I want to spend time with you," he stated simply and without agenda, but that look in his eyes said otherwise. This crazy, off-the-charts attraction between them, he felt it too.

Damn, but she wanted to go with him. She stared at his large, tanned hand stretched across the table toward her. It was a strong hand, nails neatly clipped, but not the manicured hand of a suit. "I don't know you."

"That's what I want to change." All the reasons she shouldn't take that hand and let him lead her away from the pub flitted through her mind, but faded in the arcing stadium lights of her desire to go with him.

For the sake of those objections, she whispered, "I don't know if I can trust you."

"Yes, you do." He gestured with his fore and middle fingers between them. "You can trust me because this fucking insane thing between us, I feel it too." His gaze pinned and held her. "And it's like nothing I've ever experienced in my life." His smile softened and became self-deprecating. "I need to know you, Bronwyn."

Those words played across her like a harp, and she forced her ass to stay in her seat.

"Excuse me." Alexander leaned to the table to his right.

It was the German woman from the tour, but she'd swapped her Man U sweatshirt for a white blouse with chubby, cheerful bumblebees on it. "Yes?"

"I'd very much like to take this beautiful lady to dinner, but she's wary of me being a stranger." His smile could have melted the wax off a candle.

The German woman rallied and gave Bronwyn an approving nod. "You cannot be too careful."

"What if you took a photograph of us and if she's not at breakfast tomorrow morning, you can take it straight to the police?" Alexander looked at Bronwyn and raised his brow in a question.

"Well…I suppose." The woman frowned and glanced at the man dining with her.

He shrugged and looked at Bronwyn. "Would you like to go

to dinner with this gentleman?"

"Yes." Right now more than the next breath she took.

"Good." He nodded and raised his cellphone. He snapped a picture of them together. "There, you see. Now all is good."

"For you." Alexander put the bottle of wine and two glasses on their table and offered her his hand again. "Shall we?"

Outside, the night was mild with a soft brine-laden breeze. Alexander led her down the sidewalk to a low-slung vintage sportscar. He jerked his head at it. "This is us."

Her hesitation returned, and Bronwyn stared at the car. She didn't know much about cars, but the gleaming walnut dash screamed expensive.

Hands in his pockets, Alexander waited for her to make up her mind. If Deidre were here, she would tell her life was short. She would give that great cackle of hers and wink and say, *Trust yourself, darling.* Deidre would also be quick to point out the undeniable hotness of Alexander.

He opened the door for her, and she climbed in.

Neither of them spoke as he drove them down the main street and into a more residential area. Smaller houses gave way to bigger ones, spaced more widely apart.

For better or worse, she'd made the decision to go with her gut. "Where are we going?"

"To the best place around here for food." He flashed her a smile and went back to watching the road.

Ambient light etched the perfection of his profile against the night. She'd never met anybody quite so good looking before. He was almost too perfect to be real.

He turned between a pair of stone gateposts and stopped in the circle driveway in front of a beautiful stone manor house. Rectangles of welcome light shone from the mullioned windows and the portico over the door.

She leaned forward to get a better look. "This is your place."

"Yes." He made no move to get out the car. "Once you enter

that door, abandon all hope. I have you in my evil clutches, and I shall never let you go."

"You say that like it's a bad thing."

He laughed, his teeth flashing white in the dark. "I'm going to feed you, give you a great glass of wine and get to know you."

"Okay." She returned his smile.

Inside the manor was everything the exterior promised. Gleaming wooden floors were partially covered by large rugs that deadened the sound of their footsteps. She caught glimpses of immaculate antiques, wainscoting and large oil canvases. She wanted to stop and examine everything, but Alexander led her through and into a large, renovated kitchen.

Heat from a huge range taking up one entire wall of the kitchen made it feel cozy. Light gleamed off copper pans hanging above a massive central island topped with creamy white granite. The cabinets were dark sage on the bottom and creamy white on the uppers. It was pretty much her dream kitchen.

"Here." Alexander pulled out a wooden stool at the counter and patted the seat. "You sit here while I plot your demise."

"Will I get that wine while you're plotting?" She perched on the stool and watched him move about the kitchen. He looked completely at home in the space.

He disappeared into a pantry and came back with another of those dusty bottles that she suspected were vintage. After pouring deep ruby wine into two crystal goblets, he put one in front of her and took the second. He raised the glass. "To new friends."

"To new friends." The connection hummed gently between them, turned down to a comfortable level now.

Alexander rolled up the sleeves of his shirt. Muscle and sinew flexed in his forearms as he flipped the cuffs of his shirt. "Right." He pulled a butcher block closer. "Food."

She took a sip of her wine and made a surprised hum of

delight. It was definitely not what she'd been drinking at the pub.

He looked up from chopping onions and smiled. "Good?"

"Yes." She wanted to bask in the male beauty of that smile. There was something about it that felt as if he smiled like that for her alone.

Alexander swept the chopped onions into a large pan. "So, Bronwyn, tell me all about you."

He crushed garlic with the flat of a knife blade and then chopped it. Everything about him radiated self-assurance and confidence. It intrigued her but left her feeling discombobulated. "Why don't you tell me about you instead?"

"Fair enough." His smile had a rueful edge. Garlic joined the onions, and he added olive oil as he turned to the range. And wouldn't you know it, but his ass was as perfect as the rest of him.

"Not much of interest really." He raised his voice over the sound of frying. "I'm the product of thousands of years of inbreeding to create the idiot you see before you." The smell of onions and garlic frying made her mouth water. "Overbearing mother, absentee father, privileged upbringing, insufferable sense of my own importance."

There was a whole lot more to the story than that, she'd lay money on it, but he made her laugh anyway. "Overbearing mother?"

"Complete nightmare." He put a saucepan of stock on to boil. "I'm warning you now so you can never say I didn't tell you."

It was odd, and she was pretty sure he was joking, but then again not. His eyes were darker than pitch and hard to read. A soul deep weariness hung about him, the sort that should belong to a much older person. The man in front of her couldn't be older than thirty. "Have you always lived in Greater Littleton?"

"My entire life," he said. "I was born here, raised here, and I will most certainly die here."

Again the oddness of the last part of that struck her. "Why are you so sure you'll die here?"

"It's my home." He chuckled. "And I did tell you about the overbearing mother."

"She probably won't live forever."

He laughed and said, "I'd take that bet."

"What do you do? For a living." Her sense of him being so familiar jibed with mining for information. It was almost as if she should have known the answers to the questions she asked.

"I manage the family business," he said. "We've been at it for a few years, and now it's my turn at the helm."

"Family business as in?"

"Mostly land. A few investments and businesses." He turned from his cooking and topped up her wineglass. "The pub is another of those family businesses."

Now the cringing waitstaff made more sense. "Ah. You're the owner?"

"Guilty as charged." He sipped his wine, dark eyes studying her over the rim. "Unfortunately, I haven't been there as much as I would have liked lately, and standards have slipped."

"And by land, you mean ancestral land." He was a lord after all.

"Now you have the full story." His smile warmed his eyes and she grew slightly breathless. "Your turn."

"Oh." She didn't want to talk about herself, but to delve deeper into him. Still, turnabout was fair play. "Only daughter, no father, mother died when I was three, raised by my grandmother."

Sadness crept into his expression. "I'm sorry, Bronwyn. Nobody should lose a mother that young."

"Thank you." His empathy crept under her skin and warmed her. "My grandmother raised me. She was like a mother."

He motioned her to him. "I need you to stir."

"What am I stirring?" She rounded the island to join him at the range. "And I should warn you I can't boil an egg."

"Risotto." Up close, his smile hit her like a brick to the back of the knees, as he shifted her between him and the range and put a spoon in her hand. "Stir, and when the liquid is absorbed, add another ladle of stock."

He moved away, and she immediately missed his nearness.

She stirred as he worked beside her. No question he knew his way around the kitchen. The atmosphere was easy as he chopped mushrooms and something that looked like bacon. "What is that?"

"Pancetta." He dropped the pancetta in a hot pan, and it hissed, smelling as divine as only cooking bacon can smell.

"That's fancy Italian bacon, right?"

He grinned. "Yup, but *la pancetta è poesia, il bacon la Colonna dei necrology.*"

Bronwyn almost choked on her next swallow of wine. "And you speak Italian."

"Add more stock." He jabbed a thumb at her pan. "I speak Italian, French, Spanish, Greek, German and enough Russian to argue over taxi fare." He cocked his head and smirked. "Are you impressed yet?"

"Are you trying to impress me?"

"Absolutely." He shrugged and sipped his wine. "I'm throwing out some of my best material here."

Bronwyn laughed. The easy flirtatiousness was more comfortable than the intense, breathless excitement at the pub. Perhaps it was because they were in his home, but he seemed more at ease, less...she struggled to find the right word...focused.

"Tell me about your grandmother." He removed the cooked pancetta to a plate and dropped the chopped mushrooms in the pan.

"Deidre was wonderful. We were very close." Maybe because she'd lost both her daughters young, but Deidre didn't believe one moment of life should be wasted. *You don't have another life in the closet, darling. This is the one you get, so make it count.*

"Just the two of you?" Alexander had a way of concentrating on her that made her feel like they were in a vacuum.

She found herself telling him more than she'd intended. "Actually, I had a sister too, but she died before I was born. My aunt, my mother's sister, died when I was sixteen."

"I'm more sorry than I can say." He took her hand and squeezed it. Warm tingles spread from the contact up her wrist and arm. It felt too intimate too fast, and she took her hand back.

"It's fine." She wanted to lighten the mood. "I mean it's not, but it is what it is. We don't seem to live long in my family."

"And your grandmother?"

The grief snuck up on her and Bronwyn had to blink back tears. "Last year."

"I'm sorry, little witch." He closed his hand over hers as his dark gaze nearly swallowed her whole.

Warmth from his touch spread up her arm, and she had the insane desire to press her face into his chest and have him hold her. Seeking distraction, she said, "You've called me that twice before."

"Have I?" With a last squeeze, he dropped her hand and went back to grating parmesan.

"At the statue and then at the..." Bronwyn thought back. At the pub she'd heard him whisper little witch, but she couldn't be sure he'd said it. It was confusing, so she shifted the subject. "Actually, my grandmother is the reason I'm here."

He raised an eyebrow and sipped his wine. "Tell me."

"She wanted me to take this trip and trace our roots." Bronwyn raised her glass, but she had finished it.

Alexander reached behind him, snagged the bottle and topped her glass up. "And your roots brought you here?"

"I did one of those ancestry tests and it told me I am one hundred percent English and Irish and traced me to here." She shrugged and sipped her wine. "And here I am."

He toasted her with his glass. "And I, for one, am glad you are."

CHAPTER FIVE

A ll through making dinner, Alexander kept it light and easy, disguising the compulsion that drummed through his blood like a second heartbeat. *Mine, mine, mine.* He could dress as a modern man, even ape the mannerisms and speech of one, but beneath the urbane exterior, his true self lurked: a man born in a savage time who had survived by being the strongest and the most feral.

After dinner he daren't linger. With his senses finely attuned to her, he craved her. It wasn't a polite or a gentle thing, his craving. It demanded he lose himself in her, that he take her, and in so doing, surrender himself completely to her.

He'd seriously underestimated the pull of the prophecy. He had brought her to his manor to keep her away from Rhiannon's prying eyes, knowing those same prying eyes would report back that he'd taken her home.

"Tell me what you thought of the statue." He needed to understand how sensitive this dormant witch was.

She started. "Why would you ask that?"

"You spent some time staring at it this morning. It took all of my devastating charm to draw your attention away." She was guarded around her abilities, which suggested someone had taught her to hide them. That same someone had probably saved her life.

It could be a coincidence that the sole remaining bloodline of water witches had an alarming tendency to die young. Like it was plausible that every one of them was so clumsy or careless of their own lives that they got into car accidents, fell off cliffs, drowned in calm seas—he'd been doing his homework on Bronwyn's family. Or it could be that someone had been systematically targeting and eradicating them.

Her magic smelled of honey and sage, and it clung to her like a subtle perfume. It taunted him to press his skin to hers and absorb her scent.

She turned in her seat to look at him as he drove. "Do you know anything about Sir Roderick?"

"A little." The crippling strength of Roderick's sword arm, the bone crunching impact of Roderick's punch, and Alexander most definitely knew enough to get the hell out of the way when Roderick swung that war hammer of his.

She tucked one leg under her and shifted closer. "Is that him in the statue?"

"It most certainly is." The warm silk of her skin made his mouth water. He could kiss her, pull the car over and kiss her. She would let him too, but he was not so sure he would be able to stop. Strike that. He knew he wouldn't be able to stop with a few kisses. How thrilled Mummy dearest would be to know how well that prophecy worked.

"Hmm." She wrinkled her nose like she wasn't certain. "Hermione is not sure. She said it might be him."

"I'd stake my life on it. It's Sir Roderick all right." The confines of his car made him painfully aware of how easy it would be to touch her.

"How do you know?"

That was a long story, and one that would end in her running screaming into the night, and away from him. Unfortunately for her, he was all that stood between her and Rhiannon. "Old family, goes way, way back. All the way back to good old Sir Roderick." And then he added because he couldn't resist how much it would piss Roderick off if he could hear it. "My ancestors say he was a bit of an arse."

"Bitter feuding families?" A teasing lilt lit her voice and made him want to taste it from her lips.

"The bitterest." He threaded his car through the quiet village. It was late enough for the streets to look abandoned, but Rhiannon's spies would be out there, watching, reporting.

"Do you know who the woman in the statue is?"

Maeve. Sweet, beautiful, innocent Maeve. Grief prevented him from replying immediately. The first time he'd seen Maeve, she had been peering at him through a window while he seduced another woman into doing Rhiannon's will. Even then, being so much Rhiannon's creature as he had been, the purity of Maeve had struck him. So different from the grasping creature he'd been intent on bending to Rhiannon's will, Maeve's presence had washed over him like cool, fresh spring water. Diminutive and delicate, like a spun sugar confection, she'd pierced the solid exoskeleton of blood magic Rhiannon had woven around him. With her flaxen hair and giant azure eyes, Maeve had been so much stronger than she looked. She'd have to be for the task Goddess had chosen for her.

"Maeve." He cleared his throat and repeated a name he had no right to speak. "Her name is Maeve."

Bronwyn gasped and she stared at him. "You're sure her name was Maeve."

"I am." Bronwyn chewed on her bottom lip and stared out her window. She was definitely hiding something from him about Maeve. "Why so interested in them?"

She made a dismissive motion with her hand and lied again. "It sounds like a romantic story."

"Romantic." Alexander laughed. He couldn't help it. Roderick would have given his left ball, maybe even his right as well, for it to be have been romantic between him and Maeve. Unfortunately for Roderick, the old bastard's legendary luck with women had failed him with sweet, innocent Maeve. "Sir Roderick certainly liked the ladies, but nobody would ever accuse him of being romantic."

Bronwyn leaned closer to him in her eagerness. "So were they lovers?"

"Not that I'm aware of," he said. And not for lack of wanting on Roderick's part. "Roderick was her...guardian. He looked after her."

"Did she need looking after?"

Bronwyn was so close that if he turned his head, their mouths would meet. He kept his attention on the road. "More than either of them could have believed."

"Who sculpted the statue of them?" Bronwyn sensed a story, and she wanted to know it all.

"That is impossible to say." He pulled up outside the Hag's Head and parked. Before temptation got the best of him, he hopped out of the car and came around to her side. Opening her door, he held his hand out to her. "Here we are. Back safe and sound."

He could sense them, eyes on him and Bronwyn, slithering in the dark shadows cloaking the sides of the pub.

Bronwyn put her hand in his, and he wanted to throw back his head and roar to the world that she was his. For the sake of those hungry eyes he kept hold of her hand. For the sake of the burning need in him, he kept hold of her hand.

She stopped in the light of the portico over the pub door, adorably shy and uncertain all of a sudden. "Thank you for dinner. It was lovely."

Hundreds of years—hundreds of women—spent waiting for this woman. The one woman destined to be his, and the one woman he could never have.

"My pleasure." Out there with watching eyes, he was safe to give in to the demand to touch her. He stroked the peachy smoothness of her cheek as he cupped it. "May I see you again?"

"Yes," she whispered. The wanting reflected in her eyes appeased the gnawing ache in him.

"Tomorrow." He brushed her full, beautiful lips with his. Meaning to pull back on that brief contact, his miscalculation thundered lava hot through his blood. With their lips perilously close he froze.

And then she sighed, and her eyelids fluttered shut.

Alexander lost the battle and slanted his mouth over hers. The need to taste her raged through him, and he took her mouth, his tongue claiming the hallowed space beyond her lips.

Her hands fluttered, and then she wound her arms around his neck.

He deepened the kiss, taking what was his. Desire thrummed his nerve endings and his cock hardened. Like a randy teenager, he pressed against her.

Bronwyn's body cleaved to his, and she moaned in the back of her throat.

He cupped her round, delicious arse and pulled her tighter against him. He could take her upstairs right now. Take her.

And that was precisely the problem and why, hate it as he may, he needed to stop before it raged beyond his control.

Gentling his kiss, Alexander eased them both down before breaking away.

The sight of her, mouth kiss swollen, cheeks flushed, almost undid him, but he reminded himself of the stakes to the game they played. "Good night, little—Bronwyn."

She hesitated at the door, the same desire still haunting him playing across her face. Then she turned, opened the door and let herself in. She tossed him a sweet, shy smile over her shoulder. "Good night."

The door closed, and he was alone in the quiet night. Or not. He spoke to the shadows to the left of the door. "You can go home now; there's nothing more to see."

"Very good, my lord." Clyde slithered out of the gloom. "I wasn't being a voyeur."

"I know that." Despite himself, he pitied Clyde. Rhiannon kept her minions on a short leash.

Cool night air helped clear his head, so he left his car at the Hag's Head and walked toward the green. He was playing a dangerous and complicated game. One misstep, and he could lose everything. But he wouldn't be the only one who paid the price.

He should have known the prophecy would come with its own insurance policy. His and Bronwyn's mutual fascination made sense in light of what the prophecy expected of them. In the few meager hours he'd known her, Bronwyn had already burrowed beneath his skin.

Failure had become even more terrifying.

All these sodding years, that bloody prophesy had been hanging around, mainly irritating him, and now it looked alarmingly like it might roll right along and drag him with it. Fucking hell! He'd always found the idea of being a cosmic stud service, an arcane sperm donor, distasteful and demeaning. Even now though, his cock was ready to remind him of what a splendid idea it was after all.

The night stayed fine, with a light onshore breeze dispelling any lingering heat.

As though Roderick called to him, he wandered over to the statue on the village green.

At the base of the statue, a pair of teenagers were trying to eat each other's braces off. They paid him no mind as he stopped right in front of it.

The Lovers.

Alexander laughed aloud. If Roderick would give him ten seconds before he tried to remove his head with a broadsword, they might have had a good laugh over that one.

The teenagers were still at it, so Alexander nudged the boy's foot with his toe. "Go home."

The boy tore his mouth off his girlfriend. "Fuck you, old man."

Ah, the youth. So charming. "I'm older than I look." By approximately seven hundred years. "But why don't you fuck off instead?"

The boy managed to hold his stare for an impressive two seconds before sloughing to his feet and tugging the girl up with him. "You don't know me. You can't tell me what to do."

Alexander gave him the look. The one he'd learned at dear old Mum's knee.

The teens scuttled away like hell was after them.

"Well." He took a seat at the base of the statue. The stone pressed cool against his back. "It's starting to look rather alarmingly like you and I are going to have another go at each other." Alexander couldn't remember when he'd started his nocturnal chats with Roderick. It amused him to know the other man had no choice. If Roderick had a choice, Alexander would be fighting, not chatting. "I would wish you luck, but as that will probably result in my demise, I'm sure you'll understand why I resist."

With the idea of fucking firmly off the table, fighting sounded like a grand idea. It had been a long time since Alexander had enjoyed a competent opponent. Roderick had been the last, and that had been nearly four hundred years ago. Alexander had won their last bout, which was the only reason he was still breathing, and Roderick was…well, he didn't rightly know what or where Roderick was.

It was a pity they were sworn enemies because they were probably the only two men capable of understanding each other.

"She feels you." He liked to think Roderick understood him. Sad sod that he was, talking to a stone person for company. "She feels you waking, and it's driving her batty." Not that Rhiannon and sanity had ever had more than a glancing acquaintance. "You're the only thing stopping her from getting into that castle, and if she could, she would have done away with you already."

Rhiannon's power grew almost daily, and Alexander could sense it in her, pulsing like a huge gray malevolent slug beneath her skin. "She's getting closer to breaking the ward spell."

He sat there until the chill brought him to his feet. A wonderful cognac he'd been saving since 1815 was calling his name.

"I'll be seeing you, old man." He tapped the plinth. "Sooner rather than later, if you know how to do what you were created to do."

Halfway down the lane toward his home, Alexander felt her. Dear old Mummy. The foul miasma surrounding her crept over his skin and made him want to dermabrade it off. He didn't hurry his pace. She would sense him and know he was on his way.

He let himself in through his front door, not bothering to lock it. The only person he wanted to lock out was already sprawled across a Victorian velvet chaise drinking his cognac from a pint glass.

Tonight Rhiannon had dressed old school in a wine-red velvet evening gown that clung to her body. Gems gleamed about the neckline and down the long sleeves. She smiled and held one slim, white hand out to him. "My son."

"My lady." Suppressing his recoil, Alexander took her hand,

kissed the back and bowed to her. And the royals thought they had familial formality in their homes. "You honor me with your presence."

She watched him with those pitch-dark eyes. "Do I really, Alexander?"

"Of course." Not at all, but he was careful to keep all such thoughts off his face. Fucking hell! She'd already quaffed half his bottle of cognac. He poured himself a measure and stood in front of the armchair opposite her.

She motioned him to sit, and he did.

"You had her here." She breathed deep. "I can still smell her."

"Yes." Alexander didn't dissemble, like he didn't sit without her permission.

Her eyes glittered. "Are you drawn to her?"

"Yes." More than even she knew.

"Do you want her?"

"Yes."

"Good."

She was a vicious bitch, and just because she needed him enough not to kill him, it didn't mean she couldn't make him hurt. "It won't be long before I have her."

"You haven't yet?" Exposing the delicate column of her neck, she rested her head against the back of the sofa. It wouldn't take much to slit her throat. A quick lean forward and the dagger he always kept tucked away.

"This is a different time, as you know." It would do him no good to slit her throat, however. She would heal long before she could bleed to death. He still wasn't sure how old she was, but she predated the original druids and went back to a time before time was measured. "It would go better for us if she wasn't crying rape afterwards."

"Ugh." She grimaced. "It matters not to me."

"Nor I, really." He sickened himself with his lies and half-truths. "But I judged circumspection the best course. She'll succumb to me, and I'll get the job done without anyone being any the wiser."

Her belief in him doing what she'd created him for was all that kept Rhiannon at bay. She took another long pull on her pint glass. Alcohol didn't affect her like it did humans. She was long past that point. "Does she know what she is?"

"Not at all." Alexander wished for his little witch's sake she could stay ignorant, but her life depended on him destroying her bubble.

Rhiannon stood and put her pint glass on the table. "I had not planned on some of them getting away. There might be others."

Not many and not nearly enough. The screams and sobs of that night still trod his nightmares. Being the son of Rhiannon, he'd always believed he understood and accepted evil. That heinous night, he'd found out how wrong he was. "Did you do it?" Her mood augured well for asking questions. "Did you kill her family?"

"Not me, darling," And she smiled. It was all the more disturbing for its flawless beauty, her smile. It hid a being so impenetrably dark she defied description. "But I cannot allow cré-witches to run around all over the world. That bitch is still alive, and if they start using their magic again, it will awaken her."

That bitch, better known as Goddess, the source of all life and truth in the world, and the only thing that could stop Rhiannon. Although Goddess had been asleep since her dying witches had cast a spell so powerful it had almost ripped the veil between good and evil. They had done the unthinkable and used blood magic. It was against everything Goddess was, her very essence, and it had driven her into a sleep so deep, only Rhiannon caught dim flashes of her from time to time.

The same spell had left Roderick and Maeve on the village green.

"She's the one," he said, because she would already know who Bronwyn was. "And I'll take care of it."

"Hmm?" She studied him, her lids lowering over her dark, glittering eyes. "Be careful, darling. You're a clever one, but not that clever."

CHAPTER SIX

CRÉ-WITCH CHRONICLES

Time passed as she floated, and time was lost. More time vanished and the loss coupled itself to emotion. Time became the enemy, and she was no longer alone in the void because time carried with it a panicked sense of how she needed to escape.

Perception crept into the vacuum and forced itself into her awareness. Sensory input pierced the void. First sight and then touch. It was cold and dark in the abyss. So dark and cold and silent that if she screamed it would ring endlessly. Then she smelled something. This time when the bubble floated up through the endless dark, it carried a distinct smell and the smell brought memories with it.

She remembered things lost and things no more.

This never-ending emptiness filled her with fear. She feared she would never find her way out, and she had to get out of this place that robbed her life in the relentless press of time. But this place had no ending and no beginning, and she did not know how.

It seemed to take forever to put a name to the scent. It might have taken eons, or just a heartbeat; she had no way of knowing.

She veered away from those thoughts. They terrified her. Time terrified her.

She concentrated instead on the smell and broke it into two parts, both of which had a name, lily and orange. Like pins stacked in a row, one thought, idea, concept, crashed into another and blossomed in her mind as certainty.

Not a disembodied smell at all, the lily and orange belonged to magic. It was the scent of unique magic wielded by a witch. A witch such as herself. A cré-witch. Suddenly starved of the magic, she lunged for it. It danced maddeningly out of her reach, and now she no longer floated, she waited. She waited at the place the magic had appeared for it to appear again. When it did, she would grab on to it and force it to take her home.

Home, a concept so painful it hurt to breathe.

SATURDAY MORNING MADE it a week since she'd come to England, and Bronwyn bore the heavy sense of a momentous night before. Outside her bedroom window, the sea was topped with white caps and swirled green and sapphire around the rocks.

"I think I've met someone, Dee." Even with death separating them, she never felt as if her grandmother had left her completely.

Outside the open window, gulls screeched, and a sprightly onshore breeze ruffled the curtains.

"He's so beautiful, Dee. Like he stepped out of one of those books we used to read." She and Deidre had spent hours drinking red wine and reading novels. In those novels, women met men who struck them dumb, men who made their blood heat and their pulses pound. "But there's something else there too. He's so…" She couldn't find the right word, so she used the one that came closest. "Mysterious."

Trust your instinct. Deidre had lived her life by that as well. Except her instinct hadn't helped her that morning a year ago when she'd gotten into her car and driven to the store.

After a shower, Bronwyn got dressed and made it down to the dining room. The German couple sat eating their breakfast by the window. The man smiled and waggled his phone at her.

She smiled back and took a free table. Even on such a bright day, the interior of the Hag's Head was dark and smelled faintly of stale cigarettes and beer. A massive inglenook fireplace, mantel stained black by countless fires, dominated the wall to the right of the bar. Dark wainscoting and heavy, low wood timbers added to the general gloom.

"Madam." The same waiter from last night appeared at her table. "English or continental breakfast?"

"Continental." She didn't have a good feeling about the pub's kitchen and eggs. If she ordered the eggs, maybe Alexander would appear and whisk her to his manor and whip up eggs benedict. Or not.

The waiter grinned at her, his eyes glinting with odd intensity. "Very good, madam. Right away."

"Thank you." There was something off about the waiter, and he creeped her out. He smelled odd as well, kind of sickly and putrid, like rotting vegetation.

Still grinning and twinkling, he leaned into her personal space. "Coffee?"

"Sure." The hair on her nape rose and she moved back as discreetly as she could.

To her relief, he scuttled off with her order.

She waited for her breakfast with half an eye on the door. Alexander has said he wanted to see her today but hadn't taken her number.

The waiter appeared with her breakfast: a croissant, a pat of butter shaped like a witch's hat, one of those mini pots of strawberry jam and a bowl of anemic cantaloupe. Given her insipid meal, the coffee was surprisingly good.

Too restless to stay indoors and wait for Alexander to maybe appear, Bronwyn wandered out of the pub and took a walk down the main street. Planning for this trip had not progressed much beyond getting to Greater Littleton. She'd come with a purpose and she needed to push distractions aside.

According to her DNA, her family came from this village. The closest connection she'd felt had been at Baile, and when she'd met Mags. The same Mags who had promised Bronwyn the answers she was looking for. She could grab a cab and take Mags up on the offer of tea, but that seemed intrusive. This morning, Baile gleamed pale gray above the village, beautiful and serene. It would be wonderful to find proof her people had come from there.

A bay window with mullioned glass panes drew her to the Speckled Grimoire Book Shoppe. The window displayed a Harry Potter Collector's Edition set, and a coffee table book on British castles. Toward the back, beside a handmade cardboard sign saying Local Author was a book called, *The Secrets of Baile; Fact or Fiction...or Worse.*

A book shop—excuse her, shoppe—might be a good place to look for information. The local section was disappointingly small, and she settled for a map of Greater Littleton and *The Secrets of Baile.*

Back on the street again, she headed for the green with some half-baked notion of seeing if the statue had the same effect on her today. Alexander had known a lot about Roderick and Maeve, but he hadn't told her how he knew. If the information Alexander had given her was readily available, Hermione might have had it. His offhand reference to his family being old and going way back didn't really make sense. Sure they might have all sorts of information on the town and the castle. A house as big as Alexander's was bound to have a library, right? So, if he knew the statue was definitely Roderick, why not tell the world?

Being around Alexander had befuddled her, made her thinking mist. The knowing muttered inside her. She should have asked more questions. For a woman with a mission to find her roots, she'd let prime opportunities to press him for answers pass her by.

In the clarity of morning, last night seemed unreal. Other than that kiss, and that, she remembered like a million-pixel image with her other senses built in.

Irritated with herself, she leaped on the distraction of a sign promising a local farmer's market that afternoon. Still early, barely ten, she arrived at the parking lot as the vendors were setting up. A sound like a gunshot cracked through the still morning.

Bronwyn jumped and looked around for cover.

"Bloody woman." A vendor with huge baskets of lavender blossoms rolled her eyes at Bronwyn.

A volley of bangs sounded and a dark green Land Rover careened around the corner. People scurried to get out of the way as it clattered past her on a series of farts and explosions before being aimed at a parking space and stopping with a squeal of brakes and another ear splitting bang.

The stench of rotten eggs and raw sewage hit her and made her eyes water.

Retching, a man with a crate of big red cheese wheels hurried away.

A woman leaped out the Land Rover surrounded by a pack of dogs of various sizes. They all squirmed and mobbed around her as she looked about her and beamed. "Morning."

A couple of people gave her a grudging nod.

Medium height, and curved like a 40s pinup, the woman wore low-rise jeans and a tight-fitting *Supernatural* T-shirt which read *"I'm a Dean girl, but I'm Sam curious."* Riotously curly auburn hair fought the scarf attempting to hold it back. Her eyes tilted up like a smug cat's, and her mouth was almost too full for her face.

She wasn't conventionally beautiful, barely even pretty, but Bronwyn had never seen a sexier woman. She oozed sultry earthiness.

"Oy, Niamh!" A rotund man with a fringe of hair clinging to the edges of his pate clomped across the rutted parking area toward the Land Rover. "What have I told you about these bloody dogs?"

"Morning, Denis." Niamh's wide red mouth split in a grin. "Is that a new shirt?"

Denis stopped, blushed and rubbed a hand over the placket of his beige short-sleeve button-down. "Er...no."

"Are you sure?" Slightly raspy, deep and rich, even her voice was steeped in sex. "I'm sure I would have noticed you looking like a sexpot before."

Niamh's dogs boiled around Denis. A medium size, stringy brindle mongrel stuck his nose in Denis's crotch.

Denis went puce and nudged the dog away. "Now, see here, Niamh, we've spoken about this before. You can't have all these dogs here without them being on a lead." He fended off more advances from the pack, dancing out of the way of curious noses.

"I know." Niamh sucked her bottom lip into her mouth and chewed on it. "Only, you see, Denis, if I put leads on all of them, how would I hold the leads?"

"Well...you could...I..." Denis's gaze stuck on her mouth and didn't move. "You could bring less dogs."

Niamh's eyes widened, kittenish and adorable. "I could do that." Then she looked crestfallen. "But they do so love to come with me."

"That's all very well and good." Taking a deep breath, Denis tried to get a good bluster going. "But this is not the place for out-of-control dogs."

"Hmm." Niamh stepped into Denis's space and laid a hand on his chest. "I'll think of something, Denis." She gazed into his eyes. "I promise."

Denis gaped, snapped his mouth shut, and melted. "Okay."

"Okay?" Niamh held the eye contact and Bronwyn could feel the sizzle from twenty yards away. Bronwyn would put good money they could feel it all the way on the other side of the fairground.

Denis made a strangled noise of assent. "Also, we've had some complaints about the Landy."

"The Landy or the fuel?" Another woman stepped up beside Niamh.

Transfixed by Niamh, Bronwyn hadn't noticed her climbing out of the Land Rover. The new one was also a redhead, but more copper than auburn. She stood half a foot taller than Niamh, all of it legs.

This woman was a classic beauty, her features almost cold in their fine perfection.

"It's the fuel, Alannah." Denis looked starstruck now. "It has a very unpleasant odor."

"It's the fuel of the future." Alannah gave him a sympathetic grimace. "I imagine people were not too keen on the whiff of petrol when they first smelled it either."

"I know." Niamh giggled and peered up at Denis. "It stinks to high heaven. My dogs are always complaining."

Alannah's shoulders firmed, and she stuck her chin out. "Fuel of the future."

"Is it too much to ask that they miss one Saturday?" The lavender vendor was thumping baskets around her stall. She looked at Bronwyn as if they were allies. "Nothing but chaos wherever they go."

"They're beautiful." Bronwyn couldn't stop staring.

"That they are." The lavender woman rolled her eyes. "My

nana says those Cray women were always touched by the fairies." Sniffing, she straightened and jammed her hands on her hips. "Suppose that makes sense with them being witches and all."

"Witches?" Cray women must be from the castle. Bronwyn took a step forward. Were they connected to her?

Prickles skittered up and down her spine, and the hair all over her body stood on end.

"Niamh!" A third woman stormed around the Land Rover, and for a second Bronwyn thought she was seeing double. The third one was an exact replica of Alannah, only instead of yoga pants and a T-shirt, this one had on cargo pants and a black T-shirt with *Arcane Activist* scrawled across her full breasts in bright red writing. "Niamh!" she bellowed. "Get your fucking dogs out of the Harry Potter wands."

"Bronwyn!" Wearing a yellow, green and purple tie-dyed caftan, Mags had joined the third woman and she was staring right at Bronwyn. She raised her voice across the distance. "I told Sinead you would be here, but she never believes me."

The third woman, Sinead, locked eyes on Bronwyn. "Who's she?"

"One of us." Mags beamed at Bronwyn and took a step toward her. "The one we've been waiting for."

The lavender seller threw her a dark look.

Sinead frowned at Bronwyn. "We've been waiting for someone?"

Grinning, Mags nodded.

Alannah and Niamh were also looking at her.

Alannah waved and Niamh gave her a smile that made her want to gawp.

Little Witch.

Her muscles melted. Heat washed over her skin. Alexander was there, and her heart rate triple timed it.

"There you are." Alexander stood close enough behind her

for his body heat to envelop her. His breath caressed her neck and shoulder where her T-shirt left it bare. "I thought I might have to chase you all the way back to America."

Steeling herself against the impact of him, she turned. "Hi."

"Hi." A slow, sweet smile spread over his beautiful face.

The farmer's market, Mags and the other Crays, the busy vendors, all of it faded away and it was only her and him locked in a secret moment out of time and place. His eyes darkened, and his gaze drifted from her eyes to her mouth. They were standing so close her breasts almost brushed his chest.

"Oy, Alexander." Niamh gave a shrill whistle. "Stop hogging her, and let us say hello."

"Too late." Alexander's hand rested on the small of her back. "The Cray ladies have spotted you."

"Do you know them?" Bronwyn didn't know how it was possible, but he looked even better than he had last night. He smelled delicious, like soap and freshly showered man and she wanted to roll around in his scent the way one of Niamh's dog was writhing on the grass.

"Yes." Alexander threaded his fingers through hers and tugged. "Come and meet some of my favorite girls. I suspect you'll discover you have a lot in common."

The weight of her hand in his felt perfect, the curl of their fingers as if they'd been created to do that.

Oh, Dee, I'm in so much trouble here.

Bronwyn couldn't be sure, but the breeze seemed to carry Deidre's full-bodied chuckle.

Alexander led her toward the group.

All four Cray women stood and watched as she and Alexander approached.

Panic surged through Bronwyn, and she nearly tugged her hand free and ran for it. The air about them crackled with portent, like this was so much more than five women meeting for the first time. If she didn't know better, Bronwyn would swear she was walking face first into her fate.

Niamh frowned and looked at the others.

"Yes." Mags nodded.

Alexander squeezed her hand, and Bronwyn's world righted itself again.

Trust. Deidre sounded as if she was standing right beside her. *Trust your instinct.*

Niamh grinned at Alexander. "Hey, handsome. Look at you all fresh from the shower and smelling pretty."

"Dear God, Niamh." Alexander bent and kissed her creamy cheek. "You should come with a health warning for straight men everywhere."

Niamh's husky chuckle stroked like velvet down Bronwyn's spine. "Now where would the fun be in that?"

"At least we'd stand a chance." Alexander straightened and tugged Bronwyn forward. "I have someone here I want you to meet."

"Hi." Niamh hugged her. "I feel like I know you already. Mags has not shut up about you."

Not sure how to react and sure she was developing a girl crush, Bronwyn managed a strangled, "Hi."

Alexander indicated Mags. "Of course you've already met the lovely Mags."

"I'm sorry about yesterday." Mags wrinkled her nose. "I tend to come on a bit strong. But I'm harmless." She leaned closer. "Also, that Hermione scares the shit out of me."

Alexander chuckled and bent closer to Bronwyn's ear. His warm, minty breath washed over her cheek. "Don't believe it. That sweet face hides the heart of a lioness."

"I'm Alannah." Up close she was even lovelier, with eyes an impossible shade of indigo. "And this is my sister, Sinead."

"We're twins," Sinead said, as if the double sight whammy wasn't immediately obvious.

"Sinead is an arcane activist," Alexander glanced down at her and then smiled at Sinead.

Sinead straightened her shoulders. "We have dedicated ourselves to ending discrimination against the supernaturally endowed, the dilution of magical lore through juvenile literature, the commercialization of pagan sacred sites, and fracking."

"Never mind that." Mags elbowed Sinead out the way. She lowered her voice and did a quick left-right check of the fairgrounds. "We need to talk." She peered behind her. "But not here."

"Invite her to Baile," Alexander said. "I'm sure Bronwyn would love to see more of the castle. Did you know she's here to trace her roots?"

"Why?" Sinead wrinkled her nose. "A bunch of dead ancestors aren't going to tell you anything."

"Don't be so sure." Alexander jumped in before Bronwyn could argue with Sinead. "Our past can define our present."

Bronwyn liked Mags, thought Niamh was gorgeous and Alannah seemed nice, but she wasn't so sure of Sinead.

"Yes, do come." Alannah's smile made her feel special. "We don't have many visitors."

Sinead snorted. "We don't have many visitors because we like it that way."

"Ignore the grumpy cow." Niamh rolled her eyes. "And do come and have tea. Or lunch. Lunch is better."

"Well, I—"

"Tomorrow?" Mags pressed, eager like a child with a new toy. "Come for lunch tomorrow and we can chat." She lowered her voice. "You really should come. I've seen it."

"What you got there?" Sinead cocked her head to the side and pointed at Bronwyn's book in her left hand.

Embarrassed at being caught with a book on Baile in front of the Crays, she shrugged. "I was curious about—"

"Well, I wouldn't read that." Sinead whipped it out of her

hand and tossed it into a nearby garbage can. "They make all that crap up, you know." She turned and said over her shoulder, "Come to lunch and find out for yourself."

Bronwyn wasn't sure what Mags meant by having seen it, but she would like to go to lunch, despite Sinead. "I'd like that."

"Good." Alexander raised her hand and kissed it, leaving the hot tingling imprint of his lips behind. "But for the rest of today, she's all mine."

CHAPTER SEVEN

Alexander led the way to his car. He had the top down to take advantage of the beautiful day. "Where to? I'm at your disposal."

"Water." Bronwyn didn't have to think about. "Get me close to water."

He smiled and that smile gained potency every time she saw it. "You got it."

Alexander whipped through Greater Littleton and onto a narrow road following the coastline. Wind scrambled her hair into a frenzy, and salt laden air felt heavy with possibility.

He pulled over at a small yellow wooden shack. "Fish and chips," he said. "No visit to England is complete without it."

A cheerful woman with wind chapped cheeks grinned as they approached. "Who you got there with you, Alexander?"

"Bronwyn." Alexander motioned the shack's proprietor. "Meet Beatrice, Bea to her friends. Beatrice meet Bronwyn."

"Hi." Bronwyn felt suddenly shy.

"Aren't you a pretty thing?" Beatrice looked thrilled before glancing at Alexander. "For two?"

"If you would."

Beatrice handed them their fish and chips in boxes almost too hot to hold.

"I thought you served fish and chips in newspaper." Bronwyn shifted the box from one hand to the other.

Alexander grimaced. "We did, and then health and safety got their knickers in a twist about it."

"What's this?" She peered inside her box at the creamy sauce in a small plastic tub.

"Tartar sauce. You dip your fish in it." Alexander took her hand and led her behind the shack to a narrow, grass choked path. "And now to the water."

The path wound around a rocky dune and opened on to a pebbled beach. Alexander led her to a large boulder and helped her clamber to the top. The sea had worn a flat space perfect for sitting on the top, and the sun was warm on their heads.

The crash of the tide made conversation difficult, so Bronwyn ate her fish and chips and let the peace that always came with being close to water wash over her.

Alexander was watching her with his dark eyes. Eyes that dark could hide a wealth of secrets, and she got the sense there was so much more to him than appeared on the surface. She wanted to unwrap the layers of him and find out more. "What?"

He shook his head. "You look peaceful."

"I am." She popped another chip in her mouth. "I love water."

"I bet you do." He broke off a piece of fish and ate it. "You draw strength from it."

She didn't know how he could have guessed that. Gesturing the sea, she said, "It's so powerful. It makes me feel like anything is possible."

He nodded. "There's a theory that we're all drawn more strongly to one of the four elements."

"Deidre used to say something similar." Deidre would have loved to sit right here and eat delicious fish and chips. Bronwyn hoped that some part of Deidre was here with her.

"You look sad." Alexander cocked his head.

"It's nothing." She tried for a smile, but it wobbled off her lips. "Sometimes I miss my grandmother." She gestured their surroundings. "She would have loved this."

"Little witch." His face softened, and he slid his palm around her nape. "I am so sorry for all your losses."

His hand heated her nape. His thumb stroked her neck and electrified her skin.

"Why do you call me that?" Her limbs had a will of their own and leaned toward him like a sunflower tracking the sun.

Sultry heat lit his eyes as he studied her mouth. "Perhaps because you've cast a spell on me."

Sexual awareness aside, she had to laugh. "That's really lame."

"I know." He chuckled and brought his mouth closer. "This is for me."

If last night's kiss had been an exploration, this one was an invasion. His mouth claimed hers, owned it. His tongue stroked into her mouth. His hand cradled her head and tilted her like he wanted her.

Bronwyn surrendered to the raw masculinity of his kiss. Fisting her hands in his shirt, she hung on to him as the rest of her world went up like a bonfire. His mouth, his flavor, his skin, his scent, it consumed her and she, in turn, needed to devour.

Alexander's phone rang.

With a groan, he deepened the kiss.

She didn't care that they were sitting on a rock for anyone to see. He could do anything with her as long as he kept kissing her.

His phone stopped and started up again.

Bronwyn tore her mouth away from his. "Shouldn't you get that?"

"No." He bent his head and moved in for more kissing.

His phone started ringing a third time.

"Fuck." He snatched it up and read the caller display. Alexander went still. Expression blank, he stared at his phone. His face remained inscrutable, but a whole lot more seethed beneath his unnatural silence. He looked up. "I have to go."

"Is everything all right?" Bronwyn swallowed her disappointment and stood. She brushed sand and grease from her meal on her pants leg.

"Yes." Alexander studied her face as if he wanted to map it in his mind. "Bronwyn?"

All trace of desire was gone from his face, and a chill crept over her skin. "Yes?"

"Never mind." He shook his head and his tone lightened. "Unfortunately, I have to cut this short."

Neither of them spoke as he drove back to Greater Littleton. He stopped outside the pub and stretched his arm over the back of her seat. "I'll see you soon." Leaning in, he brushed her mouth with his. "Count on it."

The day dimmed, and the wind carried a new sharpness to it. Bronwyn shivered and hurried into the warmth of the pub.

ALEXANDER STOOD beside Rhiannon's altar, facing the gathered faithful, and steeled himself to witness the pointless waste of life. Rhiannon has summoned him away from his time with Bronwyn and demanded he help the twisted two, Edana and Fiona, set this crap up.

The faithful had started gathering with sundown. He'd been watching their repulsive shit for more years than he could count, and it still turned his stomach. Actually, that was a lie, and the true gut churner lay at his door. For at least half that time, he'd stood right by her side and drank the Kool-Aid. He'd even dispensed the Kool-Aid.

The melodramatic scene would almost make him laugh, if it

hadn't hidden something so dark it oozed through the air. Rhiannon loved a good dark powers *mise en scène.*

Thick, oily smoke from hundreds of candles created a heavy haze that burned his eyes. Candles covered every available surface and littered the floor. One unwary soul had already set the hem of their robe on fire and had to be carried out. There couldn't be a candle available anywhere south of London with the number of them crammed into the old school hall.

He kept his horror on ironclad lockdown, because there was where Rhiannon wanted him, and there was where he'd be. His own miserable life had stopped meaning as much to him about the time he'd been instrumental in the murder of ninety witches. Now, he served penance. His amends were to watch and know each life she took that he couldn't prevent was another failure. It was the sole reason he was still alive, because until Goddess awakened, he was the only one who could do anything about Rhiannon.

And Goddess was waking up. Tonight's ritual was all about stockpiling power for when Rhiannon needed it. Rhiannon had seen Bronwyn meet her coven sisters today, and it had spurred her to action. If the coven ever figured out who and what they were, and Bronwyn with them, Rhiannon would need extra power to combat them. Unlike the cré-witches, whose magic was constantly with them, Rhiannon had to steal power and squirrel it away for when she needed it.

The Cray cousins had been living in ignorance, and it had kept them alive, but now Mags was tapping too close to the truth vein. Even with her largely dormant powers, she'd managed to stumble over how important Bronwyn was.

Like peering through a rain-streaked window, Mags's gift gave her occasional clarity on the future. And she'd nailed this one. Bronwyn was the future, their future, as in the future of the cré-witches. Mags knew enough to know Bronwyn was important, but not how she was important, and that knowledge could very well get all of them dead.

In the meantime, Rhiannon shored up her magic, preparing for the battle to come and moving all her pieces into place.

The old school her cult had gathered in had been abandoned in the sixties as too small to meet the community's growing needs. Rhiannon had snapped it up from the village, and the council had been only too happy to make some money out of an obsolete asset.

Nobody wanted to miss one of Rhiannon's rituals, and the crowd was standing room only. They'd heard the stories of her true power. They gathered around her, the hopeful and the hopeless, searching for something greater than their ordinary lives. They believed in Rhiannon because they needed to, and tonight she would reward that faith.

Turned toward the door through which Rhiannon would appear, the crowd's faces bore a nauseating mix of excitement and fervor. Most of them had no idea what they were about to witness. Those who did know what was going down were as lost as the dead. Stupid and clueless, the lot of them, playing at being witches, playing with forces so beyond their control.

Just like the Baile witches. They had no idea who they were or what they were capable of either. He'd befriended the Cray women, convincing Rhiannon it was to know her enemy, but he'd grown really fond of them. Mags was delightfully vague, Niamh a sexy force of nature, Alannah had a heart of gold, and Sinead defined the word intense. They didn't deserve to die, and he would do whatever needed doing to make sure they didn't.

Heat and odor of so many bodies pressed together made him long to break a window, just so he could breathe. Nobody moved, nobody complained, because nobody in their right mind would mess with Rhiannon. Especially not as her mood grew fouler every day. Drawing attention to yourself invited a world of nasty to your door.

As her son, he'd been accorded the position of "honor" closest to the altar. Behind the altar—a reconstituted desk from the science lab—six robed and hooded acolytes caterwauled some tuneless, creepy as hell chant. It made him want to make ghost noises and creepy waggly fingers. Six acolytes, evil six, mark of the beast. Mark of the psychotic bitch, more like.

With her devotion to the dramatic, Rhiannon would love it. As much as she could love anything right now.

If Roderick woke, Baile would draw from him, and her defenses would grow stronger. Maeve, as a spirit walker, could open the secrets of the caverns to this current, clueless tiny coven.

The acrid scent of urine reached him. The venerated one had pissed himself.

Completely naked, and stretched across the altar, Clyde did his best to look "worthy" and not scared shitless. Poor, stupid bastard.

Alexander didn't know where Rhiannon found them, or how she managed to persuade them to give up their lives for her. But they did, in an almost endless supply.

Nobody had held Clyde down or drugged him senseless. Stupid fucker had walked right up to the altar and climbed aboard.

Macabre shadows made by flickered candlelight danced across the wall and ceiling. The cloying stink of incense joined the miasma of sweat and piss.

Rhiannon's sycophants sucked up the air in the room with their mounting excitement. At least half of them would be puking before Rhiannon was done. Most of those and a few others would finally clue in on what sort of devil they'd sold their souls to. Too late, because Rhiannon never let go once she had her claws in.

Then there were the select few whom he went out of his way to avoid. These were the psychopaths, the sick fucks who got off on the violence and the pain. Not surprisingly, Rhiannon's favorite kind of follower. Edana and Fiona fit neatly into the psychotic category.

If he ever got a chance to meet Goddess, he would ask her what she thought she was doing when she picked Rhiannon as one of her first four. If she really was this omniscient being, how did she not see right through Rhiannon and pick someone else?

Rhiannon had turned her back on being a cré-witch when she had decided being a goddess would suit her so much better. She'd been growing in power for over two thousand years, and tonight's macabre pageantry was a complete waste of time and effort. Rhiannon could do it in a back alley as effectively, but she loved an audience.

The chanting intensified and magic—the real kind—oozed into the hall. Those susceptible to it murmured to each other. The robed choir intensified their efforts. Deluded fools that they were.

The magic came from Rhiannon, waiting outside to make her entrance. She didn't share her jealously collected and guarded power, and she certainly wouldn't allow it to be diluted amongst this many people. She liked them to think their association with her gave them power.

The truth would devastate most of them, and seriously dent her fan club. Rhiannon couldn't give them any power because she didn't have any. Not since she'd been expelled from the cré-witch coven and her connection to Goddess severed. The power she wielded was stolen, corrupted, and forced to serve her.

The hall doors flew open and crashed into the wall on either side. The woman beside him jumped, someone screamed, and a number of people gasped. Rhiannon would be eating this up with a ladle.

Edana and Fiona leading the way, another four priests behind her, Rhiannon made a slow and stately procession through the center of the hall. People dropped to their knees in waves.

Not stupid enough to be the one man standing in this orgy of worship, Alexander did the same.

Her escort wore robes in the four colors corresponding to the four birth elements. Some part of Rhiannon would always be a cré-witch, and although she'd been separated from her birth element since the moment of her expulsion, that part of her still longed for the connection.

Pure white, and almost transparent, Rhiannon's robe gave her an ethereal quality. It also showed her naked beneath it. So much more than a son ever wanted to see of his mother.

Brushed into a gleaming curtain, her dark hair hung past her hips, and he chose to focus on that instead.

She drew parallel with him, stopped and held out her hand. "My son, my pride and joy, will you not join me?"

It wasn't a request, and Alexander bowed and took her hand. He schooled his features and led her in a procession around the altar. The more he allowed his distaste to show, the worse her display would get. Positioning Rhiannon behind the altar, and facing her congregation, Alexander stepped back. Blessedly, the choir gave it a rest.

Absolute silence greeted Rhiannon. Palpable excitement throbbed through the air.

Rhiannon drew hard on her stolen magic.

It ground against his nerve endings like a toothache. He didn't know how she did it, drew that much magic. Blood magic felt like taking a rusty razor blade to your internal organs. The more you drew, the deeper the cut. Judging by the echoes he was getting, Rhiannon must be in agony.

But the show must go on.

She picked up a black-handled dagger. "Behold the holy athame."

The holy athame came from the Jamie Oliver collection, where he'd ordered it online for her.

Her congregation threw up their hands. "Behold."

Fiona's eyes glinted, and Edana's cheeks flushed. They loved this as much as Rhiannon. He thanked his good sense every day that he'd never gone there with either of them. That Roderick couldn't say the same gave him a smug sense of satisfaction.

Not looking nearly as sure of his decision anymore, Clyde kept his gaze locked on the knife.

Rhiannon leaned down and kissed him, once on each cheek, each eyelid, and his forehead. "For your sacrifice, you will be forever remembered. We will speak your name with honor, and we will raise you to be revered amongst us."

Rhiannon would barely remember his name by the end of the day if she even knew it now.

What if he didn't play along? Yeah, right, and hardly the first time Alexander had that thought. Say he did the unthinkable, freed Clyde, and the two of them made a run for the door.

At a generous estimate, they had a twenty percent chance of reaching the door alive. Assuming he could get Clyde to make a break for it, and that was by no means a certainty.

Say they got lucky and made it out the building, then what? Rhiannon had people everywhere, from the citadels of power to the worst piss-soaked alley. There was nowhere he could go she wouldn't find him, except the one place barred to him. Baile.

"My son?" She held the knife out to him, the challenge in her eyes unmistakable.

Alexander's gut twisted. She was testing his loyalty, and with more than himself to think about now, he could not fail.

At least he could make sure Clyde didn't suffer too much. It was so much worse when he'd met them before, and Rhiannon knew that. This venerated being Clyde was no coincidence.

He made the first cut at the wrist. Not too deep, but enough to start the flow of blood.

Gasping, Clyde locked his gaze on Rhiannon.

"*Eas.*" Rhiannon's eyes glittered as she called to the east. "Show me the path that opens the way."

From the acolytes, the two wearing air element yellow robes stepped forward.

Rhiannon dipped her fingers in Clyde's blood. She anointed each acolyte's forehead in turn. "I worship the dawn. I celebrate the spring. I make this sacrifice to the waning moon, and I live this as youth."

By sheer will, Alexander forced his hand not to shake as he slashed Clyde's groin. He had to cut deeper to hit the femoral artery. The trick was not to nick it too deeply or the entire thing would be over too soon, and Rhiannon would choose someone else. Maybe the next someone would not be so willing to give up their life.

This time Clyde cried out.

Alexander locked it down, hard. He couldn't help Clyde now. Clyde had made several stupid decisions that landed him there, and if their roles were reversed—or worse, it was one of the Crays on the table—Clyde wouldn't hesitate.

"*Deas,*" Rhiannon called, her voice growing stronger.

Red-robed fire-element acolytes stepped forward.

"Show me the path of coming into being."

She went through the whole anointing thing again.

Blood dripped steadily from the altar to the floor. In the front row, one of the faithful paled as she stared at the growing pool of deep red blood. A soft murmur of distress from somewhere in the crowd broke the tense silence.

It was all very well to talk about blood sacrifice, get yourself loaded on a couple of gin and tonics at the local pub and arrive for the spectacle. But only the true psychopaths could stand here unaffected as a man bled to death.

"Please," Clyde whispered.

Alexander couldn't even look at him. The time to beg for his life had come and gone. He cut deep into the second wrist.

A look of displeasure crossed Rhiannon's face. She hated to be rushed.

Tough luck, bitch. Alexander moved to Clyde's neck, ready to make the final cut.

Rhiannon sped up through her anointing of the west.

Someone retched, followed by the patter of vomit hitting the floor. It wouldn't be long before the puking chain reaction set in.

Aaand there they went.

Without looking to see if Rhiannon was ready, he slashed the carotid.

She had two minutes tops to keep torturing the poor bastard.

Rhiannon rushed through the rest of her rigmarole.

It was all bullshit anyway. She didn't need the acolytes, the audience or the whole anointing with blood thing.

Agony twisted her features as the elemental life magic fought back. It hated what they did to it and every time subduing it was like a wild ride into hell. He got a certain satisfaction from watching the magic tear into her.

Shudders wracked her body. Her audience stared in horror as the fighting magic threw Rhiannon into a grizzly sort of St. Vitus's dance.

Edana and Fiona each took one of Clyde's wrists. Pain twisted their features as they shared Rhiannon's burden.

He could have done the same, helped her, drawn from the same blood magic she did and helped her overpower the magic. His loyalty didn't, and wouldn't, stretch that far. She knew he despised the blood magic, and still she chose to test him by drawing him into it.

If she wanted someone dead, then she could pay the full price for it.

The convulsions intensified, tossing her around like a ragdoll. She tumbled to the floor, still thrashing.

Edana was on her knees. Fiona clenched her hands into fists, holding on by sheer force of will.

Rhiannon was right to fear Maeve's awakening. Maeve could teach Bronwyn all she needed to know to waken the water cardinal point.

Distressed murmurs broke from the watchers.

A pale-faced acolyte, the blood a garish streak on her forehead, stepped forward. "What's happening?" she whispered. "Is our lady well?"

"She's fine." Alexander gave her an unconcerned smile. "Shouldn't be much longer now."

Rhiannon's convulsions intensified, and Alexander motioned the choir.

Fear and fervor driving them, they broke into a chant.

Alexander dropped a cloth into the pool of blood at his feet and then stood on it. Magic roared through his body like a flamethrower and burned him from within. He dug his hands into his thighs to hide his reaction, gritted his teeth until his jaw ached.

Abruptly Rhiannon stilled. Broken blood vessels crisscrossed the whites of her eyes. Blood dribbled from her nose as she gave him a triumphant smile. "It is done."

He really hoped so. Alexander helped her to her feet and tucked the blood-soaked rag out of sight.

Rhiannon's acolytes rushed around her. Someone started the "all hail" bullshit but Alexander tuned them out.

Leaning over, he shut Clyde's dead, staring eyes. "Goodbye," he whispered. "I hope wherever you are, it's better than where you came from."

CHAPTER EIGHT

In her dream, Bronwyn sat with Deidre in their kitchen at home, a house that would be hers when she returned. It was early on a summer morning, the air sticky and hot, greenery running wild in Deidre's garden. Beyond the garden, the dark blue smudge of the sea filled the horizon.

They sat at the scrubbed wooden table in the center of their ordinary, rather drab kitchen. Deidre cradled a mug of tea between her palms and she was smiling at Bronwyn.

Even as one part of Bronwyn registered this was a dream, Deidre seemed so real to her. The lightening of her lashes at the tips, the deep smile grooves on either side of her mouth, the sunlight catching the faint peach fuzz on her top lip that she refused to wax were all so heartbreakingly familiar. Bronwyn could even smell the wood and jasmine that she always associated with Deidre.

Birds outside went quiet. Sunlight dimmed, and she and Deidre looked out the window. A large cloud moved over the sun and Deidre frowned. "That's not right."

Rolling and expanding, the cloud grew darker and thicker.

"So wrong." Deidre's favorite mug, the one with the picture

of the pillar of cats that used to make her smile, dropped from her hands and hit the table. Tea splashed over her lap and the mug rolled off the table, hit the tile floor and shattered.

Deidre stared at the cloud, now black and covering the entire sky. Her eyes widened, eyes the same shade of green as Bronwyn's. "It's coming."

Bronwyn wanted to run, but she couldn't move. She was stuck in her chair with her arms useless by her sides. She opened her mouth to scream at Dee to run, but no sound came out.

The black cloud filled the garden. Nothing moved, leaves withered on their branches and died and still the black cloud came.

It swelled through the garden and pressed against the kitchen window. The window moaned under the pressure.

Bronwyn's scream got trapped in her skull. Copper and decay made the air reek.

"Go," Deidre whispered. "She's coming for you. It's you she wants."

I can't leave you. But the words didn't come out.

"You must live." Pale and shocked, Deidre looked at her. "You are the one."

The kitchen window cracked, jagged lines shooting across the glass.

"Go." Deidre's wood and jasmine scent rose, more intense than Bronwyn had ever smelled it before. "Everything. All of it, has all been about you."

The window imploded in a shower of glass.

Bronwyn screamed and woke in her bed in the Hag's Head. Her breathing was heavy and labored, and sweat covered her body. She could still feel the oily stench of the thick black cloud,

She snapped on a light. The lopsided wardrobe faced her bed and beside it a chest of drawers of a darker veneer. The red gingham armchair in the corner still held yesterday's clothes.

Everything as it was before she fell asleep, yet she shivered.

Outside the window, a halfmoon rode the sky above the sea. And that's where she needed to be. Some people loved mountains, others liked rolling grasslands, but for her it was always water. Dee had told her she'd been swimming almost before she could walk properly. At just two, she'd apparently walked straight into the ornamental lake at a public park. Fortunately Deidre had been there to pull her out. That had been the first incident of many, and for safety's sake, Deidre had taught her to swim.

"What the hell was that, Dee?"

Of course Deidre didn't answer. Deidre had died a year ago.

Bronwyn ached for the tranquility the sea gave her, so she got out of bed and hauled on her clothes from the night before. Taking only her room key and her phone with her, she crept through the silent inn.

The night air smelled odd and clung to her skin in a way that reminded her too vividly of her dream.

Deidre had been trying to warn her of something. The knowing whispered of danger. She checked her phone. It was three fifty-three in the morning, and the village of Greater Littleton was deserted.

A stray cat sat on a wall and made eye contact, watching Bronwyn pass. Maybe going out alone at night in a strange place was not the safest thing to do, but her need for water drowned her caution.

The closer she drew to the beach, the more her sense of foreboding quieted. She slipped between a fish and chips shack and a store that in the daytime sold sunscreen, hats, and espadrilles. The stony beach crunched beneath her Chucks as she picked her way to the water's edge.

The tide foamed and bubbled up the stones toward her, ran over her Chucks and the icy cold seeped through the canvas. The air was lighter here, but lingering heaviness felt like cobwebs hanging in her face. Keeping her feet in the water, she followed the shoreline as it meandered closer to the cliff Baile perched on.

As soon as she clambered between huge boulders to a small tidal beach, silver in the moonlight, the nasty sensation disappeared, like a soap bubble popping.

Yes, Deidre's voice whispered in the darkness, so softly it merged with the gentle onshore breeze. Other women's whispers rode that breeze.

Welcome.

Sister.

Water calls, Sister.

The voices should have freaked her out, but they were strangely comforting. They pressed back the dread left by her dream.

A sane person would be running away from disembodied voices in the middle of the night, especially considering the average lifespan of the women in her family. She didn't know if the same curse, or genetics, or plain bad luck ran in the men in her family, because the men never stuck around for long enough to be relevant.

Alexander had crashed into her life so unexpectedly and with the force of a derailed train that she had to question her response to him. Was she doomed to repeat the Beaty woman legacy? Perhaps like her, the other women in her family had met a man, had this intense attraction and acted on it. Only to have him leave before the sweat was dry on the sheets.

Tucked against the cliff, a small path rose from the beach, and Bronwyn took it. Wind pushed against her back, as if it were trying to help her with the steep climb.

Bronwyn had no idea where she was going, but she knew she had to get there. Conviction bloomed in her as she followed the path snaking upwards along the cliff edge.

Abruptly it ended in the dark maw of a cave entrance.

Leaning her hands on her knees, Bronwyn stopped and caught her breath and gave her aching thighs a rest. She must have been at the entrance to the caverns that ran beneath Baile that Hermione had told them about.

She took a tentative step onto the wide ledge in front of the cave entrance. Dare she go in there? She was straight up trespassing and being that dumb bitch from horror movies, the one who went into the haunted house, followed the weirdo with a chainsaw, or was not content to say Candyman once, twice, three times or four.

"Bronwyn." Mags appeared so suddenly out of the cave that Bronwyn jumped and may even have shrieked.

"Jesus." Her heart was trying to leap out her throat. "You scared the shit out of me."

In the moonlight, Mags looked even paler than ever. She turned her face to the breeze and closed her eyes. Her expression was almost blissful for a moment. "Sorry. The dream has us both spooked."

"Dream?" Bronwyn's hackles rose.

"The dark cloud." Mags looked at her. Her eyes glowed opaque silver. "The one that's coming for you."

Bronwyn couldn't think of a single intelligible thing to say, so she stared at Mags.

"I get these dreams." Mags shrugged as if she hadn't completely blown Bronwyn's mind. "Dreams. Feelings like premonitions. Not all the time but they always come true." Mags smiled suddenly. "Like knowing you were coming."

"You keep saying that to me." Bronwyn's mouth dried.

"I know." Mags wrinkled her nose. "Niamh tells me I freak people out. Did I freak you out?"

"Yes."

"I thought I had. I was going to fix it when you came to lunch, but you're here now." Mags closed her eyes and turned her face up. A light breeze ruffled the ends of her long hair. She looked like some strange sort of moon goddess in her long pale dress.

Trust, Dee whispered. *We rest here.*

"I need answers." There wasn't space for lies between them, so Bronwyn went with the truth. "I came to Greater Littleton looking for answers."

"Hmm." Mags opened her eyes and nodded. "Best we have some tea then."

Bizarrely, Bronwyn couldn't think of a better thing to do, so she followed Mags up the stairs cut into the side of the cliff. No handrail guarded the sides, and a wrong step would send her hurtling to the rocks far, far, far beneath them.

She was frankly amazed she'd climbed that high. The tide was starting to eat its way up the beach, and she wouldn't be going home the way she'd come. A tug at her heart made her feel like she might be home after all. When she'd made the decision to come looking for answers, she'd had no idea how strange her search would get, or how emotionally draining it would become.

Alexander had not seen her later last night, as he'd said he would, and she hated how much she hated that he hadn't.

At the top of the stairs, Mags opened an arched wooden door in the stone wall and led Bronwyn into the bailey. The wall blocked the wind, and the same sense of peace and rightness Bronwyn had experienced last time she was in Baile settled over her.

"Here we go." Mags opened a door and light spilled out.

Blinking against the sudden brightness, Bronwyn followed Mags into a kitchen. It hadn't been part of the castle tour, and despite looking like a step back in time, the kitchen had a lived-in feel. A huge range sat in the alcove that had housed the original hearth. A modern dishwasher beneath the super-size enamel farm sink looked completely out of place.

That farm sink hadn't come from Restoration Hardware.

A small pack of dogs appeared through an archway and came to greet her. Of various sizes and breeds, they lolled their tongues at her and invited her to share the joke of having tea in the wee hours of the morning.

"Hey." Niamh drifted into the kitchen with a huge ginger cat cradled in her arms. "The dogs are excited about you being here."

On Niamh, sloppy track pants and an oversized *Winchester Family Business* T-Shirt managed to look movie star sexy.

Mags filled a copper kettle and put it on the range. "Tea?"

"Please." Niamh dropped into a ladderback chair and leaned her elbows on the rectangular scrubbed oak table in the center of the kitchen. "Did you drive here?"

"I walked up from the beach." Nobody seemed the least bit phased by her being in their kitchen at four a.m. "I had a bad dream and went for a walk."

"Ugh." Niamh pulled a face. "You had that too? The animals woke me from it, but what the bloody hell was that?" She looked to Mags for answers.

Mags shrugged, but a frown creased her brow. "Whatever it was, it wasn't good."

"True that." Bronwyn's agreement was enthusiastic.

"Hello, Bronwyn." Alannah slunk into the kitchen with a beautiful smile like she was hitting the Paris runway. "Your shoes are wet. There are some slippers warming by the range."

"Right." Her Converses were making puddles on the flag-stone floors.

Alannah went over to the range and brought her a pair of slippers. "Here we are."

Bronwyn took the seat opposite Niamh and slipped her wet Chucks off.

Alannah picked them up and propped them near the range. "There." She smiled. "Those will be dry and toasty before you know it."

"Thank you."

A thump sounded from somewhere beyond the kitchen. "Motherfucker! Niamh! That fucking badger is blind."

"Sinead." Alannah rolled her eyes. "I'd better get the coffee on. Would you prefer that to tea?"

"Yes, please."

Alannah looked as close to an angel as Bronwyn had ever seen, and she moved about the kitchen like she was in her domain. She shooed Mags away and got a large brown pottery teapot from a shelf near the range. "Now." She smiled at Bronwyn. "Scones, I think."

"Fucking hell, Niamh." Sinead appeared in the doorway wearing a scowl. Her hair was escaping in a snarl from an elastic band and she wore men's striped pjs. "That badger nearly tripped me down the stairs."

"He can't help it." Niamh shrugged. "He's blind."

"I know that." Sinead threw herself in the seat beside Bronwyn. "Hi."

"So then watch where you're going." Niamh cuddled her cat and stroked a dog's head at the same time. "Because, clearly, he can't."

Alannah brought a white enamel pitcher to the table along with a stack of glasses. She distributed the glasses and poured water into each. "Drink." She pushed a glass at her twin. "Coffee won't be much longer." She smiled shyly at Bronwyn. "I make my own you know."

"What?" Bronwyn blinked in the radiance of that smile.

"Coffee. Grow our own beans and roast them too." Sinead grunted. "We've got a knack for growing things."

Niamh snorted and gently placed the cat on the floor. The dogs sniffed it as it passed and then followed the cat to the hearth. They all found a place and lay down. A weasel shot out from beneath a cupboard and joined the animal family at the hearth. They all found a place like they did this every day.

Mags caught her watching and winked. "Niamh has a way with animals."

Her mind might be slow, but she was starting to get the gist here. "Dreams and premonitions." She pointed at Mags.

Mags nodded.

"Growing things." She glanced at Alannah.

"Yes." Alannah gave her an encouraging smile and carried on mixing dough in a wooden bowl. "Sinead and I have the same knack. Probably because we're twins." The kettle boiled, and she put her bowl down and poured water into the teapot. She swished the hot water around to warm the pot and tossed it away. From a tin canister, she added three spoons of tea and then more hot water. It was like a beautiful ritual to watch, and it made Bronwyn's heart hurt. Deidre had always turned making tea into an elegant ritual.

A cold nose nudged her thigh, and Bronwyn looked down into the melting brown eyes of a retriever.

"You're sad," Niamh said. "She can feel it."

"And you're good with animals." Bronwyn put her final piece of information into place.

Alannah brought cups to the table and then the teapot. She put a mug of coffee in front of Sinead and then Bronwyn. It smelled like pure heaven, and Bronwyn took a deeper sniff.

"Milk?" Alannah laughed. "Or do you like cream like they do on the telly?"

Bronwyn laughed with her. She didn't know how she could not. "Cream please."

"I'll get it." Sinead shoved back from the table. "Shit!"

Her glass toppled over, and water ran across the table.

Bronwyn's hand shot out, and she reached for honey and sage. The combined scents hit the air and the water stopped running and sat still on the table.

They all stared at the static water that should be running off the side of the table.

"Well, that answers what you're doing here." Alannah dropped a cloth on the water. "Sinead and I draw earth. Mags is air, and Niamh is fire. We always did wonder why none of us drew water."

Water calls, Sister. One of the voices on the beach had said that. Bronwyn wasn't sure what this all meant, but inside, her confusion stilled and cleared. Like a door thrown wide, enlightenment streamed in, and Bronwyn knew she was exactly where she needed to be.

What she didn't know was why. "I'm supposed to be here," she said. "There's something here I'm supposed to do."

Mags rolled her eyes. "That's what I've been telling you."

CHAPTER NINE

B ronwyn made it back to the Hag's Head after lunch. Niamh dropped her off in the farting, smelling Land Rover and left with a cheery wave and a hoot as she gunned down the road, causing a couple of teen boys to leap for the sidewalk and safety.

Entering the dim, dark wood wainscoted quiet of the pub, Bronwyn had the surreal sense of walking in someone else's life for the last few hours. She felt like she'd bought a lottery ticket expecting to win a ton of money but had won her own island instead. It was super cool to be the winner, and the island was so much more than she ever believed she would win, but the course of her life had shifted, and she needed to catch up.

She was a witch, and if the Cray women were to be believed, and she totally did believe them, she was a cré-witch. According to Sinead, her entire family must have been cré-witches, going generations back. It was so much more than she'd thought she'd find. Knowing others like her were there, in Baile Castle, made her feel she could claim who and what she was for the first time in her life without the inner wince.

"I'm a witch," she whispered as she climbed the creaky stairs to her room. She'd always known her affinity for water, and Deidre had guessed there might be witches out there who drew from the other three elements, but now she knew for sure.

In the kitchen, she'd watched as Niamh drew a spark from the air, how Mags could get the air to move about them, and seen for herself the massive explosion of plants in Baile's kitchen gardens. When Deidre had died, she'd felt the loss of her grandmother, but also the loss of the one being in the world who was like her. Now she knew there were at least four others like her, and that meant there could be more.

Little witch.

"Bronwyn." Alexander emerged out of the gloomy shadows in the upper hallway.

Her nape prickled and the familiar wash of heat swept her body. "Alexander."

"Yes." There was a tautness about him that put her on guard. "I've been waiting for you."

That news made her happier than it should have. With all the other revelations she was having, it didn't seem a good time for romance, but whenever he was near, she yearned to get closer. "I've been at—"

"Baile. Yes, I'm aware." He stuck his hands in the pockets of his dark gray dress pants. "Are you free now?"

"I was going to take a nap." It had been one day since she'd seen him last, but she wanted that time with him back. For an insane moment, she was almost overcome by the desire to invite him to join her for that nap.

"I wish I could," he said, as if she'd spoken her thought aloud. He took her hand in a firm, warm grasp. "But I need to speak to you."

"What is it?" She curled her fingers around his. Her hand belonged in his. Even as the thought came, she shoved it aside. Having these thoughts about a man she'd only recently met and barely knew was insane.

"Little witch. Bronwyn." His dark eyes carried a weight of sadness so heavy she didn't know how he bore it. It reached inside her and wrapped around her heart. "You have to know..." He cleared his throat. "Take a drive with me."

Whatever else he had been about to say, the thing he didn't say, that was the thing she wanted to hear. Being with him was so confusing and exhausting. Emotional currents swirled and eddied around them, and with the dream and wee-hour tea parties, she'd barely slept the night before. "I really am tired."

"I know." He cupped her cheek in his palm. "None of this is fair to you. Come for a drive with me."

When he asked with his heart in his eyes like that, she could deny him nothing. "Okay."

"My lord." A chambermaid appeared at the top of the stairs with a pile of snow-white bedlinen in her arms. "Do you need anything, Miss Beaty?"

"No, thank you, I was—"

"Make up Miss Beaty's room, Stella." Alexander wrapped his arm around her waist. He pressed her against his side and planted a hot kiss on her neck. "We'll be back shortly."

"Right you are, my lord." Stella's eyes gleamed. "That is excellent news, my lord."

Bronwyn's skin tingled from his kiss, but at the same time, it weirded her out. To her way of thinking, they were nowhere near the sort of intimacy he'd implied to Stella. Also, why the hell was he bothering to share any detail of their relationship with Stella?

"Come." He slipped an arm around her shoulders and led her down the stairs.

He took her around back of the pub to where his car waited in a small parking lot wedged between buildings. Opening the door for her, he motioned her inside.

"What was all that about?" Bronwyn pointed to the pub. "And you keep calling me little witch." She held up a hand to stop him from speaking. "Don't tell me it's my imagination. I've had about all the strange shit I can take right now."

"I know." Sighing, he scrubbed a hand across his face. "But come for a drive with me, and I'll answer your questions."

Once she was in the car he drove through the village and took the road to the castle. As far as she knew, this road only went one place.

Bronwyn turned in her seat. "We're going to Baile."

"Eventually," he said and kept driving.

More riddles and half answers. "Alexander." She put as much steel as she could into her voice. "Pull over. I want those answers now. I've just left Baile. I can't go back there now."

"Can you give me ten more minutes?" He glanced at her. "Then you'll understand."

Fool that she was, Bronwyn nodded.

When they reached Baile's drawbridge, he pulled the car to the shoulder and climbed out.

Bronwyn got out before he could come around to her side.

Sadness was back in his eyes, and she wanted to cry for him, and for some strange reason, she wanted to cry for her too.

"Little witch." He cradled her face. "I call you this because that's what you are."

She started that he knew that. She'd only fully admitted the truth to herself this morning. "I don't..." It seemed best to say nothing so she trailed off.

"You are a water witch," he said and kissed her forehead. "And unless I miss my guess, you are a healer as well."

Fear tiptoed into the bright, sparkly cocoon he wove around her with his touch and his words. He shouldn't know these things, couldn't know these things. "Who are you?"

"Give me a second on that one." He trailed his lips to her cheek.

It was hard to think past the touch of his lips, and the gentle scrape of his beard. "Why?"

"Once I tell you who I am, you will never look at me the same." He drew back and his gaze searched her eyes. "I want to remember the way you're looking at me now forever. I want to see the man I wish I was reflected back at me."

"I don't understand." Tears prickled behind her lids. It sounded like he was saying goodbye, and it felt that way too. They hadn't even gotten to know each other, and he was walking away. The wrongness of him leaving resonated through her. "Tell me."

"Your ancestor came from here." He nodded toward Baile. "Almost four hundred years ago, she would have been a member of this coven, and a healer."

"You can't know that."

"But I do know this, my little witch. And so much more." He kissed her, a soft brush of his mouth over hers. "I know because healing is hereditary, and when I touch your hands, I can feel the power in them. I know because when you reach for your gift, I smell the honey and sage of it. I know because I was there."

"Eh?" She must have misheard him. Either that or he was nuts. "This isn't funny."

"I'm guessing your ancestor was away from Baile the night the coven was attacked." When she tried to pull away, he tightened his hold on her face. "Healers were often out of the castle. She might even have had a coimhdeacht with her, and he got her to safety. Either way, she escaped the coven massacre and went to America."

"Let go of me." He must have been making fun of her desire to connect with her heritage. All this crazy talk and using words she didn't recognize. "I want to go back now."

"You can't go back." He shook his head. "I lied to get you into the car." Jerking his head at the car he said, "I have your packed bags in the boot."

Outrage swept through her and she wrenched away from him. "I...what...what the hell!"

"I was hoping you would stay at Baile this morning, because that's where you need to be, behind Baile's wards." He looked as sane as the next man, but the crap coming out of his mouth was certifiable.

She marched around to his trunk and popped it. Like he'd said, her suitcase and carry-on were in there. "Son of a bitch. You had no right to touch my stuff. What the hell is wrong with you?"

"Listen to me" He grabbed her by the shoulders and gave her a small shake. "You're going to need to listen and do it well."

The nerve of the asshole. She didn't find him one bit sexy now. "Listen to me, you moth—"

"If you don't get inside Baile's wards, and stay there, the same thing will happen to you that happened to your grand-mother, your sister, your aunt, your mother." His gaze bored into her. "The same thing will happen to you that happened to all the women in your family."

"Are you threatening me?" Pulse spiking, fear thrummed through her.

"No, sweeting." His face gentled. "I'm trying to save you."

"From what?" When he didn't speak fast enough for her, she planted her palms on his chest and shoved. "Talk!"

He barely rocked back. "Goddess cannot wake until she has a witch from each element. We thought all the water witches were extinct, but you were in hiding."

She had questions, so many, and yet her brain couldn't form the right words into sentences, so she gaped at him.

"It took Rhiannon time to find you, but she did, and she's been killing the women in your family who manifest the gift. One at a time, until you're the last one left."

Her feet didn't feel solid around her and the cliff, the sea, his face all blurred and swirled. She thought she might faint. "You can't know this. This can't be true."

"You are the last water witch, Bronwyn, and without you, Goddess will never wake." He pulled her into his arms. "You're going to have to get over your freak out, because we're out of time, and there's more you need to know."

She fought his hold. If she heard any more, her head might explode. "There can't be."

"Listen to me." He held her against him, refusing to let her struggle free. "You must listen to me. If you keep walking around in ignorance, it will kill you. And you cannot die, little witch. I will not let that happen."

"Why?" She stayed stiff in his hold, but the betraying softening was already invading her muscles.

"Because the way you feel when I'm around. This impossible fucking craving to be close to me, I have it too." He kissed the top of her head. "You are my destiny, Bronwyn, and I'm only now grasping the full extent of that."

His words, the startling sincerity of his voice, reached inside her and quieted her.

"I was created for you," he said. "And I've been waiting all these years for you. I had no idea when I found you that I would crave just to be near you."

"Please." She pressed her face into his neck. Not sure what she was asking of him, but sure that she needed it like her next heartbeat.

"Ironically, it's because I was created for you that I can never have you."

It was crazy, but he broke her heart with those words. "You can, I'm right here. I don't understand most of this, and I'm terrified, but you're the only thing I am certain of."

"You can't be." He drew back far enough to look at her. "You belong first to Goddess, and she needs you, and the rest of us need Goddess. Without her, we're fucked."

Bronwyn didn't get half of what he was saying. She only got that he was walking away from her before they'd even started. A tiny part of her brain registered she wasn't asking the questions she should be asking. That she was focusing on the wrong thing.

"There's a prophecy," he said, his beautiful eyes intent on hers. "The son of death shall bear the torch that lights the path. And the daughter of life shall bring forth water nascent and call it onto the path of light. Then they will bear fruit. And this fruit will be the magick. The greatest of magick and the final magick."

"That has nothing to do with me." She shook her head, but she couldn't shake the sick feeling he was telling the truth.

"You are the daughter of life." He smiled. "And I'm the son of death. In your heart, you know it's true."

She stared at him. Deidre and her dream flooded back to her.

"There are forces that want the child we would create." Alexander laughed, but it held no real humor. "Our child will be the greatest and the final magic, and there are forces that will kill to control that child."

"This is nuts." It seemed such a gross understatement that it made her laugh. Once she started to laugh, she couldn't seem to stop.

"The story Hermione told you is true." He spoke over her hysterical laughter. "Almost the entire coven was massacred in one night. They were massacred by the same being who wants our child. She tried to overthrow Goddess that night, and she failed. Since then, Goddess has been dormant, but that you're here now is a sign she's ready to awaken."

"You keep talking about a goddess." She battled her bizarre laughter under control. "I don't even know who that is."

"She is who you serve." His expression grew wistful. "She is why the cré-witches came into being. Your coven sisters will tell you about her."

Sadness, soul deep mourning, pierced her. There had been many more coven sisters and they were all gone.

Alexander growled and shook his head. "There's so much to tell you and not enough time for all of it." He cleared his throat. "You think you came here to find your past, but you're here because you're fulfilling a deeper purpose in a game that is bigger than both of us. You're here to save the cré-witches by waking up Goddess." He raised her hand and kissed it. "And Goddess must wake."

"You can't be serious about this." She felt stretched taut beneath her skin. "Where does that prophecy thing fit into this?"

"They have dovetailed into one person. You." He shrugged. "Goddess always did like a neat plan."

Her mind refused to absorb the information. Words were being fired at her like missiles, and they exploded around her and shattered her world. "This isn't real."

"It's real." He tightened his grip almost painfully on her hand. "And you're out of time. Rhiannon knows you're here, and she knows how to get to you."

"Rhi—what are you talking about?" And then, like she was a complete fucking girl, tears streamed down her face. She didn't even know why she was crying, but it all felt too much.

"I know this is a lot. Strangely enough, that will be the least of my sins against you when you come to make sense of all this." He gripped her shoulders. "For now, understand this. I have never wanted to flout my fate more than I do now." And he kissed her.

Hot and hungry, he devoured her mouth with his.

She tasted the despair and desperation in his kiss, and she wanted to take it away.

Then he released her and looked beyond her.

Niamh and Mags walked through the gatehouse surrounded by Niamh's usual collection of animals.

"Mags knew you would be here, and the animals sensed Bronwyn," Niamh said. "What's going on Alexander?"

"Bronwyn can tell you." As if it hurt him physically, he grimaced and stepped away from her. "She's had a shock, and she's going to need you when she recovers." Alexander unpacked her luggage from his trunk and put it on the road in front of Niamh. "Take her inside the wards and keep her there." His face was so cold it made her shiver. "If she leaves, she's as good as dead. Don't doubt it for a second. In your library, I want you to look up Rhiannon. When you find that information, know that she's back, and she's stronger than ever. There's a fight coming, and you ladies need to wake the fuck up in a hurry and get ready."

CHAPTER TEN

"On the subject of waking the fuck up." Alexander stood at the base of the statue. In his long, long—and really, it warranted a third—long life, he'd come to a couple of realizations. Firstly, people didn't really change. For the most part, they recycled the same patterns of greed, lust, envy and fear. Those who broke the pattern were few and far between, and generally ended up getting devoured by the masses.

Secondly, life had highs and lows, but most of living took place in the endless plain of nothing in particular running between the troughs and peaks.

And thirdly, the one he was about to shove into motion, was that life presented you with defining moments. The problem being, life didn't announce them with trumpets and streamers. You had to recognize defining moments to act on them. Generally, they popped into your conscious mind, often as a splendidly bad idea with gruesome and repellant repercussions.

He put his leather satchel down and dropped his head back to stare at the sky. He'd always loved the night sky. Stars littered the darkness like pinpricks of hope in a vast fabric of heinous. Dear Goddess, he was getting maudlin. You would think after all these hundreds of years, he'd have had his fill of living. He didn't know how normal people did it with their precious few years.

Standing before his defining moment, all he could think was he'd never gotten the girl. He hadn't, and now wouldn't get to ride into the sunset with Bronwyn, white hat firmly in place. As a concept, he could live with it, but since meeting Bronwyn—knowing the warmth of her skin, the taste of her kiss—it seemed a damn shame.

The night of the coven massacre, Goddess's first three had used what residual power they had to cast a spell from the shadow realm, drawing Baile's wards far enough onto the village green to protect the petrified forms of Roderick and Maeve. Baile shouldn't be allowing him this side of her wards, but it was another of those mysteries he didn't have time to unravel. Gritting his teeth against the blood magic backlash, he pulled the athame from the bag. Clyde's blood was still on it and resonating blood magic. If the poor bastard had still owned a soul, he would have been able to see Alexander use his life force for some good.

The athame was bad enough, but the cloth he'd used to soak up the blood shrieked so loud it wouldn't surprise him if Rhiannon could hear it. By the time she worked it out, the job would be done, the die cast, and his true allegiance revealed.

He ran the athame's wickedly sharp blade over his palm. In a sort of hypnotized horror, he watched his blood mix with Clyde's on the blade. It dripped through his fingers to the pale gray concrete plinth. Rhiannon didn't know that Baile would let him past her wards. If she had known, without a doubt, she would have used his ability.

"Air," he whispered.

Wind rose in protest, the element trying to escape his mastery, flattening the grass on the green and shaking through the leaves of the oak trees.

Bronwyn. Tiny and fiery and pure of purpose to her gleaming cré-witch soul. His little witch and his defining moment, his fork in the path, the cattle prod up his pampered arse to get him to act. After tonight, nothing would be the same again. Tonight, he declared a side and drew his line in the sand.

Blood flowed freely down his wrist to his elbow and Alexander wrapped the cloth with the dead man's blood around it. Blood magic hacked through him like a rusty scythe.

"Water." The agony of blood magic made his head swim. Rhiannon was so much stronger than he.

Dimly the tide crashed into the rocks on the beach. A water fountain across the green bubbled into life and shot a stream of water into the air.

Alexander brought water into line with air and wound them in a ribbon of power. He took the dark oozing force of blood magic and fed it from the power ribbon.

"Earth." The ground beneath his feet shuddered. The elements were things of life that recoiled from death magic. His head pounded and his heart raced as he gripped earth and wound it with air and water.

Above him, the dark cloud of blood magic rolled into being, and reached its obliterating tentacles for the strongest source of life magic, the statue.

The three elements struggled against his mastery. Clyde's corrupted blood stopped his hand from healing, and he bled freely, the entire cloth soaked now and dripping, droplets hissing and smoking as they hit the earth.

Alexander pulled on his remaining strength. "Fire."

Streetlamps around the green flared and exploded in a shower of sparks.

The four elements wove tighter and tighter into the power thread. His breathing was labored, and he grew lightheaded as he forced the two magics together. Lifting his bleeding hand, he pressed it against the stature. "Wake up, you son of a whore. We're out of time."

———

MAGIC. *It reappeared so suddenly she was not ready for it. It was not magic as she knew it either. This magic grabbed for her with harsh grasping fingers. Tainted fingers that rampaged like fever through her body. The torment hammered her, and she screamed for it to stop, but nobody heard her in the void.*

Magic ripped at her belly, and she tried to make it stop, but it kept coming in relentless waves. Not content with her belly, the magic fastened around her heart as well, then her throat, and climbed to her forehead and tightened in an excruciating band.

Magic bored into her mind and tore open her memories. She had a name, and her name was Maeve.

Deeper dove the magic and yanked more memories to the surface.

There had been danger, so much danger they had feared for their survival. The end of the cré-witches had come. The final thirteen had stained Goddess with their blood magic and sent her into stasis.

They gathered around her, the dead thirteen, their souls now wraiths hanging between life and death for all eternity. Forever silenced, forever cut off from Goddess, never to reincarnate again.

Gray and disembodied, they stared at her through hollow gray eye sockets. They had stood guard for her all through her long sleep.

How long?

Colleen had been there, and Lavina, with poor damaged Hester. They had given their souls to protect her.

Years sped past her in a confusing blur of images, sounds, and smells.

Rhiannon had ripped through the wards and brought death and destruction to Baile. For the sake of their future, Maeve had been chosen to do this.

She reached for Baile, for some sense of the castle, but there was nothing there. Panic increased her heartbeat. She was alone in this endless nothing with a strange, foul magic pulling at her.

Blood magic. The same thing that had put her here, but subtly different. Her element of fire rose like a shining red rope and wound about her.

Gritting her teeth against the pain, Maeve quested toward fire. Fire would never hurt her. Fire demanded she wake. Fire had been alone for too long, dormant, misunderstood and abandoned. It reached ravenously for the power in her and lit her from within.

Maeve touched on the blossoming magic. Lily and orange pierced the abyss. The other magic was still there, still pulling, but lily and orange dominated it now, shoving it away from her.

She didn't know what awaited her at the end of the dark tunnel she traversed. Ahead, fire pulled her and lily and orange rose to assist her. Her magic, the touch of it infinitely sweet and dearly missed.

Would Rhiannon be waiting for her at the end of this tunnel? Could Roderick protect her? Her heart beat faster at the idea of Roderick.

Roderick, her coimhdeacht, whom she had only begun to appreciate. Her last memory was of Roderick, looking into her eyes, his strong arms holding her, as he threw himself into the void with her. Please, Goddess, grant that he had survived the void. She pushed lily and orange into the bond.

Silence. Dead echoing silence.

And then...there. So indistinct she might have missed it. She sensed him. A new sensation took hold of her and shook her. Laughter. Of course, Roderick was there. Roderick was far too stubborn to leave her, and she could not imagine an existence without him.

A sound thumped in her ear. It itched. Then it came again,

vibrating through her head, and she did not care for it. The sound grew stronger, more insistent and settled into a steady rhythm.

Da da dum.

It was her heartbeat, growing stronger with every moment. Air rushed into her chest and forced her to take the first real breath in she knew not how long.

MAEVE OPENED HER EYES. She drew night air into her lungs and registered unfamiliar smells. The grass beneath her hands was familiar, and she dug her fingers into it. Something was smothering her, and she pushed to get free.

A groan sounded in her ear.

"Roderick?" Her voice rasped, unused and strange to her newly awakened ears.

"Steady," a man spoke. The voice sounded vaguely familiar, but she couldn't place it. "You're on the village green."

Roderick's chest rose and fell against her back as he drew in a gigantic breath. "Blessed."

"Coimhdeacht." Her guardian protector, the man who had linked his life with hers for as long as she lived. "Roderick."

Above them the moon hovered in a cloud-strained sky. She blinked at the brightness of it, so beautiful she wished she could touch it.

"Maeve?" Roderick's muscles twitched and rippled against her. "You are well?"

"I believe so." She touched her face and found reassurance in the familiar tilt to her nose tip, the curve of her lips, the line of her brows and the cut of her jawbone. Whatever else she found, she was still Maeve. And she was awake again.

No sense of the foul miasma of Rhiannon's magic lingered about her, but someone had woken her. She could sense the source of the strange magic standing to the left of her, and Maeve turned her head.

A man with dark hair crouched beside them. He looked pained, his dark eyes blazing at her. She knew this man. Her gut twisted. She feared this man.

Roderick sensed her fear, she felt him grow alert through the bond. He pushed her behind him and lunged forward. Muscles unused sent him crashing to his knees in front of Alexander.

"Whoreson." Roderick rasped painfully. He reached for his sword but overbalanced and crashed into the ground.

The foul magic vanished, and Alexander laughed. "It's been a while since someone called me that. I rather think I've missed it."

"I'll kill you." Roderick growled and struggled to all fours. He stayed there panting. Through the bond, his pain lashed at Maeve, more than she believed any being could bear.

"I'm sure you will." Alexander handed them a strange transparent vessel filled with clear liquid. "Water. You'll need it."

Roderick recoiled from it. "You think I would drink anything you offered."

"Right." Alexander shook his head. He tipped the vessel to his lips and drank. "See? And really, as much as I've missed our spats, you're going to have to get yourself and your witch behind Baile's walls."

"Baile." Roderick quested for the castle. He frowned. "Where is she?"

"She's there." Alexander handed them the water again. "But she needs you about as much as you need her right now."

Swaying and lurching, Roderick managed to rise into a crouch. He reached an arm behind and kept her against his back. "I don't need steel to kill you."

"That's debatable." Alexander raised his brow.

It was unfair that such a beautiful face concealed a soul so evil.

Alexander glanced behind him. "As much as I'm loving this reunion, we really need to hurry things along." He shoved the water at her. "Drink the water, Maeve, and get that tunnel open."

Roderick grabbed the water vessel and sniffed it. He raised it carefully to his mouth. "It smells odd."

"That's plastic you're smelling." Alexander smirked. "Getting up to speed with this century is going to be a mind fuck I wish I could witness."

Roderick glowered at Alexander but spoke to her. "If it's poisoned get yourself to the tunnel."

"But—"

"No argument, Maeve. Not this time." Roderick sipped the water.

Maeve held her breath.

He took another sip. Then he gave a grating laugh. "It's water."

Handing it to her, he scowled at Alexander. "You woke us?"

"You left me no choice." Alexander shrugged. "Baile needs you. The witches need you, warrior. Your work has only just begun."

"My work ends with you dead," Roderick said.

Alexander nodded and stood. He held out his hand to Roderick. "Fair enough, but why don't we start with something less ambitious. Standing, perhaps?"

Maeve sipped carefully. Cool and wet, water slid down her throat and brought tears to her eyes.

Alexander put his shoulder beneath Roderick's and raised him to standing. Then he reached for her.

"Don't touch her." Roderick lunged between them and would have fallen if Alexander hadn't caught him.

"You help her then, but get her up, and do it now." Alexander glanced behind them again. "The amount of magic this is putting out will have her on her way."

Rhiannon. The name resounded in Maeve's mind, and she shivered. Taking Roderick's outstretched hand, she got to her feet. The pain in her unused muscles made her eyes water and she could barely support her body. She clung to Roderick for balance.

"A few steps and you'll be able to sense Baile." Alexander had his arm around Roderick's waist as he dragged them both forward.

The wards prickled over her skin, but they hit Roderick like an anvil. Through the bond, she felt the influx of sensation rush through his bone, muscle and sinew.

Roderick threw his head back and roared his agony to the skies.

Covering her ears, Maeve tried to absorb what she could through the bond. With the pain came strength as well. Already Baile healed and revived her beloved and favorite son.

Roderick's vitality bloomed rapidly, reached for Baile. They snapped into a tight loop, Roderick and Baile, feeding and regenerating each other.

Stretching his muscles, Roderick finally stood straight and tall, the unassailable coimhdeacht sent to protect her. He turned to her and cupped her face. "Take from me, Maeve."

He controlled the rush of power through their bond, feeding it to her in a slower and kinder stream. She grew thirstier and sipped the water and offered the vessel to Roderick.

He took a tiny sip and gave it back to her.

"More." She nudged him with the vessel. It crackled and buckled in her grip but didn't break. She had no idea what manner of stuff this plastic was, but it was strong and malleable.

On the far side of the wards, Alexander watched them with a strange whimsical expression. He caught her eye and his normal inscrutable mask slid into place. "Hello, spirit walker. It's been a long time."

"How long?" Roderick glared at him.

Alexander raised a brow. "Unfortunately for me, not a conversation I'm going to have with you. Get back to Baile. Now."

He turned and jogged away.

Roderick flexed his arm muscles and arched his back. He winced, and Maeve felt the pulse of lingering discomfort.

The green was surrounded by so many buildings, many of them ugly and crude, but the church was still there, and she motioned toward it. "Should we?"

Roderick raised his brow at her in an expression she hadn't even realized she'd missed. "I think we must."

***

BRONWYN WOKE as her forehead hit the table. "Ow."

It took her a moment to orient herself. She was in the Baile library. After Alexander had dropped her off, she'd come with Mags and Niamh to find out more about Rhiannon.

Bronwyn had no idea how long she'd been asleep. In the predawn gloom casting shadows over the stone walls and floor, her knowing prickled beneath her skin, and she looked about for what had triggered it.

With three floors of shelving on either side of a bank of windows facing the sea, the library presented a daunting number of books, but no other people. Opposite the great floor-to-ceiling windows gaped a walk-in-size hearth.

Click, who-ha-hoo, click, vrrrt.

Wearing a tatty Tasmanian Devil sleep shirt, a woman perched on the back of a three-seater leather sofa to the left of her. The woman's long gray hair was a tangled mess that hung past her waist. Her big green eyes were fixed on Bronwyn. She made another clicking sound and turned her head to the side and kept going, way past the point a normal head should turn.

Bronwyn was warming up for a good scream when the door

opened and Niamh stamped in. "You're awake. Alannah was getting the kettle on."

"Er...yes." Bronwyn didn't know how the strange woman was perching on her haunches like that.

"Roz!" Niamh addressed the woman. "I told you I would introduce you to Bronwyn."

Roz hopped off the sofa, stuck her arms out behind her like she was flying and ran from the room.

"Well." Niamh gave her a bright smile. "I see you've met Roz."

"I—"

The floor shook and Bronwyn grabbed her pen before it rolled off the table.

"Sodding hell!" Niamh stuck her arms out to keep her balance as the floor rumbled and shook around them.

As suddenly as it had started, it stopped.

"Was that an earthquake?" Bronwyn hadn't heard of England having earthquakes.

"I don't know what that was." Niamh held on to the back of a chair and peered into the gloom, as if waiting for the quake to come back.

A door banged, and they both jumped. Then another door and another, until the entire castle was echoing with door bangs.

"Is this normal?" After that awful scene with Alexander yesterday, Bronwyn was all done with bad surprises.

Niamh shook her head, eyes huge in her pale face. "I have no idea what's happening."

A subterranean groan rumbled through Baile.

"It's Baile!" Sinead burst into the library with Alannah on her heels. "She's...alive."

"Alive?" Bronwyn said at the same time Niamh yelped, "She?"

This had all the makings of a horror movie.

"Definitely a she," Alannah said and beamed as if she'd won the lottery. She motioned Sinead. "We can feel her."

Not sure what to make of any of it, Bronwyn clung to the table edge. "I'm confused."

"You're confused?" Sinead rolled her eyes. "I was born in this castle, have spent my whole life here, and I've never known she had an awareness."

Niamh chewed her bottom lip. "You're sure this is the castle you're sensing? There was that time with the mushrooms—"

"Oh, yes." Alannah nodded and grinned. "She feels...old."

"And solid," Sinead said. "Also I get the sense she's happy."

This was starting to feel a whole lot too much like a Halloween haunted house. Only real. And a castle. "What the hell does a castle have to be happy about?"

"She was missing something. Longing for it." Alannah frowned and got a far off look in her eyes.

Niamh leaned forward and peered into her face. "Are you talking to Baile now?"

"It's a someone." Mags flit through the door already dressed in a maxi skirt and peasant blouse. Her hair was brushed and shining, and she looked wide awake. "It's a someone Baile has been missing."

"You can talk to her too?" Niamh frowned. "Why can't Bronwyn and I?"

Bronwyn was not at all sure she wanted to speak to Baile.

"No." Mags scoffed and rolled her eyes. "I saw him earlier tonight." She fluttered a hand around her head. "I had a vision whatsit."

"This someone is a him?" Bronwyn seemed to be the only one keeping track of the facts here.

Mags nodded. "Oh yes, definit—" She cocked her head. "Wonderful! Our visitors are almost here." She turned and looked over her shoulder. "We should probably gather in the kitchen."

CHAPTER ELEVEN

S till not sure what she was doing in the kitchen, Bronwyn took a seat at the table as Alannah made tea. At least Baile had stopped shaking things.

Cheeks flushed and eyes sparkling Mags paced the kitchen, peering out the window and then through the archway into the rest of the castle. "I'm not sure where they'll come from." She giggled. "This is super exciting."

"Will they want tea?" Alannah paused with a spoon of tea leaves hovering over the teapot. She frowned. "I have some poppy seed loaf left but it's not to everyone's taste."

"It's a tad…dry." Sinead pulled a face and shrugged. "But everyone likes tea." Then she glanced at Bronwyn. "Except maybe for you. Is that because you're American?"

"I like tea." They were missing the point. "I just pref—never mind." Somebody had to keep them all focused. "Who is this visitor, and what do they want?"

"Not a visitor." Sinead took a deep breath. "He belongs to Baile, like he's part of her."

Alannah added a couple of extra spoons of tea to the pot. "We'll definitely need biscuits."

"Do we have any of that lemon cake you made?" Sinead got up and brought cups to the table. "That was delicious."

"I do." Alannah bustled over to fetch a cake tin from the Welsh dresser against the far wall.

"At last!" Mags ran over to the kitchen door and opened it. "Hi!"

A man and woman stood on the other side. They were dressed in what looked like some kind of historical dress and staring at the occupants of the kitchen.

Bronwyn stared right back with the rest of the Crays.

"Hello." Alannah found her voice first. "You should come in."

The man stepped into the kitchen.

The hearth fire flared, and Baile shook and groaned, but it did have an oddly joyful note to it.

The man put his hand on the doorjamb. "Settle down, girl."

He had a deep, raspy voice and a strange accent that sounded nothing like the other accents of Greater Littleton.

"Wait there," he said to the woman and strode deeper into the kitchen. "I am Roderick. Who are you?"

Nobody answered his question. For her part, Bronwyn was still stuck on his name. "Roderick?"

"Aye." He nodded his dark head, and his pale blue eyes swept the kitchen and everyone in it. "If you're here, it means you are cré-witches."

"Ye-e-es." Niamh stared at the man. She frowned and raised a hand. "When you say Roderick—I really only know of one Roderick—now I'm confused."

"Roderick?" The woman at the door wore a long, old-fashioned dress. And by old-fashioned, they weren't talking the seventies. Not the nineteen seventies anyway. Her blond hair hung in a thick braid over one shoulder. She was short and slim with darkly lashed blue eyes. Bronwyn put her at about her own height of five foot nothing. "Can I come in yet?"

"I need to ascertain your safety first, Blessed." Roderick's tone had Bronwyn's eyebrows heading for her hairline. And she'd thought Alexander was bossy. She needed to focus.

Holding out her hand and stepping forward, Mags said, "Hi, I'm Mags. Well, my full name is Magdalene, but nobody calls me that."

"Seer?" Roderick stared at her.

"Um...okay." Mags shrugged. "Can we get back to the Roderick thing?"

"What year is this?" As Roderick glanced around the kitchen, his gaze stuck on the range. "Where is the kitchen hearth?"

Alannah stepped aside and motioned the range with her hand. "They put this in a while ago. It takes some patience to get the hang of it, but once you do, it's marvelous."

"Hmm." Roderick prowled the kitchen while they all stayed stuck to the spot and watched him.

Bronwyn grabbed her courage and cleared her throat. "Umm...I think I speak for all of us when I ask if you could explain who you are and how you come to be here."

"I am called Maeve." The pretty blonde waved from the door. "And we came through the tunnels from the church to the caverns."

It couldn't be the Maeve from the statue, but that was not a name you heard all that often. Perhaps Bronwyn had hit her head harder on the table than she thought.

"There are tunnels from the caverns to the church?" Sinead straightened her shoulders. "How come I've never seen those?"

Maeve shrugged and looked at Roderick. "I really cannot say."

"Blessed! I have already spoken. Wait there." Roderick held his hand up to her, and Maeve snapped her mouth shut.

"Big bossy person." Sinead squared her shoulders. "If you speak to her like that again, you and I are going to have an issue."

"And you are?" His pale blue gaze stuck on Sinead with disconcerting intensity.

Sinead didn't flinch. "I'm Sinead, and that's my sister Alannah."

Alannah nodded and held the teapot aloft. "Tea. I was just making a pot."

The man switched his gaze to Bronwyn. It made her feel stripped to her bra and thong.

"Bronwyn." She pushed to her feet, not liking how much sitting put her at a disadvantage. "Bronwyn Beaty, and I know how I got here, but you still haven't answered my question as to how you got here."

"I am Roderick of Baile," he said.

Baile rumbled beneath their feet and Roderick smiled. In all the excitement, she hadn't noticed until he smiled how good looking Roderick was. Tall as well, with a pair of shoulders that looked like he could take the world's problems and tote them around for a bit.

He wore breeches and a cream shirt that fastened at the neck with a leather tie. Long, full sleeves did nothing to disguise the muscle beneath. If Roderick suddenly turned nasty, he could do some damage.

"The only Roderick I know of is the one who built Baile," Bronwyn said. "The original owner."

"Nobody owns Baile." Roderick chuckled. "But she did allow me to put stone and mortar together to create her."

Bronwyn sat down again. The blood drained to her feet, and she had to breathe deep. "I'm afraid that's impossible."

"Blessed." He smiled at her like she was a cute kid who made him laugh. "Nothing is impossible when magic is involved."

"Magic?" Niamh breathed the word on a sigh. "Is that how you're here?"

"Roderick." Maeve jammed a hand on her hips. "I can see

there is nothing dangerous about these women. They are cré-sisters."

Roderick hovered by her side as Maeve stepped into the kitchen. "I am beginning to think we have been gone for a long, long time." Her gaze lingered on the dishwasher and the fridge. She skimmed Alannah and stared at her sleep pants. "A very long time."

"Perhaps." Roderick looked at Bronwyn. "What is the year, Blessed?"

She didn't get the blessed business but at last a question she could answer. "Twenty twenty."

"What?" Roderick stilled.

Maeve paled and leaned into him.

His arm went around her immediately. "Did you say twenty twenty?"

"Yes." Maybe she could have broken that a bit gentler. "Two thousand and twenty."

Roderick gaped at her.

Maeve stared at her and whispered, "I think I need a cup of tea."

"Tea!" Alannah beamed at Maeve. "That I can do."

Sinead nodded. "With lemon cake."

Bronwyn had to keep reminding herself not to stare. But there really wasn't a behavioral precedent for having tea and some excellent lemon cake at a hair shy of dawn with a man and a woman who had been a statue for nearly four hundred years.

Even thinking about all the impossibilities of the situation made her glad she was sitting down.

"This is wonderful." Maeve ate Alannah's cake in three enormous bites. For a small woman, girlfriend could eat. "Cook makes, I mean used to—" Her face creased into an expression part pain and part confusion.

"It may even be the same recipe." Alannah smiled at her reassuringly. "There is an old recipe book that's been in the kitchen since before my grandmother's time."

Roderick side-eyed the cup of tea Alannah put in front of him. "Let us begin with who is king."

"No king. Not really a queen either." Sinead was clearly a rip the Band-Aid off type of girl. "I mean the queen and the rest of the royals are still around, but they don't rule or anything."

"Except for Meghan and Harry," Alannah said. "And they're not dead or anything, but they're not really still around."

"I beg your pardon?" Roderick glared at her. "What else do they do but rule?"

"They do charitable works, raise awareness of issues." Alannah had the mixing bowl out and was working more baking magic. "They're a great tourist attraction."

Roderick sat back in his chair and gaped at her. "And who rules the country?"

"The people." Bronwyn leaped into the gap. "For the people, by the people."

"Eh?" Roderick blinked at her. "Everybody dispenses law on everybody else? Has the world gone mad?"

"Obviously not." Sinead rolled her eyes. "The police dispense law."

"The civil administration dispenses the law? Now you are speaking foolishness." Roderick snorted. "Woman, I think you do not understand how matters work."

"Are you being serious?" Sinead scowled at him. "And I know how things work a fuckuva lot better than you, mate."

Maeve gasped and choked on her tea.

Roderick looked thunderous. "Watch your mouth, Blessed."

"You watch yours, fossil." Sinead got to her feet, jammed her hands on her hips and stuck her chin out.

"I see manners have been lost along with womanly decorum." Roderick frowned at Sinead.

"We also lost the sexist bullshit along the way." Sinead snorted and stared him down. "You have a lot to learn, big guy. I'm gonna love teaching you every bit of it."

Maeve put a hand on Roderick's arm. "Perhaps we should let them explain?"

Breaking his glare-off with Sinead, Roderick grunted and nodded.

Sinead glowered for a few more seconds and took her seat. She jabbed her fore and middle fingers at her eyes and then at Roderick. "Got my eye on you, big man."

Roderick raised a brow at her, and turned to the table. "You may begin."

Bronwyn settled in for a long conversation. And one that blossomed with every new piece of information revealed. It took an entire lemon cake to get to the spread of democracy. By which stage Maeve was looking shell-shocked.

"I think that's probably enough new information for now," Bronwyn said. "The rest might be easier to cover on a need to know basis."

"Hmm." Roderick hadn't spoken since they'd broken it to him that women now voted. His hotness factor seriously dimmed with every sexist statement out his mouth. Bronwyn tried to cut him some slack, but Sinead looked like she had made it a personal mission to bring him into this century.

Maeve folded her hands carefully on the table in front of her. Thus far, her biggest revelation had been the dishwasher and the fridge. She was beyond fascinated, and Bronwyn looked forward to introducing her to the washer and dryer and the vacuum. "May I ask you a question?"

"Go ahead." Alannah put a plate of chocolate muffins on the table.

"The magic." Maeve looked confused. "I cannot sense any magic."

Roderick looked at her. "Nothing?"

"Very little." She chewed on her lip, picking at the edge of the table with her fingernail. "There is always magic at Baile."

Bronwyn leaned closer to Maeve, along with the Cray cousins. It suddenly occurred to her that Maeve would have even more answers for them. "There are only a few of us left."

"Only you?" Sadness filled Maeve's eyes. "Are there no more witches?"

Roderick covered her hand on the table with his. Sexist and arrogant he might be, but his tenderness with Maeve went a long way to diluting that.

"There's Roz." Niamh pulled a face. "But that's it."

Bronwyn had almost forgotten about Roz. In a morning packed with weird, Roz and the sofa perching would have to take a number. "The women in my family never lived very long."

Alexander's revelations were still too painful for her to approach. He'd loaded their final interaction with so much information she needed time to sift through it.

"Our mothers were sisters," Mags said. "There were four of them, including Roz."

Sensing the same sadness that dogged her, Bronwyn asked, "What happened?"

"They died in a car crash," Niamh said. "Fifteen years ago."

"I'm sorry."

Alannah touched her shoulder. "Our grandmother raised us, but she passed five years ago."

"What's a car?" Roderick's frown grew deeper and deeper.

They'd get to that, but Bronwyn wanted to know how Roderick and Maeve had ended up as a statue. "Were you here when the village attacked the castle?"

Maeve recoiled and gasped.

Putting his arm around her, Roderick nodded. "Rhiannon had turned half the coven to her side. We did not see it coming."

"Rhiannon." Niamh glanced at her. "That name keeps cropping up."

"Alexander said we need to do our research about her when he brought me here," Bronwyn said.

Roderick growled, a sound so menacing Bronwyn wanted to put more distance between them. "There is a reckoning to be had between that whoreson and me."

"What do you have against Alexander?" Mags chuckled. "He's a good friend."

"Friend!" Roderick pounded the table with one huge fist. Cups rattled in saucers and a glass of water nearly went over. "You are a cré-witch. Alexander is not your friend."

"No." Maeve shook her head vehemently. "No. Alexander is...evil."

Bronwyn was glad she hadn't brought the prophecy thing up. The Alexander she had experienced had been confusing, enthralling, and thrilling, but not evil. She couldn't think of him as evil, but Roderick looked adamant.

"Evil?" Niamh gaped at them. "Maybe we're not talking about the same person?"

"Tall, handsome, dark hair, dark eyes?" Maeve looked hopeful.

Mags sighed. "We're definitely talking about the same person. He's always been very nice to us."

"Indeed." Roderick looked angrier than Bronwyn had ever seen another being look. He leaned his fists on the table and got in Mags's face. "Like he was nice to the ninety women he murdered. Witches like yourselves. And the thirty good men who were my brothers in arms who died trying to protect those women."

Alexander had never said anything to her like that.

Heavy silence blanketed the kitchen.

"Okay." Bronwyn cleared her throat. Her head spun, and her chest ached. She didn't want what Roderick said to be true. It made no sense for her to have reacted to Alexander the way she did if what Roderick said was true. At the same time, there were enough commonalities between what Alexander and Roderick said for her to need to know more. She needed to put her heart aside and let her head take the lead. "I think there's a lot we don't know."

CHAPTER TWELVE

Maeve stood in her old bedchamber and felt like an interloper. There were things she remembered that hadn't changed, but the connected room—bathroom the other witches had called it—was new.

Her head throbbed with all the new she'd heard today, and she knew there was so much more to come. Outside her casement, the sea looked the same, but the village was easily three times larger than in her time.

There were noises that broke the peace, and they made no sense to her. Growls and purrs of big silver things that flashed through the sky and sped along the roadways. She couldn't remember the words they'd given her to put names to those noises.

The other witches, the new ones, had all gone about their business and even though she was tired, Maeve avoided the large bed in the center of her chamber.

Even knowing it was silly, she didn't want to close her eyes because she was afraid she wouldn't wake again. Or worse, wake four hundred years later in a world that made no sense.

Through the bond, she could sense Roderick prowling Baile.

Even the castle felt different, as if it were covered in woolen batting that stifled it.

Roderick's presence came closer and then a soft knock sounded on her door.

"Come in." She leaned against the casement and stared at the sea.

Roderick stood behind her and studied the view with her. "At least that much is the same."

"Yes." It was comforting having him near. "They thought Alexander a friend and knew almost nothing about Rhiannon."

"It worries me." Roderick leaned his shoulder on the window embrasure. Mellow sunlight played across his coimhdeacht markings on his arm, the patterns and swirls etched on his skin telling the story of his service. She was now marked on his skin beside the other witches he had served before her. "It also makes no sense Alexander woke us and helped us into the tunnels."

That didn't make sense to her either. "He doesn't smell anymore."

"Smell?" Roderick frowned down at her.

"The blood-magic stink," she said. "He used to have it, and he doesn't anymore."

Roderick sighed. "I know not what him not reeking of blood magic means. Along with a number of other things that make no sense to me."

"You are not alone in that." Maeve dared reach behind her for his hand. Their bond had been so new that she had not yet accustomed herself to having a coimhdeacht, let alone being comfortable with him before that hideous day, the one her mind veered away from.

He took her hand. "You did not want to sleep?"

"No. I'm afraid." His markings flared brighter umber at her touch.

He nodded, and he knew because of the bond, but also

because he had been frozen with her all these years. "Want to go for a walk?"

"Where to?"

He shrugged. "Let us explore our new now together."

Still holding her hand, Roderick led her back into the hallway outside her chamber. "Baile is…there." He grimaced. "But not as she used to be. I can sense her, but she does not thrum in my blood."

"Why?" The carpets beneath their feet hadn't aged. Drawings, paintings and samplers made by witches who had made Baile home decorated the walls. She stopped at a beautiful charcoal sketch of a horse in motion. Sadness gripped her like a fist in her chest.

Roderick tightened his clasp on her hand as he reassured her through the bond. There were often times when having another human feel every emotion you had, able to peer inside your mind and heart and see what you kept concealed, was intrusive and uncomfortable. In moments like this, however, Roderick's bond to her was a blessing. She would never feel lonely again. She would never have to explain how she felt or what she thought.

Pressing her head to his shoulder, she stared at the sketch. She remembered the day they had hung it. To her, that day seemed three weeks ago. Even though it was unnecessary, she said, "Colleen, she drew that."

"She had a keen eye." Roderick's light blue eyes filled with shared emotion. "I have been thinking perhaps Baile is so quiet because all the coimhdeacht are gone."

His sadness throbbed between them, grief for the men who had fought by his side and were now dead. "All of them?"

"Aye." His sadness coiled around her heart, and she wanted to shed the tears he never would.

She wrapped both her arms around him and kept her head pressed to his shoulder. "Not all the coimhdeacht are gone."

"No, not all. But I am the only one left."

"For the new ones, this picture is painted by a witch dead for hundreds of years." Maeve touched the corner of the picture frame, seeking that tangible connection to Colleen. "We only saw her yesterday."

"We should do something," he said. "We could go to Birgit's mound and release their spirits to the Far Isle."

Tears threatened, and Maeve blinked them back. "I would like that."

"Let us to the caverns." He tucked her arm in the crook of his elbow and gently tugged her away. "I cannot feel Goddess either."

As the marks on Roderick's arms, which had been worn by all the coimhdeacht, told the story of his life and his bonds, so the thousands of sigils in the caverns below Baile marked the lives of witches past.

Maeve was spirit walker, the only one a coven could have, and it was her job not only to place the sigils on the cavern walls, using shells, fossils and crystals, the sigils that held the key to a witch's spirit, but she could walk amongst them after their death.

Roderick was right. She couldn't sense Goddess, either. Even the vague notion that Goddess might be no more was too much to contemplate, so she kept it tucked in a tight mind box even Roderick couldn't penetrate.

The sun slid behind a cloud, but the air was warm enough not to require a cloak. Not that Maeve would know where to start searching for one.

Sand crunched beneath their feet as they crossed the bailey. Images flashed through her mind. Hester being dragged by her hair. Blood covering the stones they walked across.

"Don't." Roderick glanced at her, his jaw taut. "It does no good. Remember them as they were before that day."

Before he had become coimhdeacht, Roderick had been a

knight and a good one. He had seen battle and death countless times before being granted this land. "Is that what you do?"

"When I can." His chuckle lacked humor. "It does not always stop the specters from haunting me though."

"It will help if I can meet their spirits." Maeve waited for Roderick to open the door in the bailey wall that guarded the stairs to the caverns. "If I can see them whole again and in a better place, perhaps I can forget how they got there."

He nodded. "That would be good for both of us."

Maeve thrust her sadness aside. When she walked with the dead, she would see her sisters again soon.

As they descended stone stairs to the cavern entrance, wind tugged at her skirts and hair. Women of this time wore very different clothing. Breeches even, and she planned to adopt their way of dressing as soon as she could.

As she stepped into the caverns, the entrance felt different, dark and still.

Nothing.

The sigils did not wake to her presence as they should. For her, as they were for everyone else, they were patterns on the wall made of fossils, shells and crystals. It was like missing a limb. "No."

"Do not despair," Roderick murmured. Through their bond she could sense him questing for Goddess and she knew not if he sought to comfort her or himself.

They walked deeper into the first cavern. It was so dark she stumbled over a rock.

The sigils had always cast a soft ambient light for her, enough for her to see her way.

Baile was muted, Roderick couldn't sense Goddess, and now the sigils remained dormant. She couldn't reach the witches who had passed. Maeve refused to even consider the possibility the sigils might be forever dead.

Maeve called fire to her and clicked her fingers. Fire rose, as did her magic, scenting the air with lily and orange, but the upswell of power fell short. Fire's response was a trace of the power she should be able to wield. "My element is..." She couldn't quite put it in words. "Like a candle barely burning."

"It must be tied to Goddess being so hushed." Roderick took the lead, seeming to see better in the dark than she. He led her through an arched doorway into another chamber and then another beyond that. Even Maeve had never explored how many chambers ran beneath Baile. She had only worked in the caverns with sigils on the walls. "If you can sense fire it means it is still there but weak. Like Baile."

Not wanting to ask her next question, Maeve's nerves tightened around her lungs. "And Goddess?"

"Same." Roderick frowned in concentration. "She is there but not there."

"Then not dead." And Maeve drew enormous comfort from that. If Goddess was still amongst them, there was hope. Goddess was life, and from life flowed all blessings and good. Cré-witches had been created in her image, made conduits of her magic, to serve life and the life within humanity.

Their footsteps were loud in the silent caverns. In the past, when Maeve had visited, the sigils had always hummed or chimed when she was near. She stopped and pressed her hand to the wall.

Silence greeted her. Where the sacred grove should have been was now a vast emptiness. Her presence rippled through the dead space, growing wider as it spread in circles from the point of contact.

A breath of breeze stirred the dark.

Sister.

Spirit Walker.

Her dead sisters' voices came from down a long, dark tunnel, so soft she could barely hear them. But at least they were still there, so she indulged in the victory. If they were there, then she could still walk amongst them. "I need to reach them," she said. "They need me."

"Aye." Roderick led her through the caverns into the central cavern. "I think we are needed for much in this time."

In the center of the central cavern lay Goddess Pool, absolutely still in the dark cavern. Maeve could barely make out the water as darker matter within the gloom.

Roderick stopped at the edge of Goddess Pool and plunged his hand into the water.

Light, the same icy blue as Roderick's eyes, burst through the pool.

Maeve reeled against the sudden brightness.

Light blazed and then dimmed to creamy phosphorescence. Goddess's voice, old and brittle as cracked parchment, said, "*Roderick?*"

"My lady?" Roderick crouched beside the pool with his head bowed. "I serve."

"*Roderick.*" The voice strengthened. "*You are come at last.*"

"I have come, and I serve." He glanced at Maeve. "I stand with my Blessed."

Light flickered in the water and then brightened. "*Good.*" The light dimmed and Goddess's voice weakened. "*It is almost too late. Magic is almost gone.*"

"You need magic." Truth crashed into Maeve. Magic came from Goddess, but it also fed Goddess, like the cord between a mother and her unborn child.

Water flared brighter.

And Maeve knew the why of all of it. Why her sisters had given their lives to send her and Roderick into a frozen state. Why Baile had exhausted her magic to keep them sheltered, and why they were alive at this time. Her coimhdeacht stood near, so tall and strong, and here to work by her side. When Roderick had bonded to her, she had been confused and disbelieving.

Why would a spirit walker need a warrior guardian to protect her when she never left Baile? "It's the magic."

Goddess had known all along. Maeve would need Roderick to protect her in this new time when nothing was as it had been, and they needed to forge everything from new. Goddess had gifted her the strongest of all the coimhdeacht, the one who could succor Baile. She was the spirit walker, and her dead sisters held the key to all the magic of cré-witches who had come before, and Maeve sensed they would need it all. "It's our magic." It bore repeating because it was all they lived for now. "We need to bring it back."

CHAPTER THIRTEEN

Rhiannon had no idea what he'd done. Yet. Alexander knew this for certain because he was still breathing and attending her demand for an immediate meeting. Even her desire to control the prophecy might not be enough to save him if she ever found out the part he'd played in waking Roderick and Maeve. Fortunately, he didn't see either Maeve or Roderick sharing that tidbit with her. Roderick hated him, but that paled in comparison to how Roderick felt about Rhiannon.

She would find out eventually, so he was living on borrowed time. For now, however, it was enough that Bronwyn was behind Baile's wards, and Roderick was around to keep it that way. He couldn't prevent the sting of *if only* when he thought of Bronwyn. It was as it was, and thinking otherwise would get her killed.

"When did they wake?" He thumbed through his cell for the latest on the mysterious disappearance of *The Lovers* statue from the village green. Speculation around who, what, when and why ran the gamut from esoteric to entertaining.

Edana and Fiona huddled in the corner of Rhiannon's living room looking like they wanted to be anywhere else.

Alexander empathized, but Rhiannon had called this meeting, and none of them were foolish enough to not attend.

"Late last night." Edana gave him a melting look. He would have thought she'd have given up on him by now, but she was nothing if not relentless.

Fiona, the far wiser of the two, kept her attention on a fuming and pacing Rhiannon. "More like the very early hours of this morning."

Edana glared at Fiona, who made a face back. Even they wouldn't bicker with Rhiannon in a froth. It was safe to say Rhiannon had not taken the news of Roderick and Maeve being awake well.

"We need to keep a lid on this," he said. In these days of cell phones and the internet, keeping magic under wraps was imperative, and Rhiannon looked about a heartbeat away from incinerating the village. Another constant in his long life was the way people reacted on discovering witches and magic were real—they didn't like it. A lot.

Keeping her gaze on the main danger source, Fiona nodded. "I've got that in hand."

"Have you?" Rhiannon halted midpace, her eyes flashing fury. "Like you had Roderick and Maeve in hand. Remember?" She stalked a paling Fiona. "The little spirit walker wasn't going to be a problem." She jerked her chin at Edana. "This pretty toy was going to keep Roderick busy."

Fiona bowed her head. "You're right, mistress. We failed you." She side-eyed Edana. "I was given to understand Roderick's attachment was of a more lasting kind."

With that, Fiona tossed Edana under the bus, reversed, and drove over her again.

Paler than her white sundress, Edana stared at the floor. Her lips moved as if she was praying for her life. Alexander wished her luck with her prayers. Certainly no good or loving being would be listening to them. Pretty—no beautiful—but vain and stupid, Edana had done her fair share of havoc wreaking.

"He preferred the spirit walker to me," Edana whispered.

Alexander would have made the same choice as Roderick. Not Edana's match in physical beauty, Maeve radiated purity. He had only met her a couple of times, and not under ideal circumstances, but Alexander would have chosen Maeve over Edana any day of the week and twice on Sundays.

On a growl, Rhiannon paced to the other side of her cluttered living room.

More like a clamber and trip, because Rhiannon never threw anything away. Countless treasures from her obscenely long life filled her house to bursting. Every now and again he snuck one out and sold it. Rhiannon had learned how to use a credit card but gave no thought to how that credit card got paid off. It was in everyone's best interests to keep her contentedly tottering around in Louboutins. "Where is the water witch?"

"I'm not certain," he said and the interrogation light swung his way. "I've been making considerable progress with her."

Always ready to defer blame, Fiona sniffed. "Really? Holding hands and tongue tussling isn't going to get the job done."

"I'm aware of that." The trick to Fiona was never letting her see your weakness. "Not that I'd expect you to grasp this, but seduction is a subtle pursuit more than a bellowing charge."

Fiona flushed and scowled at him. She could glower all she liked because they both knew he had what Rhiannon needed.

Rhiannon wove around an upholstered Tudor chair, tripped over a leg and gave it a vicious kick. "I'm missing something."

"In terms of?" Alexander winced for the chair. He got up and moved it out of her way. The chair would pay off her Fortnum & Mason's account this month if she didn't kick the shit out of it first.

"They woke up."

The look of pure rage she gave him had Alexander stepping

closer to the door. His gut clenched. Now that her rage was more manageable, her brain had kicked in. "I'm aware."

"So, how the fuck did they do it?" Snatching up a seventeenth century brass lantern clock, she hurled it against the wall.

Alexander really wished she wouldn't do that. Bribing new minions with flashy bits of metal and bling took an ongoing injection of capital. "You think they had help?"

"What else?" She eyed an extremely rare fourteenth-century English pewter openwork pricket candlestick.

Alexander moved it out of her line of sight. "They've been stirring for some time. Didn't you tell me that?"

"Stirring." She growled. "But nowhere close to surfacing."

"Ah." Alexander braced himself. Last time the subject of Maeve had come up it had cost him a truly exceptional fifteenth-century Norman walnut revolving book stand that he'd earmarked to cover her latest Harvey Nicks spending spree. Not keen to field more nasty demands from Harvey Nichols' credit department, he kept his tone conciliatory. "But there's not much she can do without being able to access her gift. Your magic has gotten stronger and stronger."

The certifiable look drained from her face, and she almost smiled. "You're right. While she has been sleeping, I have been using my time well. They have no idea what I'm capable of."

"Does anyone?" He made sure to color his tone with the right amount of awe.

"No." She preened and then snapped her fingers. "Bring me the bowl."

Fiona brought her favorite iron casting bowl and placed it on a really lovely Charles I west country oak refectory table.

Blood magic hung in a thick, oily miasma around her and oozed deeper into the room. Alexander stood as far back as he could to mitigate its effect on him.

"What are you doing?" He eased closer to a window and cracked it open. Blood magic grated against his skin.

Eyes closed, dripping blood from her slashed palm, Rhiannon frowned.

It wasn't unusual for her to simply ignore him. Alexander often wished he could do the same to her.

"The wards," she murmured. Her frown deepened and then disappeared. Her eyes popped open. "Fucking Roderick being awake has strengthened them."

"Are you sure?"

She gave him a look of such derision that had he not been well used to them, his feelings might've been hurt. "I created those wards." Contempt dripped from her voice. "I created them, and I can do with them as I will."

Not quite, but he wasn't stupid enough to correct her. Rhiannon had cast the magic that raised the wards, but they were anchored through Roderick and his connection to Baile. He had a pet theory that back then, when Rhiannon had been one of the original four witches called by Goddess into service, she'd linked Roderick to the wards as a way to bind him to her. Alas, Goddess had not shared Rhiannon's plans and Roderick had been bonded to Tahra.

"I need not tell you what is at stake here." She scowled at him.

"No, you don't." His entire life, he'd lived and breathed her need to vanquish Goddess. His very existence was in service to her ambition.

Hand dripping blood all over the Aubusson carpet, she closed on him. "Make sure you don't fail me with the water witch."

"I won't." He met her gaze without flinching. It was only a matter of time before the delicate dance of smoke and mirrors he'd been doing came to an end. "I've made myself a friend of Baile's witches."

Rhiannon narrowed her eyes as she stared at him, trying to see into his mind. He wished her luck with that. He hadn't allowed her to penetrate his shields in hundreds of years. "You are only of use to me in a limited capacity, son."

"So you keep reminding me." It had been even longer since he'd felt any filial affection for her. "I know what I'm doing. I'm good at this."

"Yes, you are." She smiled, and it was disturbingly beautiful in what it hid. "Women like you."

He shrugged. She'd made sure of that when she'd conceived him. "She's already smitten."

"Good." She threw herself into an armchair and pressed her bleeding palm into the fabric. "You will need to move fast now that Maeve is awake. We don't want her teaching your witch how to wake up the cardinal point."

"Does Maeve even know about that?" Not since the first four had been called had the cardinal points been an issue. They'd been created by the first four, one for each element, but in the history of the cré-witches, they'd never been allowed to go dormant like they were now.

Rhiannon made a face. "Roderick may. Goddess always adored him."

"She always did have questionable taste."

That drew a chuckle from her. "It's interesting that you say that." She stood suddenly. "I want that witch, and I want that castle."

"I'm working on both."

"You have a week." She slammed out of the room.

It wouldn't have done him any good to protest a week wasn't long enough. Frankly, he was amazed he'd kept her at bay this long. With Baile growing stronger and the wards with her, Rhiannon's patience would run out faster.

"Don't fuck it up." Fiona sneered as she cleaned away the casting bowl.

"Really?" He adjusted his cuffs. "But think how much fun you would have if I did."

Edana leered. "I'd ask her to give you to me."

"How tempting." His cock shriveled at the mere suggestion.

Alexander let himself out of her house into the quiet of Greater Littleton's premier residential street. Her house was surprisingly small and lacked Rhiannon's usual desperation to parade her importance and wealth. But it had once been a rectory, and it amused her to live in it now. Only he and the twisted two knew about the rectory. The rest of her minions saw her only when she chose and never in her lair.

A headache pinched behind his eyes. All his plans were mere distractions, a way to buy time. If he could stall Rhiannon, he could maybe ensure Bronwyn's safety. If Bronwyn was safe the cré-witches could wake the water cardinal point. If water was activated, Goddess might begin to regain her power and be able to oppose Rhiannon. *If, if, and fucking if.*

He turned the corner onto the main road and walked toward the green.

Police cars still clogged the roads around the green, and yellow police tape surrounded the broken plinth. He doubted there was police procedure for a missing statue.

"Isn't it dreadful." Hermione appeared at his side, eyes on the police action. "Who could have done such a thing?"

"Do the police know any more?"

She shook her head. "It's like it vanished."

It was exactly like that.

"I'm sure there's a plausible explanation," he said. And there would be. It amused him how, in this time, people contorted themselves to produce logical and scientific explanations for magic. Their faith in science gave them the delusion they were in control. They had no idea what a master puppeteer Rhiannon really was. Even he didn't know the extent of the spread of her tentacles through the power structures ruling the modern world.

Three uniformed coppers were working the scene. They moved about oblivious to how the wards shifted their perceptions. Whenever they moved closer, the wards altered the reality to make them believe they were standing in a different place. Alexander could see the shimmer of the wards and the reality they concealed. As they strengthened, the wards would make it so people could see Baile, travel toward it, and somehow never make it inside the castle. The raising of the wards had been some of Rhiannon's best work.

The only time the villagers had breached the wards was when he and Rhiannon had made it so they could. On that fateful day in 1645 when he had first discovered Baile would allow him past her wards.

CHAPTER FOURTEEN

CRÉ-WITCH CHRONICLES

Bronwyn woke the next morning to that feeling of something momentous having happened. The way, as a child, you'd wake up Christmas morning, and in that moment before you opened your eyes, you knew that day was going to be a special one.

Whrrrr, click, click, who-ha-hoo-ha-hoo.

The momentous-day feeling was replaced by one of being watched, so she cracked her lids open.

Roz perched on the end her bed. She cocked her head and studied Bronwyn. Smacking her lips, she did that sickening head swivel. *Who-hoo?*

"Morning, Roz."

The Tasmanian devil sleep shirt had been replaced with a cleaner and newer Tweety Bird sleep shirt. The tangled nest of Roz's hair would need a pair of pruning sheers, possibly a high-powered hose.

Click-click-whrrrr. Roz ducked her head and appeared to be studying her feet. She sat up suddenly, a mouse dangling out her mouth.

A grown woman eating a mouse was all kinds of wrong. Bronwyn shuddered.

Dangling by its tail and scrabbling tiny splayed nails through the air, the mouse twisted and pivoted.

Roz slurped up an inch of tail.

Getting her dry heaving under control, Bronwyn managed an inside voice. "What are you doing with the mouse, Roz?" She couldn't express how much she wanted to be wrong about what Roz was doing with the mouse.

Roz cocked her head, jerking the mouse into a limbs akimbo frenzy.

"Niamh." Bronwyn yelled. She was so out of her lane here. Her voice took on a hysterical edge. "Niamh!"

Roz worked her lips, and another inch of mouse tail disappeared into her mouth.

"No." Bronwyn's feet hit the floor, and she hissed at the cold stone. Hobbling closer to Roz, she kept her arms clearly in view. "Do not eat the mouse, Roz."

Another pursed lip suck and more tail disappeared.

"Niamh!" Bronwyn slammed her little toe into the corner of the bed. "Ouch! Motherfucker! NIIIIAAMMHHH!"

Niamh stumbled through her door, hair in a wild red tangle around her head and shoulders. "What?" She caught sight of Roz and recoiled. "Ah, bollocks. That is so wrong."

Two dogs and a three-legged badger followed Niamh. The badger disappeared under Bronwyn's bed. The dogs joined the fun, tails wagging as they yipped and danced around Roz.

"Do something." Bronwyn's gaze fixed on the shrinking tail as she rubbed her injured toe on her standing foot.

Niamh crept closer and hissed at her. "Don't panic her."

"Never mind that. Get the ..." Bronwyn ran out of words and waggled her finger at the terrified rodent. "Get it out of her mouth."

"Roz." Niamh inched closer to her aunt. "Give me the mouse."

Roz turned her head to Niamh. A two-hundred-and-seventy-degree twist that made Bronwyn's stomach lurch. "She should not be able to do that."

The smaller terrier-type dog gave a straight-legged spring in his attempt at the mouse.

Roz had reached the thick part of the mouse tail now. One big gulp and it would be *Hasta La Vista, Speedy*.

Niamh grabbed the two inches of mouse body and locked gazes with Roz. "Drop it," she said. "Drop it right now, Roz."

The terrier sprang and yapped its agreement.

Roz bared her teeth at Niamh.

The mouse squealed.

The other dog leaped onto the bed and lunged for the mouse.

"Get off my bed," Bronwyn bellowed at the dog.

It ignored her and made another attempt at the mouse. Seeing its companion making headway, the terrier joined him on the bed.

Niamh tugged on the mouse.

Roz narrowed her eyes and then snapped open her mouth.

"Thank you, Jesus." Niamh stumbled back with the mouse cradled against her chest.

Roz shimmied her shoulders and hopped off Bronwyn's bed. She drew level with Niamh and hissed before sauntering out the door.

Robbed of their prey, the dogs leaped off the bed and joined Niamh.

Niamh stared after Roz. "We have got to do something about her."

"Maybe Maeve will know something." There was only so much a girl could take, so Bronwyn shoved Roz to the back of her mind. "Did a statue really wake up yesterday?"

"I don't know if we could call it waking up." Niamh's eyes sparkled. "But two really old people arrived in our kitchen."

Bronwyn liked the *our* in that statement. "We should go and check on them."

"Maeve's not in her room." Niamh looked guilty. "I may have spied on them earlier."

"May have?"

Niamh giggled. "Definitely did. Had plans to hover over her bed like a total creeper. I still can't really get my head around her being real."

"If she's not in her bed, where else would Maeve be?" Bronwyn would probably have also lurked around like a psycho.

"Barracks," Niamh said. "Or that's what my grandmother called that part of the castle."

Bronwyn pulled on some socks for her icy feet. She didn't suppose heating the castle would be easy. "Barracks? As in an army?"

"All castles have them." Niamh shrugged. "Ours were for the coimhdeacht."

"The what now?" Bronwyn had caught something that sounded like kweev-duct.

"Roderick was the first of them, and they were supposed to live in the barracks. We thought they were a legend, to be honest." Niamh rolled her eyes. "Men who were called by Goddess to serve as protection for the witches. There was something about being bonded to each other." She shrugged. "It all sounded like a fairy tale. I don't remember the details."

"A bond, like marriage?" Roderick and Maeve had certainly seemed to be close. He hovered around her protectively.

Niamh shook her head. "No. I'm not really sure but more like a you protect me and get superpowers for it, sort of thing."

"Superpowers?" Really, at this point, the litany of whacked shit in her life should be drowning her. Bronwyn was amazed she hadn't started dribbling or perching on beds like Roz. "Like super strength or x-ray vision?"

"It sounds stupid when you put it like that." Niamh poked her arm. "Now get dressed so we can go and spy on our walking fossils."

Bronwyn dived into her underwear and went with jeans and a sweatshirt. Bunching her hair into a ponytail, she followed Niamh downstairs into the great hall.

They moved past the red cordon that Hermione had detoured. "I had to call Hermione and cancel the tours." Niamh grimaced. "She was really not happy. Although the disappearing statue has definitely generated more interest in the village."

"Right." Canceling the castle tours made sense, given the newest arrivals at Baile. Roderick and Maeve's appearance would have made a good story for Hermione's tour patter. However, not a story anyone would believe.

Niamh took her to an arched wooden door that had to be fifteen feet high and nearly that wide. Thick slabs of metal reinforcing said you weren't getting in there unless you were invited.

Bronwyn tried to remember. "Was this part of the tour?"

"I haven't been here in years." Niamh pressed her palm to the door. "I hope you don't have a thing about spiders."

Bronwyn baulked. "Why?"

"Never mind." Looking far too innocent, Niamh turned the door handle.

The door swung open as if it had been recently oiled and revealed another corridor. A bank of windows ran along the left of the corridor, and from there, they could see clear to Greater Littleton. The flagstones shone as if recently polished, and the wood wainscoting reflected a warm sheen.

"Huh." Niamh blinked at the corridor. "Last time I was here…" She took a ginger step beyond the door.

Bronwyn wasn't moving without more information. "Last time you were here, what?"

"It was dusty." Niamh took another couple of steps. "Full of cobwebs."

"Maybe Roderick cleaned it." Bronwyn followed her.

Niamh looked unconvinced. "That's a lot of cleaning."

On the wall opposite the windows—windows with sparkly clean glass—large tapestries depicted battle scenes. Lots of swords and knights and horses...and a couple of dragons. Surely there weren't...

At this point, it was really looking like it might be wiser to go with shit and not question too closely.

At its end, the corridor widened into six broad stone steps leading down to an arched double door, heavy with metal studs and braces. "Were they expecting some kind of attack?"

There was a definite warlike decorating scheme going on in this part of the castle.

Niamh stopped in front of the door. "We were never allowed to go further."

"Why not?" Bronwyn had a brief, and worrying, fantasy of opening the doors and Smaug flying out.

"Here goes nothing." Niamh turned the handle and shoved. "Oof!" Her shoulder collided with the doors. "These are bloody heavy."

Putting her shoulder beside Niamh's, Bronwyn joined in shoving the doors open. Once they got them moving, they swung open smoothly.

Welcome.

"What?" Bronwyn looked at Niamh.

Niamh blinked back her. "What?"

"You said welcome."

"No, I didn't. You did." Niamh paled. "Didn't you?"

"Nope." Bronwyn shook her head. Running like hell seemed like an option.

Niamh's dogs surged past them down the corridor. The terrier looked back and barked at them.

"They wouldn't go if it was dangerous," Niamh said and took a couple of hesitant steps before stopping. "You coming?"

"Is no an option?" It took a few deep breaths for Bronwyn to trust Niamh's pack and follow them through the doors into an open space. Weapons. Everywhere she looked. Swords, pikes, lances, axes, that stick with the spiked ball on the end that she didn't know the name of. Crossbows and longbows, quivers full of arrows, and daggers of all shapes and sizes. Everything you would need to wage a medieval war, and all of it gleaming like it had been neatly cleaned and hung up that morning.

Niamh's low whistle broke the silence. "They all look brand new."

Four wooden tables, each with two benches neatly tucked beneath them, took up the center of the room. You could probably seat eight to ten per table.

"So these kweev-whatevers were soldiers?" Bronwyn had wandered into a medieval re-enactors wet dream.

"Coimhdeacht." Hands behind her back, Niamh stood in front of a bunch of swords on the wall and stared. "Kind of. More like elite bodyguards, each individually sworn to protect one witch."

If witches had magic, then why would they need protecting? But she was beginning to feel like a preschooler with all her questions, so she tucked that one away for later.

An archway, doors standing open, led into an even bigger room. Oval shaped with a sandy floor, one wall was entirely made of windows facing the village. Nobody could approach the castle without being seen from the parapet outside the windows.

Again with the martial decorating theme. Less ornate than the ones in the other room, weapons hung on the walls, whilst others sat in open wooden crates stacked against the wall. A crate of wooden staves provided a clue.

"This must be a sort of practice room," Bronwyn said. Again, it looked as if someone could step on the sandy floor and pick up a sword.

Through another door, they followed Niamh's dogs. Rows of open doorways stretched on either side of a central passage.

They peered into the nearest one. A large canopied bed dominated the room. Beside the bed, stood a wooden cabinet, and at the foot, a large wooden trunk.

On the bed, Roderick and Maeve lay sleeping. He was on his back, and she was tucked against his side, head on his shoulder.

"It must be a kind of married thing," Bronwyn whispered to Niamh.

Niamh studied the pair. "They certainly seem to be close."

"We are not married." Roderick opened his eyes and looked at them. He raised one dark brow in question. "Is something amiss?"

Niamh stared back at him. "I don't know, is there?"

Bronwyn was really glad she wasn't the only one floundering through all of the new revelations. "We came to find you," she said. "In case you needed anything."

"Roderick?" Maeve blinked awake. She sat up and frowned at the bed. "I must have fallen asleep."

Roderick smiled at her. "You did. We came here after the caverns."

"Niamh?" Mags called from outside. "Are you and Bronwyn down here?"

"In here," Niamh bellowed back, loud enough to make Bronwyn wince.

"It appears I am to entertain the entire coven in my bedchamber." Roderick sat up and rubbed his hands over his face. It really was a very handsome face, especially with the light dusting of stubble over his square chin.

The wicked ink scrolled over his forearm was a deep russet brown. Bronwyn wanted to study it closer.

Mags trotted into the room, smiling. "Couldn't stay away either, hmm?" She grinned at Maeve and Roderick. "I have so many questions. I woke up in the middle of the night, and all the things I want to know wouldn't stop going around and around my head." She giggled. "Eventually I had to get up and write them all down."

Roderick looked appalled, and Bronwyn empathized.

"Good morning." Alannah appeared in the doorway with a tray in her hands. "I brought coffee." She raised the tray to show them the cups on it. "But then I couldn't remember when coffee first came to England, and maybe you didn't know it or like it."

"So, I brought the tea." Sinead eased past her into the room with a second tray.

Something passed between Maeve and Roderick. Bronwyn couldn't see or hear a damn thing, but she sensed they communicated in ways she didn't understand. Yet.

"Coffee." Roderick sent Alannah a looked of near desperation. "I know coffee."

"Told you so." Sinead put the tea tray on the chest at the end of Roderick's bed. She motioned to it. "Help yourself."

Alannah had included a plate of cinnamon rolls and one of blueberry muffins. She caught Bronwyn looking at the baked goods and shrugged. "I bake. Mostly when I'm stressed."

The next few minutes passed in getting everyone provisioned.

Niamh's dogs jumped onto the bed, and she perched on the edge.

Sitting on the bed seemed far too personal, so Bronwyn made a space for herself next to the tea tray on the chest.

"So." Sinead dragged the word into several syllables. "What happens now?"

It was as good a question as any to start.

Roderick sipped his coffee and sighed. "It's good."

"I roast my own beans." Alannah leaned closer to him.

Sinead took a seat beside Maeve. "And I grind them."

Maeve blinked at her and nibbled her cinnamon roll.

"Maeve and I made some discoveries last night." Roderick slipped into the role of leader, and they all let him. "Firstly, and most importantly, Goddess is alive. She's weak, but she's alive."

The others nodded as if this meant something to them. Bronwyn added it to her mental list of questions she would space out over time.

"She's real?" Alannah grew misty eyed.

Roderick gaped at her. "Of course she's real. From whence do you think your power comes?"

"They don't know." Maeve touched Roderick's arm. "I believe she has been near silent since we went into stasis. Perhaps they were not taught what we all knew from the cradle."

Roderick nodded. "Good point." He turned to look at them. "Goddess gave the cré-witches their powers, so they could serve humanity on her behalf. The stronger your powers are, the stronger she is."

Bronwyn had read about this the other night in the library. "She called four witches first. A guardian, a healer, a seer." She stopped to think what the fourth one was.

Maeve helped her out. "And a warden. We believe Goddess has called four again."

Alexander had told Bronwyn about Goddess when he'd dumped her at Baile. Wherever he was, she couldn't help but hope he was all right. Her continued connection with Alexander had to be wrong, given all that Rhiannon and he had done to the coven.

"I'm not sure we really have any powers." Niamh looked to the other Cray women for support. "I mean, I can sense what animals want, and I have a way with them, but that's not really a power."

"You're a guardian," Maeve said. "You have the power to share the minds and spirits of animals."

Niamh blinked at her. "Cool."

"And you're the seer." Maeve turned to Mags. "You can scry people, see into the future, predict things."

"I do get dreams." Mags frowned and chewed her lip. "And sometimes I know when somebody is going to arrive or the phone will ring."

Roderick reached for more coffee and another muffin. His third, if Bronwyn wasn't mistaken. It must take a lot of fuel to run all that muscle and bone.

"Wardens." Roderick jerked his head at Alannah and Sinead. "They seem to share a blessing."

"That happens with twins." Maeve smiled at Alannah and Sinead. "Not often, but it does happen, and you are warden witches. Your province is the earth and growing things."

Alannah looked at Sinead and laughed. "We do like gardening."

"Which brings us to you." Roderick looked at Bronwyn. "You're a healer."

Bronwyn looked at the Cray women and then Maeve. She didn't fit in there. "I wasn't raised in Baile."

"It doesn't change what you are." Roderick shrugged. "But if you were not raised here, and you are new, it adds to our growing evidence."

"Of?" Bronwyn asked.

"Rhiannon," he said, like the name tasted toxic to him. "Only Baile and Goddess stand between her and whatever she wants. They have both grown weak, so she must be preparing to attack."

Maeve paled and gripped his arm. "We barely survived last

time with a coven of ninety witches and a full complement of coimhdeacht."

It must have been awful for Maeve and Roderick to witness the coven massacre. What to her and the Cray cousins was a page in history, to Maeve and Roderick had been the loss of friends and loved ones.

"We need to assess our strengths and weaknesses." Roderick looked grim. "There is no time to lose. I must become familiar with this time."

"I can help you with that, brother," a man said as he popped up. One moment the space beside Alannah was empty, and the next, a tall, dark-haired man dressed like a pirate had materialized.

"Fuck!" Niamh leaped off the bed.

Sinead shrieked and jumped in front of her frozen sister.

Mags passed out, and Bronwyn started laughing. A ghost! A motherfucking ghost to add to everything else. Whelp! Why the fuck not?

CHAPTER FIFTEEN

B ronwyn's time in England was running out. Her return
ticket was booked for a week from today, and she really
didn't want to get on that plane.

From her window this morning, the sea was a calm blue
with lazy, undulating swells.

Yesterday, they'd left the ghost—Thomas, yes, he had a name
—talking to Roderick. Not a thought she'd care to verbalize too
often, and definitely not outside the castle, but Thomas had
undertaken the job of catching Roderick up to this century.

Bronwyn wished him luck with that. Roderick had been
born in a time when men were thugs, and the thug with the
biggest sword won. Considering that, he really wasn't doing too
badly with modern gender politics. Sinead had undertaken his
enlightenment.

Sitting in a pool of sunlight in her casement, she took her
time brushing her hair. Dee would have been right at home. "I
hope you're keeping up, Dee, because every day brings a new
surprise."

In the kitchen, Alannah would probably have breakfast
going, with a grouchy Sinead giving her a hand. With her pack

of animals, Niamh would already be sitting at the table, main-lining Twinings English Breakfast tea, and having strange nonverbal sorts of communication with her menagerie. Mags would appear when the meal was almost done, and Sinead would bitch at her. It wouldn't bother Mags one bit, and she'd tell them all about what had kept her up late into the night.

It had only been a few days since Alexander had just about tossed her and her stuff into Baile, and already, being there felt as familiar as if she'd grown up in the castle.

She leaned her head against the deep stone of the embrasure. It was warm beneath her cheek, and if she concentrated, she could sense the pulse of sentience that was Baile. It reached out to her in welcome and made her feel like she was exactly where she should be.

An entire life of being an outcast in the town where she'd been born, and now, she'd stumbled on her true home. Life, however, didn't work that simply, and she couldn't drop every-thing and move into a castle in England. She had a house in America, and a life. Not much of a life, but one nevertheless.

"You really would love it here, Dee." It broke her heart that Deidre hadn't seen Baile. God, she would have loved how ancient everything was, and gotten the hugest kick out of the other witches. Never mind what Deidre would have made of Roderick and Maeve.

The other witches, and Roderick, seemed to take it for granted she would stay. Even Thomas the ghost had an opinion and was firmly in the her staying here camp.

Then there were all the questions around Alexander, and she'd give anything to be able to talk her concerns through with Dee. She hadn't heard from him since he'd dropped her there. It was pathetic, but she missed him, and he was never far from her mind. If she concentrated, she even had a vague sense of him.

As she unpacked the layers of magic and mystery around Baile, she got more confused about Alexander. He'd been instrumental in the deaths of so many witches. She hated that about him, but at the same time, she couldn't lie to herself about her response to him. Even knowing who he was and what he'd done, she felt the pull to be near him. It was like he'd burrowed into her being, and she couldn't dislodge him.

She'd done enough research to know Roderick hadn't been overreacting about Alexander, and he would for sure lose his shit if he suspected her feelings, ambivalent as they were. Niamh and the modern witches liked Alexander and had experienced a completely different man than the one Roderick and Maeve remembered. Niamh said he'd pretty much always been around, being friendly, even giving them a hand now and then at market.

What they'd uncovered thus far about Rhiannon did not make the prospect of more Alexander in Bronwyn's future probable. Sadness welled inside at the idea of never seeing him again. Then there was that crazy prophecy, and she needed to sit down with Roderick and talk about the prophecy, but with revelations flying at them like mosquitoes in July, it was hard to concentrate on one thing.

"Hey." Niamh stood in her doorway, accompanied by a squirrel clinging to her pant leg, the usual dogs and a one-eyed cat. "Those look like some heavy thoughts."

"I was thinking about leaving." Bronwyn tried to keep it light, but a lump lodged in her throat at the notion of not being here anymore.

Frowning, Niamh came and sat beside her. "You're leaving?"

"I have to. Eventually." Bronwyn petted the cat that had crawled into her lap. Animals at Baile never fought or tried to eat each other. Other than Roz, that was, and she shoved that memory away. "My ticket is booked, and I have a home and a business to get back to."

"Business?" Niamh gently pried the squirrel off her leg and put it on the floor. "I never asked what you do in America."

"It's a family business," Bronwyn said. "We make herbal remedies, shampoos and lotions, that sort of thing."

"Of course you do." Niamh chuckled. "You're a healer after all."

"It's weird, you know." There was an excellent chance Niamh knew exactly what she was about to say. "Our family all had these talents or gifts, and we never put it together that they might be more than a useful ability."

"I'm a guardian witch." Niamh shrugged and grinned. "Which means I have an affinity for animals." She nodded at her current pack. "I should be able to ride around inside their heads. I mean, I've read about guardians in the library. Tahra was the first one."

One of the original four witches called to service. The others had been Brenna, called as a seer; Deidre, called as a healer; and Rhiannon. Rhiannon had been the original warden, her gift the same as Alannah and Sinead. According to Roderick, she had gone bad and tried to usurp Goddess. She had attacked Baile in the sixteen hundreds, and that attack had resulted in the deaths of nearly the entire coven, and Roderick and Maeve going into stasis. Hermione had been more accurate than she'd realized with her tour guide patter comprised of rumors and half-truths.

The cat padded over to Niamh and curled in her lap. "I thought they were cool stories," Niamh said. "Family legacies that had been exaggerated and romanticized over time."

"Instead, the opposite is true." The Beaty family had told the same kind of stories. How her great great grandmother could always tell the sex of an unborn baby, or the way great great great aunt Heather could take anyone's headache away, and according to Dee, how Bronwyn's mother had always known exactly where it hurt before the person told her. Myths and poetic story-telling Bronwyn had assumed. "We don't even know the half of what we should be able to do."

"What do you make of all we've found out?" Niamh looked at her. "Do you think it can be true?"

Relief that someone else felt the same made Bronwyn laugh. "I'm having a real hard time with it, to be honest. I keep looking at Roderick and Maeve and thinking they might be villagers with a good act."

"The statue is missing," Niamh said. "It's all over the village."

"It's…" Bronwyn didn't have the word.

"Unbelievable," Niamh murmured.

"Yeah." Bronwyn fixed her gaze outside the window. "I almost can't believe if we drove past the green the statue wouldn't still be there."

"Right?" Niamh straightened and her eyes gleamed. "We could always go and take a look. To make sure."

Bronwyn needed to be clear she'd understood Niamh right. Nobody had come right out and said it, but they were all on unofficial lockdown with Roderick holding the gate keys. "You mean take a look at the missing statue? On the green? In the village?"

"Uh-huh." Eyes sparkling, Niamh chewed her bottom lip and nodded.

"Do you think that's a good idea?" Alexander had been crystal clear on her staying put. Then again, at some point she would have to leave Baile, even if it was to get to the airport.

Niamh pulled a face. "I really don't know, but I can't see what harm it can do."

"Alexander seemed to think I was in a lot of danger from Rhiannon." Bronwyn had read enough about Rhiannon to know a threat from that quarter was not good. Roderick had driven the point home.

"Yeah." Niamh brightened. "But she'd have to know you were out of the castle for you to be in any danger, and we can slip out without anyone knowing."

They could sneak away, and getting out of Baile might help clear her head.

"We can go after breakfast." Niamh nudged her shoulder with hers. "It'll be our little secret."

Alexander's dire warnings rang in her memory, but she was tired of trying to make sense of all the new and crazy revelations and she just wanted to do something normal. Like go for a drive with a friend. "Let's do it."

Niamh grinned. "We can be there and back before anyone even knows we've left Baile."

It was ridiculously easy for Niamh to lift the Landy's keys from the peg beside the door and tuck them in her pocket. After breakfast Alannah and Sinead went to putter in their garden. Mags drifted off to wherever Mags went when she got that misty look in her eyes, and Roderick and Maeve returned to the barracks for more lessons in catch up with Thomas.

As they drove across the wards, Niamh shivered and turned to her. "Did you feel that?"

"Yeah." It was like feathers over her skin.

"It's always been there." Niamh accelerated down the hill like Roderick was chasing them. "But it's gotten stronger since Roderick arrived."

It was a glorious summer day and Bronwyn rolled down the window and let the wind tangle her hair.

Niamh drove down the hill and turned away from the village green.

"Where are we going?" Bronwyn looked behind her at the green growing smaller. From this angle she couldn't see the place where the statue had stood. "I thought we were going to look at the statue."

"We are. After." Niamh nodded and glanced at her. "But I thought we could pick up a few groceries at the same time."

That seemed harmless enough and gave them a perfect excuse for their outing. "Okay."

"I always get someone to come with me." Niamh pulled a face. "I hate going alone."

"You hate shopping?" Bronwyn stared at her. "Doesn't that mean you lose your girl card or something?"

"There's shopping for fun stuff." Niamh pulled a face. "But it's not the shopping; it's the people."

It took five minutes in Tesco to see what Niamh had been speaking about. Niamh was a magnet for men and women, and they got pissy when they couldn't get near her.

"Niamh." A tall, thirty-something man near as dammit hurdled the display of oranges and popped up in front of them. "How are you? Haven't seen you around."

"I'm good, Neil." Niamh gave him a polite smile and stepped around him.

A woman with two children passed them. "Hi, Niamh." She smiled, and her children waved. The younger started to whine about wanting to play with Niamh, and his mother hushed him with an apologetic smile.

Neil followed them to the bananas. "Have you given any more thought to dinner?"

"I have, Neil, and I can't at the moment, but I'll give you a ring." She selected a bunch of bananas and put them in the shopping cart. "Alannah hates it when I buy fruit or veggies," she said to Bronwyn. "But she can't grow bananas, and I really love them."

"It doesn't have to be dinner." Neil dropped into place beside Niamh. "We could do coffee or tea or a drink if you prefer."

Niamh's smiled tightened. "Okay, Neil. I'll give you a call."

"When?" Neil jostled Bronwyn out the way. "Because I don't want to miss your call."

"Hey!" Bronwyn refused to give ground. She was short, not invisible.

"You said you'd call last time." Neil's gaze fixed frantically on Niamh. "And then you didn't. I have a life, you know,

Niamh. I can't stand around Tesco waiting for you to show up."

"Actually, standing about Tesco waiting for Niamh to show up is not a life." Alexander turned the corner into the produce section, his attention locked on Neil. "The lady has answered your question, and as a gentleman, accept your dismissal with grace and leave while you still have some dignity."

Bronwyn's heart triple timed it, and she tried not to stare. He was such a beautiful man, and his presence filled the empty place inside her she'd been saving for him. It made no sense that someone that beautiful could front for so much evil.

Little witch. He looked at her and smiled.

Sadness and longing in his smile made Bronwyn want to weep.

"Alexander." Niamh sighed her relief. "Nice to see you."

"It's always nice to see you, Niamh." Alexander gave Niamh a smoldering smile, but it was superficial and nothing like the smiles he gave Bronwyn. There was something so palpable between her and Alexander, like they were two halves of the same whole. If Bronwyn believed in the prophecy, that would be one explanation, and one that left her tasting disappointment. She didn't like the idea of him only being drawn to her because of a prophecy that was outside his control.

"And Bronwyn." He took her hand, turned it over and kissed her palm. "I didn't think to see you here."

Sensation shot through her. The effect he had on her crackled beneath her skin. The thought of never seeing him again made her want to puke. "Niamh asked me to come with her."

"Right." Alexander stared at Neil. Neil blushed and scurried away. Alexander's manner changed to aloof as quickly as if a switch had been flipped and he dropped her hand. "And whilst I understand why Niamh prefers company when she leaves Baile, I can't condone you ignoring my warning."

That ripped her out of her erotic haze. "It's only a quick trip for some groceries and to see the missing statue."

"You can't leave Baile," he said, serious as a freaking heart attack. "I told you and Niamh that, yet here you are."

"She can't stay locked in Baile forever. Besides, nobody even knows we're here." Niamh scowled at him. "And what the hell can happen to us in Tesco anyway?"

"I know you're here, and you're being naïve if you think I'm the only one. You're a witch, your magic leaves a psychic resonance." His face hardened, and chill invaded his voice. "You can't afford to take chances. And the danger is specific to Bronwyn."

Cold slithered down her spine and made Bronwyn shiver. "I'm not sure what to believe that comes out your mouth anymore."

"Really?" He turned to her, and he was pissed, his dark eyes like onyx, power surging and snapping in the air about him. "Then let me reiterate the salient points." He leaned close enough to almost touch noses with her. "You're in peril. Rhiannon wants you, and you won't like what she has planned for you. Once she's done with you, she will kill you and take the child of the prophecy." He spoke quietly but deliberately. "She will get rid of you like she got rid of your entire family." Straightening, he turned to Niamh. "And once she's done with Bronwyn, she's coming for the rest of you. You don't have to take my word for it; ask Roderick. He will tell you exactly what Rhiannon is capable of."

This was a side to Alexander she hadn't seen, and it chilled Bronwyn to the bone. Niamh had gone pale and stared at him as if she'd seen a ghost. "Who are you?"

Alexander straightened. "Honestly, Niamh, that should have been your first question when we met."

"I'm asking you now." The scents of basil and strawberries

came from Niamh as she used her magic. "You deliberately befriended us."

"Good," Alexander said. "Use your magic to help you delve into me. Go deeper."

Niamh frowned, and her magic stroked over Bronwyn's skin. "You're old. Really old. You shouldn't be alive."

"More," he whispered. "Use your magic, Niamh. Use it every chance you get and flex it like a muscle. Goddess needs that from you. You have the ability to see within all animals, including humans. Look deeper."

Niamh frowned, studying him. Her eyes went opaque and the scent of basil and strawberries strengthened. "Shit!" She leaped away from him, eyes huge. "You're her son! You're Rhiannon's son, and you're...different."

"Well done." Alexander snarled. "Roderick will tell you to stay the fuck away from me, and you really need to listen to him." He turned back to Bronwyn. "I'm the son of the woman who wants to possess you, use you, and discard you. That should be enough to keep you clear of me. Now get behind those fucking wards before she pinpoints where you are."

Trying to ram these new puzzle pieces into place, Bronwyn stood frozen and blinked at him. Alexander being Rhiannon's son was so, so much worse than anything she'd imagined.

"Take her straight back to Baile." Alexander turned to Niamh. "And both of you stay there."

Numb, brain gears spinning, she let Niamh hurry her out of Tesco and into the Land Rover.

Bronwyn's heart beat so fast it felt like it could leap out of her chest at any minute. A son's loyalty lay with his mother.

"Shit!" As she drove, Niamh gripped the steering wheel so tightly her knuckles whitened. "I had no idea. He was always this charming, amusing man who never seemed to chase me around like the Neils of this world."

"He's Rhiannon's son." Saying it aloud didn't make it any

easier to grasp. Later when she could process this she would have questions about every interaction she'd ever had with him, every word, every touch, every look. He'd always said he felt the same thing for her that she did for him, that the connection between them was real for him too. How could she trust any of what he'd said to be true if he was Rhiannon's son?

"We need to tell Roderick what he said about Rhiannon being after you." Niamh winced and sent them careening around a corner. "He's not going to be happy about any of this. I kind of understood before, but I really get why now."

"Roderick must have known who Alexander was all along."

Niamh ground the gears as she accelerated around the green. "Of course he did. That's why he got so rabid about us not having anything to do with him."

"It also explains why Alexander was part of the cavern massacre." Speaking her thoughts aloud scraped Bronwyn raw and she wanted to weep. "Alexander does whatever his mother tells him to do."

They didn't need to go looking for Roderick when they got back to Baile. He stood outside the kitchen, arms crossed, wearing an expression so similar to Alexander's that at any other time it would make her laugh.

He waited for Niamh to turn off the engine and approached the Landy like he meant to beat the shit out of it.

"We're sorry." Niamh hopped out first.

Feeling like a coward, Bronwyn climbed out and went to stand behind her. Roderick was just a guy, a bossy one who looked good and mad, but still flesh and bone. Maybe.

"You left the castle." He folded his arms and glared down his nose at them.

Feeling a bit like being in the principal's office, Bronwyn tried to pull herself together. "We only went for a quick trip to Tesco."

"Who is Tesco?"

Niamh snort laughed, caught Roderick's blistering lack of amusement and sobered. "It's a shop. A food shop. For buying food. We were gone less than five minutes."

"Baile provides." Roderick said. "You do not leave this castle like that again."

"It was a mistake." Niamh gave him her sultry smile. "We're sorry, Roderick." She put her hand on his chest. "We understand now and it won't happen again."

Unlike Denis at the fairground or poor deluded Neil, Niamh's smile bounced right off Roderick and he continued to glower. "You do not leave the safety of the wards on your own."

"Look, we know you're upset." Niamh dropped the charm routine and went with calm reason. "And you have every right to be. We should never have left, but Bronwyn's had a bit of a shock and could we deal with that first?"

"What has happened?" Roderick pinned Bronwyn with a glacial blue stare. "Are you hurt?"

Nowhere that showed she wasn't. "I'm...fine."

"Is she?" Roderick looked at Niamh.

With an apologetic glance at her, Niamh shook her head. "No, she's not. We just found out Alexander is Rhiannon's son."

"How?" He pinned Niamh with that stare.

Some still functioning part of Bronwyn wanted to kick against his authoritarian attitude, and had she been less shaken by Alexander's revelations she might have. Maybe. Roderick was kind of intimidating.

"Ummm..." Niamh cleared her throat.

"Blessed." His voice rumbled through his broad chest. "I am responsible for your wellbeing and continued existence. We cannot afford to lose one witch. I need the truth."

Niamh squared her shoulders. "We ran into Alexander while we were out. It was a total accident—"

"You ran into Alexander?" The way Roderick said his name made Bronwyn's nape prickle. She thought he was angry before;

now he was livid. His complete stillness radiated fury from every large, muscular inch of him. "Where?"

"Tesco." Niamh took a step back, caught herself and bellied up again. "Near the cauliflower."

"Florets not whole cauliflowers," Bronwyn clarified.

"I made it plain that Alexander is not a friend and you should stay away from him." Roderick spoke in the sort of forced calm you would use on a child you found poised to attempt free flight off the roof. "He kills witches and enjoys it."

"I think him not being a friend is a bit of a massive understatement." Niamh scrubbed her face with her palms. "You could have said he was her son."

Roderick opened his mouth, shut it and nodded. "You are right. I am not always clear on what you witches do and do not know." He grimaced. "Or how much to divulge all at once."

"This is all so confusing." Niamh's voice wobbled and Bronwyn saw a touch of her confusion and upset reflected in Niamh's eyes. "I've always liked Alexander. He was lovely and so nice to us, and funny and charming." Tears dribbled down Niamh's cheeks. Her dogs appeared from the kitchen and surrounded her, pressing against her legs. "Now I find out he's her son, and he's ancient. Like ancient like you're ancient." She crouched down in the center of her pack and drew strength from them. "And you say he was here that day, and killed all those witches, but he's never hurt any of us. In fact, he's always gone out of his way to be nice to us. And right now, in Tesco. He yelled at us to get behind the wards and to stay away from his mother. Why would he do that if he wanted us dead?"

Roderick's tone gentled and he crouched in front of Niamh. "What did he say?"

"He said I was in danger, and he was most specific about it being me." Bronwyn found her voice. "He says Rhiannon wants me, real bad, and I won't like what she wants, and when she's done with me, she'll get rid of me. Then she's coming after the others. He told me, more like ordered me, to stay behind Baile's wards." She risked poking the bear. "I'm as confused as Niamh and then there's this insane pro—"

"The prophecy." Maeve took the word out of her mouth as she came through the kitchen door and stood beside Roderick. "It's the only thing that makes sense."

"You know about that?" And she'd been scared to bring it up in front of Roderick, but if Maeve knew, Bronwyn would bet her life Roderick knew too.

Niamh glanced from one to the other of them. "What prophecy?"

Bronwyn was going to let the oldies do what they should have already done and tell the rest of the coven about the prophecy.

Roderick and Maeve glanced at each other, doing that communicating without words thing again. "How are you doing that?"

"Eh?" Roderick barely glanced at her.

"Speaking to each other."

"We're bonded," Maeve blushed as she said it. "I can hear his thoughts, when he lets me, and feel what he feels. He can do the same with me."

Bronwyn shared an *ah-ha* look with Niamh.

"Wait!" Niamh held up her hand like she was at school. "I could see inside Alexander a bit. Are we bonded?"

"Not!" Roderick grimaced. "But you're a guardian, so you have an affinity to all creatures, including murdering whoresons who deserve running through with steel."

Clearly, Roderick didn't share their ambivalence about Alexander.

CHAPTER SIXTEEN

F our more days until she had to catch a plane home, and
with all of them holding firm on the not leaving Baile
thing, she had no idea how she was going to manage that.
Bronwyn was also no clearer on whether she wanted to be on
that plane back to the States or not. Actually, that was a lie. She
wanted to stay, but she couldn't drop her entire life in the States
and shack up with a bunch of strange witches in England.

Or could she? Deidre would have been all for it. Perhaps
Deidre had wanted this for her all along. Dee probably hadn't
known about the English witches, or else their family might
have run for the safety of Baile before any of their avoidable
deaths.

Her anger rose sharp and clear. The Beaty women didn't
have an unfortunate way of dying young at all. Instead they had
a determined enemy trying to ensure they didn't live. Well, she'd
gotten her answers about why her family died young. Rhiannon
had killed them, and now she wanted Bronwyn.

Last night she, Roderick, Maeve, and the Cray women had
sat in the kitchen and dissected every word of Alexander's. Well,
Roderick had done the dissecting. The rest of them had

provided information and eaten the excellent dinner Alannah had served. They'd also tried to stay out of Roderick's pissed off arc. All except Sinead, who was determined to modernize his thinking.

A knock on her door brought her back to the present.

"Hi." Alannah peered around the doorjamb. "Feel like joining a rescue mission?"

As opposed to sitting here and brooding? "Damn straight I do. Who are we rescuing?"

"Maeve." Sinead put her head next to Alannah's. When Sinead wasn't wearing her habitual scowl, it was nearly impossible to tell them apart. "We've got to do something about that dress of hers."

"I think it's all she has." Alannah looked crestfallen. "She wears it every day."

Bronwyn hadn't really given it much thought, and the distraction opportunity was more than welcome. "I guess she didn't pack for the journey they undertook."

"We should find something for Roderick too," Sinead said. "But I can handle that."

She looked delighted by the prospect, and Bronwyn had to laugh. "You're going to torture him, aren't you?"

"A wee bit." Sinead smirked. "I mean, he could do with a bit of torturing, don't you think?"

"Just a wee bit." Bronwyn made a tiny gap with her thumb and forefinger. "All that medieval manliness does make me want to put him in his place."

Alannah laughed. "Which is where exactly?" She motioned Bronwyn to join them. "He owns Baile, or as near to owning Baile as anyone can, and he was the first coimhdeacht. That makes him everybody's...great great great grand-something." She cocked her head. "Is he even related to any of us?"

"Probably." Sinead looked struck by the idea. "I'm going to do a bit of digging through the library. There are lots of personal journals in there. Want to bet me I find Roderick manwhoring his way through quite a few of those?"

"Um…no." Bronwyn had listened to what Hermione had said about Sir Roderick. Even though she had been talking about a mythical man at the time, there was probably still some smoke to the fire around Roderick and the women of Baile.

Alannah carried a large canvas tote with her as they walked down the corridor. "Maeve is a little shorter than us, but we can alter anything to fit her."

"Hang on." Bronwyn ran back to her room, grabbed a pair of jeans and rejoined them. She held up the jeans. "Something to add to the cause. From one short girl to another."

Maeve answered their knock on her door and blinked at them. With her blond hair and blue eyes, she oozed Disney-fairy prettiness. "Hello. Is everything all right?"

"Yup." Sinead held up a tote like Alannah's. "We come bearing gifts."

"Oh?" Maeve's face lit with interest as she studied the bag.

Alannah gave Maeve her lovely, serene smile. "We thought your look could do with updating."

"My look?" Maeve glanced from one to the other of them. "I'm not sure what that means."

"Your dress." Bronwyn didn't want to cause offense. "We noticed you're wearing the same one you were unfrozen in."

Maeve's face fell. "Yes. I need to make another, but with all that's been happening—"

"You made that?" Sinead stared at her. "Like yourself?"

"Ye-e-es." Maeve looked at Sinead as if one of them had lost their marbles and both of them knew who it was. "How else?"

"We buy our clothes now." Bronwyn held up the jeans. "These are mine, but I have another pair like them that I prefer. Same size and style, but I just like them better than these."

Alannah gaped at her. "Isn't it amazing how that always happens?"

"No, it doesn't." Sinead shook her head at them. "It's all in your min—"

"Those are breeches?" Maeve flushed as she stared at the jeans. "I'm not sure I dare."

"Of course you do." Sinead upended her bag on Maeve's bed. "Now we have a few other things for you to choose from. If you can sew, that solves the problem of them being too big for you."

Maeve approached the bed slowly. "Are all those for me?"

"The ones you like," Alannah said. She blushed. "But first we need to deal with the…er…undies."

Maeve looked confused for a second and then blushed alongside Alannah. "Oh."

"This is a bra." Sinead rooted around in Alannah's bag and came up with a lilac lace bra. "Actually the full word is brassiere, but nobody uses that anymore. Niamh has those huge knockers, but we guesstimate you are a similar bra size to Alannah and me."

Frowning, Maeve studied the bra. "There's not much to it, is there?"

"How much more do you need?" Sinead turned the bra to her and studied it. "Boobs go in the cups and the straps hold them firm. You don't need any more than that."

"I suppose not." Maeve kept her hands behind her back. "Is this what everyone wears as underthings now?"

"Well, these and knickers."

"Knickers?"

"What Bronwyn calls panties." Sinead hauled out a couple of packs of panties. "These have never been opened." She tore a pair out the pack and held them up for Maeve.

Maeve stared and then giggled. "Those are tiny."

"You're tiny," Sinead said. "And there will be no wearing of granny panties on my watch."

"What?" Maeve wrinkled her nose and looked ridiculously adorable.

"Never mind." Alannah came to her rescue. "Let's get these on you first and see if everything fits. Then we can try some clothes." She motioned the bed. "Anything catch your eye?"

Maeve swung to Bronwyn and pointed. "The breeches. I want to wear the breeches."

THE NEW WITCHES all wore those breeches, and Maeve had been coveting them since she'd first seen them. They clung to a woman's legs and bottom in a way that both scandalized and intrigued her. One would not have to worry about stepping on those, or trailing skirts through the mud. Even if they did leave your hidden parts exposed.

"We call these jeans," Alannah said. "Nearly everyone wears them, because they're so comfortable, and you can wear almost any top with them. It depends on what look you're going for." She handed the jeans to Maeve. "Of course, we'll get you your own clothes, but these should do for now."

First Maeve got into the underwear. The bra was simple enough, and Bronwyn did the fastenings for her. The panties were tiny and made her blush, but she wanted to get to those breeches, so she forged ahead.

The jeans fit. The fabric felt rough against her skin, but the jeans allowed her a surprising freedom of movement. She walked across the room, then back again taking longer strides.

"What do you think?" Bronwyn had a strange way of speaking that had taken Maeve a day or two to accustom herself to. "They look great on you."

"Really?" She peered over her shoulder at her bottom. It appeared very round and very there. "Does everyone's bottom stick out so far?"

Bronwyn laughed. "Did you just ask if your ass looks fat in those pants?"

Then Alannah and Sinead laughed as well, and Maeve found nothing funny in what she'd said.

"Sorry." Bronwyn caught her expression and sobered. "It's an old joke, and then the first thing you asked..." She waved a hand. "Never mind. We'll get to all the stuff eventually."

"You look gorgeous." Alannah handed her what looked like a chemise with impossibly thin straps. It was covered in the prettiest little flowers, however, and Maeve liked how cheerful it was. "Try this on."

"By itself?" The fabric was awfully thin, and in the right light, a person might see right through it.

"No." Sinead pointed. "You wear the bra under it."

"Or not." Niamh slunk into the room. "If you'd like to drive Roderick out of his tiny, Cro-Magnon mind, you could wear it without."

"Niamh." Alannah giggled. "He's not that bad."

Sinead snorted. "No, he's worse." She turned to Maeve. "Is he always so bossy?"

"No." The need to defend him roared through her, but the truth couldn't be denied. "Well, yes, but he is the first coimhdeacht and that is—was—a position of considerable power."

"Huh." Sinead wore a crafty look on her face that augured ill for Roderick's wellbeing.

It felt disloyal to say out loud that she was rather looking forward to Sinead taking on Roderick. It had been too long since Roderick's authority had been challenged. These women might be her friends. They were already her coven sisters. The thought pushed her loneliness back far enough for her to draw a deep breath. It felt like the first true breath she'd drawn since she woke in that time.

The shirt fit loosely, but she did like the way her bare arms and shoulders looked. "It's very daring for the daytime."

"Sister." Niamh grinned and tucked her arm through Maeve's. "Let's have this conversation again in a month or two."

Niamh had the same undeniable sensuality Edana had displayed, but there was a warmth to Niamh that Edana—may she rot in hell—had never possessed.

"There." With a smile, Alannah stepped back. "All done. Are you ready?"

"Not really." If she appeared like this, people might laugh at her. Roderick might not like it at all. Which should not bother her one bit. Indeed, if Roderick did not like her jeans, he could walk around in skirts. On that thought, she followed Alannah out of her chamber.

MAEVE WATCHED THE STRANGE ONE, Roz, as the woman made her odd clicking and whirring sounds and then scuttled out of the kitchen. "What ails her?"

"We're not sure." Niamh wrinkled her nose. "But she thinks she's an owl."

Certain she had misheard, Maeve stared at her. "She what?"

"Thinks she's an owl." Niamh heaved a sigh. "She wasn't always like this."

Sinead snorted. "Come on, Niamh, Roz has always been a bit weird."

The way they used words in this time was different as well. Maeve didn't think Sinead meant that Roz had the power to influence destiny. "Do you know her blessing?"

They all stared at her.

Had she said something odd? "Like I am a spirit walker." She pointed to Niamh. "You are a guardian, the twins are wardens, Bronwyn a healer. Blessings."

"Argh!" Bronwyn smacked her head with the heel of her palm. "That's why Roderick calls us Blessed."

Slack jawed, the others stared at Bronwyn.

"I can't believe we didn't make that connection," Sinead said.

Mags wandered into the kitchen, grabbed a piece of bread and ate it. She left again without a word. Seers were like that, locked in their own minds. Time was a circular concept to a seer—

"Locked in her own mind." Maeve had heard rumors about witches who had shared Roz's fate in the past. "Does Roz have your blessing?" She looked at Niamh. "Is she a guardian?"

Niamh thought it through. "She could." She pulled a face. "To be honest, I never had much to do with her when I was a child."

"It makes sense if Roz was like Niamh." Alannah nodded. "I remember Sinead and I had a cat called Cupcake who liked Roz so much better."

Sinead held up her hand. "For the record, I didn't choose the name. I would have gone with Ragnarok."

Rolling her eyes, Niamh said, "No wonder the cat preferred Roz."

"Well, what would you have named her?" Sinead ruffled up. She was passionate and outspoken like Lavina—like Lavina had been.

"I don't name them." Niamh shrugged. "They sort of put a picture in my head and that's how I think of them."

The others stared at her as if they had never heard the like. Maeve was starting to grasp how much these new witches didn't know, and it terrified her.

"I had no idea," Alannah said.

"You never asked," Niamh said. "And I never questioned it. It's always been something I do."

Maeve let that simmer in her mind. There was a truth there that escaped her at the present moment. "What element is Roz?"

"I don't know," Niamh said. "She's been like that for so long we don't know much about her."

Alannah sighed. "Poor thing. We really should do something about her."

"The healer can help," Maeve said. In her experience, healers could do almost anything given enough experience and natural magic.

Bronwyn straightened in her seat. "I can?"

"Well, yes." She now understood Bronwyn had come from somewhere far away from Baile, which was why she spoke as she did. "Once your vows are spoken and accepted."

All gazes snapped her way and stuck.

That missing truth hovered frustratingly closer, and Maeve tried to grasp it. "When you take your vows to Goddess and she accepts your service is what I meant." They still looked baffled, so she added, "The free will around being Blessed, that you can choose to spend your life in service to Goddess or not."

"So-o-o." Sinead took a deep breath and glanced at the others. "I know who Goddess is."

"Of course you do." Maeve laughed. Sinead really did have an irrepressible sense of humor. Except nobody about the table was laughing with her. "Don't you?"

"Of course we know who Goddess is." Alannah had the kindest smile that lit its recipient from within. "Although, up until recently, we assumed she was a legend connected to Baile. A bit like...gosh, I don't know...Athena or a valkyrie or Xena or something."

Maeve had no idea who those other women were, but that truth she was chasing inched closer. Her horror outstripped everything else, however. "Goddess is not a legend; she's real."

"Well, we know that now." Sinead folded her arms. "You can hardly blame us for not taking Goddess more seriously before. No offense, but you people thought the earth was flat."

The earth was flat, any fool could see that, but Maeve chose a different battle. "If you did not believe Goddess real, then you did not ever reach her through Goddess Pool." Desperation tightened her voice. "Did you?"

They all stared at her.

Bronwyn cleared her throat. "Why don't you tell us about Goddess? Start from the beginning and take it slow."

"I think I must." Dear Goddess, if they knew nothing, then Rhiannon had succeeded in her horrific plan. The day she had murdered the coven, she had buried magic and Goddess forever. "We don't know when or why Goddess came into being, but she did, and she created all you see about you."

"Wow!" Sinead grimaced. "The church must have loved you back in the day."

"Not at all." Again she had the feeling she'd missed the point, but this was too important to stop now. "In times long past, things were peaceful and harmonious. We lived with nature and she provided all we needed. Then came two brothers who fought."

The others listened, rapt.

"One of whom wanted what the other had, and they fought. The envious brother killed the other in what we call the original wrong."

"I like this version so much better than the paternalistic bull-shit I grew up with," Bronwyn said.

Sinead held up her hand. "Right there with you, sister."

They smacked their raised palms together.

"Carry on," Alannah said.

Mags appeared in the doorway. "Oh good, I thought I'd missed it." She took a seat at the table and beamed at everyone. "Maeve is about to tell us something we all need to hear."

Maeve had yet to meet a seer who wasn't peculiar.

"These brothers." Bronwyn sat forward. "They weren't called Cain and Abel, were they?"

The brother's names were hardly the important point to her story. "I have no idea, but the older killed the younger because of envy. It was the first time Goddess had seen such ugliness amongst her worshippers, and it made her angry. She withdrew from the world." Her audience hung on every word she uttered. If it were not so frightening how little they knew, Maeve might have been flattered. "Goddess is life, and the taking of life is against all that she is. It is why we, as cré-witches, can never use our magic to harm, even under fear of death."

They all looked at her as if they knew none of this.

"After a time, Goddess missed her creation and felt remiss for having abandoned it." This was a story told to every baby witch from the moment they could understand it, but not these witches, apparently. "She returned to find the darkness hidden within her creation had grown and almost choked out her essence. She called the first four witches to her service, to remind and guide her creation back to a time when they were in harmony with the essence of life."

Alannah shook her head. "I had no idea…"

"This is much bigger than anything we thought we were." Sinead glanced at Alannah.

"Oh, we're the remnants of a dying order," Mags said, looking strangely cheerful as she said it. "We're the ones who need to defeat Rhiannon." She made a helpless palms-up gesture. "At least Bronwyn is going to get the ball rolling on that."

Bronwyn stared at Mags. "Say what now?"

The prophecy! Bronwyn was the daughter of life, and no doubt, Alexander was the son of death. This was the battle, the true battle, at which the victor would be decided. She and Roderick had been sent here, to this time, to weight the scales in the favor of life.

Sitting at the kitchen table, almost four hundred years out of her time, Maeve finally got the answers to questions she'd posed before she and Roderick were spelled into stasis. So much of her previous life had been uncomfortable and inexplicable. A spirit walker raised to her full power so much younger than any other, a loner with few friends and fewer who understood her, suddenly the bonded mate of the most powerful coimhdeacht of all time. This was why. This was their purpose. She'd been right when she told Roderick they needed to bring magic back, but her task was bigger than she could have guessed. She had to teach these new witches how to be witches.

From their conversation thus far, she could guess none of them had ever been through any of the binding ceremonies required of a witch. If they had known nothing of Goddess, then it stood to reason they had never bound themselves in service.

That infuriatingly insubstantial truth slammed into her with the force of a steel spike; Roz was lost to the magic, warped, because more witches than Maeve's mind could grasp had been wielding magic without Goddess to ground and steady them.

Maeve had been wandering around in a fog since Alexander had wrenched her out of a statue and pushed her back behind Baile's wards. The fog cleared, and her first step was obvious; the new witches needed to make their pact with Goddess. Goddess needed them, and they needed to understand the power she represented.

CHAPTER SEVENTEEN

Bronwyn, along with Alannah, Sinead, Niamh and Mags followed Maeve across the bailey to the sea wall. She'd be lying if she said she wasn't excited. They were going to do some magic.

Wield some magic?

Cast some magic?

Make some magic?

She was spending a lot of brainpower finding the right verb. Mainly to keep the nerves at bay. All her life, she had been able to do stuff, inexplicable stuff that she had to keep hidden. Coming to Baile and meeting the Cray cousins had been a revelation. There were other people in the world like her and her family.

"So, how does this work?" Sinead had been firing a steady stream of questions since they'd left the kitchen.

What Maeve was talking about, and suggesting they get involved in, was on a whole new level. Maeve wasn't talking about being able to touch somebody and sort of absorb their pain or hurt. Nope, Maeve called her a healer and said she could heal. Like Lazarus kind of healing. Well, not quite waking the dead, and she was really glad that wasn't possible because... zombies—but taking someone's disease into herself and passing it into the earth.

Her gift would enable her—again she had only Maeve's word to go on here—to locate injuries and disease in a body and fix it, like some kind of metaphysical mechanic.

She was so deep in thought she almost tripped over one of Niamh's badgers, who had come along for the party.

The badger glared at her.

"Sorry," she said.

Mags fell into step with her. "You're not going back to America."

"Eh?"

"America." Mags gave her a serene smile. "You're not going back there. You're staying here."

Bronwyn narrowly avoided another badger tripping. "I haven't decided yet."

"I know." Mags didn't seem at all bothered by Bronwyn's opposition. "But you will."

According to Maeve, a seer like Mags should have the ability to see past, present and future. All the time. Mags was odd enough without adding that to the mix.

"Is it difficult sometimes?" People always thought they'd like to know their future, but sometimes it was better not knowing. If she'd known she would lose Deidre so soon, it might have messed with the time they'd had together. "There must be stuff you wished you'd never seen."

Mags winced. "There is, but I don't tell people about the bad stuff." She looked sad. "They'd only try to change things, and that never works out well."

"Of course they do." If she'd known, she might have warned Deidre not to get into her car that day, and she might have Deidre with her now. Deidre might have lived to see Baile and meet the other witches.

"But time doesn't work that way," Mags said. "You can't change one thing and expect it not to change everything else around it. Everything is interconnected."

Bronwyn still would have tried to save Deidre. But then she might not have come here with her inheritance.

"Say I told you there would be an accident and a baby would die." Mags said, chattier than normal today. "You'd want to save the baby, right?"

Bronwyn sensed a trap. "Uh-huh."

"But what if that baby grew up to be Hitler, would you still want to save the baby?"

"Obviously not."

"So you see." Mags shrugged. "Everything is so woven together that for as long as we're tethered to this physical realm we're in, we can only see time as linear and how the events along that line affect us."

"And when you see the future, what do you see?" Bronwyn accepted Mags's point, but she knew she wouldn't have been able to stop herself from trying to prevent Deidre's death.

Mags sighed. "It's mostly frustrating and comes to me in flashes that aren't very clear. It leaves far too much to inter-pretation."

"Maeve says you can fix that by bonding with Goddess." A concern raised its head. "I really hope this bonding thing isn't going to involve blood. I can't condone anybody cutting them-selves on purpose."

Maeve opened the sea door and led the way down the stairs to the caverns. The stairs were steep, and Bronwyn was glad she'd first climbed them in the dark. She might not have used them if she had seen clearly how high they rose and how far the drop off the side was.

Wind tugged at their hair and clothing. Like a sail, Mags's caftan snapped against her legs.

Crossing the threshold into the caverns, Bronwyn shivered.

She felt…something, a watchful presence. Not in a creepy way, but there nonetheless.

"These sigils represent witches who journeyed to the sacred isles." Maeve ran her fingertips over the elaborate embedded patterns on the cavern walls. "As a spirit walker, it is my task to put the sigils upon the wall, and my gift is the ability to access the dead through them and walk amongst them."

Bronwyn shivered, more intensely this time. The idea of walking amongst the dead made her uncomfortable.

As if sensing her reaction, Maeve turned to her and smiled. "As a healer, what I do often works contrary to your blessing." She glanced at the sigils, a reverent expression on her upturned face. This was Maeve's place. She was more present here than any other place Bronwyn had seen her thus far. The patterns on the walls had real meaning and significance to Maeve.

When she'd first ended up in the caverns, Bronwyn had had no idea how extensive the network of caves really was. She got it now as she and the others followed Maeve from one cavern to another. Arched doorways and corridors connected the caverns, many of them also covered in patterns—sigils. They were not decorative but represented the women of her bloodline. Cré-witches past, who had come before her and known what she was about to learn.

Maeve led them into a cavern that was larger than the rest. It also had more sigils on the walls, even up and over the ceiling. In the center of the cavern was a pool, glowing gentle luminous silver.

"Goddess Pool." Maeve stopped beside it. "And also the cardinal point for the water element." She gave Bronwyn a loaded glance as if it being the cardinal water point would somehow mean something to her. "It's also the nearest point at which we can communicate with Goddess from Baile."

Niamh tiptoed to the edge and peered into the water. "This pool is full of magic?"

"Not in and of itself." Maeve joined her. "It's a portal, a door that needs to be opened to access the magical powers of the water element." She nodded at Bronwyn. "Your element."

"I'm fire," Niamh said and then grimaced. "At least I think I am. Where's the cardinal point for fire?"

Maeve shrugged. "I really don't know, and I'm also fire. Before, when I lived here all four cardinal points were active. None of us knew where they were because we didn't need to know."

"There must be something in the library," Mags said. She shook her head. "I've been spending more and more time in there. You wouldn't believe how much information is sitting on those shelves, and we had no idea."

Crouching by the pool, Maeve stared into its depths. After a while, she sighed and glanced at them. "She's there. I can sense her, but she's too faint for much more than the vague sense of her being there."

"Should I try?" Bronwyn really didn't know how any of this worked, but she'd like to try something.

"You could." Maeve frowned at the water.

Bronwyn crouched beside her. "What should I do?"

"Umm." Maeve frowned. "Spell casting was not my blessing. I only ever watched other witches cast in their blessings. Reach your awareness into the water."

"Okay." Bronwyn stared at the water.

From this close, it was more a very pale blue than silver. The surface was as flat and clear as a mirror. Her face stared back at her. "I'm not sure what I'm doing," she said. "I don't feel anything."

Maeve pursed her lips.

"What about how you stopped the water in the kitchen?" Alannah joined them at the edge. "Do what you did then."

"I'm not sure what I did." Bronwyn tugged that memory to the forefront. "The water was running and I just—"

"Look!" Alannah nudged her.

A small ripple broke the pool's surface.

"Do it again," Maeve said.

Bronwyn reached within, the scent of honey and sage rose around her. Another ripple broke the water's surface, the same as the one before.

"Well," Maeve said. "Now we know for certain you're a water witch."

"Alexander knew that too." Bronwyn had almost forgotten her first conversation with him. "How could he have known I was a water witch?"

"I don't know." Maeve looked worried. Then her face cleared into a smile. "But I do know who can get Goddess to speak with us." She beamed at them. "Roderick. She always talks to Roderick."

MAEVE DIDN'T KNOW where Roderick had spent his time the last few days, or what he was doing. He was always there, within her. Through the bond, she knew he was aware of her and he was well. Now that she was more accustomed to it, it was a state she could exist in indefinitely. He didn't bother her or irk her; he was just a constant presence—comforting and safe.

She reached down the bond to him.

His question pulsed back at her, and she opened her senses so he could see where she was. She formed the desire for him to join them and combined that with the sense that she needed something from him.

Immediately he set out toward her. Her sense of him strengthened as he drew closer to the caverns.

"Ah!" Mags turned to the entrance. "Roderick is here."

Three heartbeats later, he came through the entranceway to the central cavern.

If Mags could use this much of her blessing without access to her element, it augured well for her power when they could connect her to her element.

"Blessed." Roderick inclined his head to the gathered witches. "You have need of me?"

"Yes." Maeve stood so he could see her. "Goddess is so dim—"

"What are you wearing?" Roderick gaped at her. His gaze raked her from top to toe, and his lip curled. "You look ridiculous. You need to cover yourself, not flaunt your body for all to see."

"Oy!" Sinead got in front of him. "You have no right to speak to her like that, you absolute prat."

He didn't, and Maeve stood like a puppet and absorbed the blow of his words. She wanted to cry. She wanted to shout at him that she didn't look ridiculous. She wanted to run and hide.

His remorse surged through the bond, but her hurt ran deep and fresh.

"I'm with her." Alannah squared up to him beside Sinead. "You need to make this right, and do it now."

"Maeve?" He tried to sidestep Alannah, but she got in his path.

"You go near her without an apology, and I'll rip your balls off and shove them down your throat."

Up until that point, Maeve would have sworn Sinead was the more aggressive twin, but it appeared as if riling Alannah had dire consequences.

"You take that back and beg for her forgiveness. Make it good, or I'll make you sorry you were born."

"Dickhead." Niamh glared at him. She put her arm about Maeve. "The only magic in this cave today is your arse in those jeans. Trust me on this."

Roderick stared at her. Regret was written on his face, but she didn't need to see it to know he felt it. Their bond overflowed with his emotion. Regret, chagrin, and…something else. Something animal and potent, undeniably sensual.

"What is that?" She didn't realize she had voiced the question until he responded.

Roderick looked at her, gaze intent and loaded. "You know what that is. You can feel it." He turned his attention to Alannah. "I am deeply sorry for what I said to Maeve. She shocked me wearing those clothes. We come from a different time, and while I am accustomed to you wearing things like that, I did not expect it from Maeve. It took me by surprise, and I misspoke myself."

Alannah folded her arms and glared. "Is that it?"

"She looks…" He pushed a hand through his hair and looked at her. "Can we speak of this alone, Maeve?"

With all she could sense going on inside him, that was probably a good idea. "I think that would be for the best." She looked at her allies and defenders. "Would you mind leaving us alone?"

"I don't know." Sinead poked Roderick in the chest. "I still think we should toss his arse out of here."

Roderick raised a brow and stared down at her. He used a phrase he'd picked up from Thomas. "You and whose army?"

Maeve kept her gaze on the other witches trailing out of the cavern. With Roderick silently standing in front of her, she was acutely aware of him, and all they didn't know about each other, and all the things unsaid between them.

Before disappearing into the next-door cavern, Sinead turned and jabbed her fore and middle fingers at her eyes and then at Roderick. "I'm watching you, motherfucker."

Roderick flinched. "She has a mouth on her."

The free swearing was taking her time to accept as well. It wasn't that they hadn't always used swear words, but not as freely, and Sinead certainly had a colorful way of cobbling her profanities together. Mother and fucker were not two words Maeve would ever have placed together.

"Maeve?" Roderick had moved to within a few inches of her, which forced her to peer up at him, and it made her feel at a disadvantage.

She took a step back.

He reached out and caught her hip with one hand. "Let me say this."

His hand warmed her skin though her breech—jeans as she waited for him to continue.

"Sinead is right to chastise me for what I said."

Chastise seemed too mild a word for Sinead's outburst, or the one by Alannah and finally Niamh. As a spirit walker, she'd always been more isolated from the coven than the other witches. In this time, she had already experienced more support and companionship than the time she'd been born in.

"You look astounding, Maeve." His cool blue eyes warmed from within. "You robbed me of thought and left me saying the first stupid thing that made its way out my mouth."

The look in his eyes tugged at something within her. A warm, melty sensation swirled in her belly. "I'm trying to find my feet in these times."

"I know that." He grasped her other hip. "And you're doing it so much better than I."

"No, Roderick—"

"Yes, Maeve, and that's why the breeches—"

"Jeans, and men wear them too."

"Jeans." A slight smile softened his serious face. "I'm adrift in these times, Maeve. I've lived for so long and seen so many different things, but this..." He shook his head. "I could never have predicted all that has occurred, all they've built and invented, all their technology." He said the word slowly and carefully as if it felt strange on his tongue. "Thomas has been helping me bridge the distance, closing the gap."

"They have created many marvelous things." She wanted to touch him, and she placed her palms against his chest. Even with their bond, the physical touch brought a warmer connection. "And much has changed. But Roderick, much has not changed. People are still people with all their beauty and foibles. Beneath their new clothes, they are still women and men."

"Perhaps not." Roderick grimaced. "Thomas is attempting to explain trans and gender fluid to me."

"Eh?" It was like he was speaking a foreign tongue.

"Never mind." Roderick tightened his hands at her hips. "When I came in and saw you looking like one of them, I panicked. I felt like I was losing my last connection to things I knew and understood."

"Oh, Roderick." He allowed some of what roiled within him to seep into their bond. "You are always so strong, so resolute. It never occurs to me that you might have your travails."

"Of the two of us, my witch, you are the stronger." He shook his head when she tried to deny it. "I can swing a sword, fight, kill. But you are my anchor in this time, all that remains of what we have lost."

"*Coimhdeacht.*" Whisper soft and sweet, Goddess's voice echoed from the pool. "*She is your reason for being here, and together, your purpose is mighty.*"

"Goddess." Roderick dropped to his knee.

It took Maeve a moment to react she was so shocked. Then she yelled for the others. "Come quickly!"

They all tumbled around the corner as if they had been hiding behind it listening.

Despite being the smallest, Bronwyn reached her first. "What? What did he do?"

"Goddess." Maeve pointed to where Roderick still remained on bended knee. "She spoke to him."

"What?" Niamh blinked at her, took a tottering step toward Roderick and leaped back again. "I don't know what to do."

"*Blessed.*" Goddess's voice was barely above a gentle breeze, but the effect was instantaneous. As one, they sank to their knees on the cold, hard cavern floor.

The new witches paled and stared at the pool.

Sinead's mouth worked but produced no words.

"Mother." Maeve bowed her head.

"Mother," the others intoned and copied her actions.

"My Blessed," Goddess's voice sounded a little stronger. *"The dark one spreads her stain across this world. She creeps into all areas of power and influence and her strength grows daily."*

Maeve dared a question. "What would you have us do, Mother?"

"You must act," Goddess said. *"I have called my new four. You must bond your magic to me."*

CHAPTER EIGHTEEN

Bronwyn couldn't sleep that night, and judging by the baking spree Alannah was presently in the middle of, neither could she.

"Hey." Bronwyn managed a smile as she sat at the kitchen table. "Guess you're thinking about what happened this morning."

Alannah frowned into the bowl she was stirring so vigorously it shook her entire body. "I don't see how I can't. Also, Sinead snores and keeps me awake."

The twins shared a suite with two bedrooms and a central living room. Maeve had told them the suite used to belong to the coven leader, Fiona. The same coven leader who had betrayed the coven to Rhiannon.

Thinking about Rhiannon inevitably brought her thinking round to Alexander, and she'd resolved to stop that shit.

"Want some tea?" Alannah jerked her head at the kettle.

Like a dose of the clap, Bronwyn wanted tea. "Don't you have anything stronger? Or is that kind of against coven code or something?"

"Bloody hell, I hope not." Alannah put down her bowl and

disappeared into one of the back pantries. She came back with a bottle of whisky and plunked it on the table. "Glasses are behind you. Pour me one while you're at it."

After Goddess had spoken—her brain capillaries were still exploding over a speaking deity in a pool in the middle of a cave —they had returned to the castle to discuss it.

Mags had been all for going ahead with the bonding right there and then. Her confidence was somewhat reassuring, but not enough to persuade the rest of them to drop and bond on the spot.

Sinead had been the most vociferous about waiting. She wasn't keen to take part in a ceremony she knew nothing about, with a deity she'd only realized recently wasn't symbolic, to achieve an outcome she didn't understand or trust.

What a wuss. Bronwyn snort laughed into her whisky.

"Cheers." Alannah tapped her glass against Bronwyn's. "Tell me." Her eyes sparkled with mischief. "Does this sort of thing happen often when you travel?"

It struck Bronwyn as inordinately funny and she started laughing. There was only so much one girl could take: ancient prophecies, men who you weren't supposed to fall in love with, evil witches, talking ghosts and deity-infested pools.

Alannah joined her, and their laughter escalated until Bronwyn was thumping the table and Alannah was struggling to stand.

"God." Bronwyn's laugher abated. "I have no idea what to do."

Alannah nodded. She got it without Bronwyn having to explain. "It goes without saying that you're welcome to stay. Forever if you like."

"You have to stay." Maeve entered the kitchen, swathed in a high-neck, full-length nightgown. With her hair in a long braid down her back, she looked like a Victorian girl. "Without you, Goddess doesn't have her four."

"I know that." And the vice that had been around Bronwyn's chest since she'd first heard Goddess speak tightened. "But it's not that simple. There are all kinds of things to consider, my house in the States, my store."

"Passports. Citizenship." Alannah tossed her whisky back. As it hit her belly, she wheezed and screwed her eyes shut. "Wow! Was that ever awful." Her eyes popped open and she held her glass out. "More."

Bronwyn topped her up then offered the bottle to Maeve. "Can I get you a glass?" She motioned the nightie. "Although, in that getup, I might get arrested for serving alcohol to a minor."

Maeve blinked at her.

Bronwyn tried again. "You look too young to drink."

"Oh!" Maeve grabbed her own glass and joined her at the table. "I'm twenty fo—well, no, I suppose not." She downed her whiskey without blinking. "I'm closer to four hundred."

Bronwyn refilled all their glasses. "You look good for your age."

They all giggled, Maeve harder than most. "Yes, but it does make me officially the oldest living virgin in history."

"You're a virgin?" No way Bronwyn wasn't following that lead.

Alannah sat forward. "So, you and Rod—"

"No!" Maeve squeaked and blushed. "Never!"

"I thought for sure you had." Bronwyn glanced at Alannah who nodded her agreement.

Maeve took her next shot as fast as the first. "It's because of the bond. It creates...intimacy between us."

Bronwyn snorted. "You keep telling yourself that, sister. The rest of us will enjoy watching Hot Rod and his blue balls stomp around Baile."

Blushing, Maeve giggled so hard she snorted. "The way you speak is so funny."

"She's American," Alannah said, and then shook her head as

Maeve opened her mouth. "Nope. No history lessons tonight. Tonight, we get drunk and do girl talk."

Bronwyn raised her glass and toasted both of them. "Also, no magic talk, no Goddess talk and no prophecies." And definitely no inconvenient feelings for woefully inappropriate men talk.

"Hear! Hear!" Alannah took her shot and shuddered.

MAEVE HADN'T REALLY HAD friends in the coven before. Her blessing was a solitary one and dealt with death. Nobody really liked being around death that much, not even her, and she understood it wasn't an end but merely a transition into another state.

Another thing she wasn't familiar with was being drunk, and she definitely thought she might be. An hour or so—she wasn't so sure of her timeline anymore—since she'd joined Bronwyn and Alannah, and the kitchen was blanketed in a warm, fuzzy glow, or perhaps that was happening inside her. Who could tell?

Bronwyn squinted at her. "This must be so weird for you."

"You keep saying weird." Maeve blinked until Bronwyn's face stopped being blurry. "I don't think you mean weird."

Frowning, Bronwyn replenished their glasses. Something must have happened to the whisky because it was way farther down than it should be. "Of course I mean weird. Weird is weird."

"Not in my world." And that made her laugh because she wasn't entirely sure where her world was. Her head felt heavy, and she wanted to put it on the table and let the soft, warm cloud she was floating on take her into sleep. "I'm so tired."

"Hmm?" Alannah smiled at her. "You should sleep."

"I don't sleep."

Bronwyn blinked. "Why not?"

"Can't." She could rest her head on the table for a minute. The wood was cool beneath her cheek. "Scared."

"No." Alannah reeled back in her chair. "What are you scared of?"

"Not waking up again." Her eyelids dragged toward each other and stayed closed. "Like happened before."

"That's bad." Bronwyn hiccupped. "Does Hot Rod know?"

Hot Rod! That was such a silly name, and she giggled. Roderick would get all grim faced if she called him that. She might call him that anyway. "Roderick knows everything. Everything." She waved a hand above her head to be sure they understood how much of everything. "I can't hide anything from him. Well, I can." She pushed herself up on her elbows. "But I did that before, and it didn't end well."

Alannah and Bronwyn leaned toward her, waiting. If she told them, they might not like her. Then again, they should hear the truth. "He nearly died." The memory had her reaching for the bottle. She slopped whisky into all three glasses. "He nearly died because of me." She blinked into the amber courage giver in her glass. "I didn't listen to him. Then they tried to drown me. He came to rescue me. Because he had to. No choice." Poor Roderick. He really had gotten the worst witch to watch over. "It's what they do. The coimhdeacht." Her new friends didn't look like they hated her, and she had their total attention. "Witches first, them second. That's why they all died here that day. They saved the witches first."

Sighing, Alannah patted her hand where it lay on the table. "I can't imagine how awful that was."

"It was." That day was the other reason she didn't sleep well. When she closed her eyes, the memories of those few weeks flooded her mind. "It all got bad so fast."

"Oh, honey!" Bronwyn blinked back tears. "You can tell us if you like."

"It was Rhiannon." Even now, saying that name made her

wince. "And Alexander. He tried to get the villagers to put me in the water. Trial by Water, you know."

Alannah nodded. "If the witch drowned, she was innocent. If she floated, the devil saved her, and they killed her."

"That's not fair." Bronwyn scowled. "I really hate that all those women died." Sighing, Bronwyn refilled their glasses. "I really wish I didn't know that."

"Me too." The grief threatened to engulf her. "I grew up with them. They were my coven sisters. Rhiannon was looking for a way in, and somehow, she got Edana and Fiona to betray the coven. Why would they do that?" She looked at Alannah for the answer. Other than when she was shouting at Roderick, Alannah was gentle and sweet and wise.

"I don't know, love." Alannah took her other hand. "Maybe she promised them more power or immortal life or something."

"It must have been the power." Maeve liked having her hands held like this. It comforted her. "The immortal life we have. Well, not actual immortality, but as close to it as we can get."

Bronwyn gaped at her. "Huh?"

"The magic." She still couldn't believe that she, of all witches, would be the one to teach the new witches. Goddess, if they knew her better, they would be as shocked as she was. "It prolongs your life. The longer you use it, and the more you use it, the stronger you become."

Bronwyn gave this some thought. "What if you fall down the cliff?"

"The magic can heal you." Before they went tossing themselves off cliffs, they needed to be clear on the next point. "If it can heal you faster than your injuries could kill you, then you're fine. If not..." She shrugged, because she was certain they were getting the point.

"Cut off your head?" Alannah swiped her throat with her thumb.

"Depends how fast you bleed," she said. "If you're Rhiannon

and have been around for thousands of years and have used…"
She couldn't find the right word. "A huge amount of magic, then
she might survive."

"Jeesh." Bronwyn blew a hair tendril out her face. "Does that
go for Roderick and the"—she waved her hand—"whatever
he is?"

"Yes." At least she assumed it was similar. "When he came to
save me that time, he almost died then. Alexander cut him with
his sword." She motioned a cut across her ribs, abdomen and
thighs. "But he was old, even then, and his healing saved him."

"Boy, can I pick 'em." Bronwyn filled up their glasses and
then stared at the empty bottle. "What did you do? That nearly
got Roderick killed."

Maeve winced. It sounded even worse when someone else
said it. "The healers wanted to go to the village. There was a
plague, and they wanted to heal the sick." She pointed at Bronwyn. "When you take your vows, you will always be wanting to
help people. Healers care, and they can't stop themselves.
Anyway." She took a deep breath. "Fiona said nobody could
leave the castle, but I knew a way they could. Roderick told me
not to, but I did it anyway."

"He must have been mad." Bronwyn whistled.

"Why?" Roderick had never been addled to her knowledge.
"No, he was perfectly sane."

"Not mad." Bronwyn giggled. "Mad like angry. Pissed."

"Furious. Enraged." Alannah nodded.

"He was awfully bossy about me not going." She remembered that part clearly. "But after Thomas and the others
rescued him from the village, he never said anything to me
about it. In fact, he said witches are witches and he was used to
that."

"Thomas is the ghost." Alannah blushed as she told Bronwyn
that. "The one we saw in the barracks." She turned to Maeve.
"What was he like? Thomas?"

"Ah!" She had liked Thomas a lot. Roderick had gotten jealous of Thomas flirting with her. "He was charming. Handsome." She smiled at the memory of Thomas's wicked smile. "And the most dreadful rake." She shook her head. "He was bonded to Lavina, and she was a lot older than him. She didn't seem to mind all the other witches sharing his sheets."

"Oh." Alannah's face fell. "A manwhore."

Maeve had never heard that expression, and it made her laugh. "Roderick was one too. A manwhore."

Bronwyn snorted. "Hermione will be delighted."

"Who's that?"

Bronwyn waved her glass. "Never mind. Doesn't matter."

Maeve finished her last whisky and sighed at the empty bottle. "We need to get you Goddess bonded."

"Nope." Bronwyn thumped the table. "We're not talking about that now."

Maeve shrugged it off. "Fair enough." Because she was enjoying not having to face Rhiannon and her relentless attacks on Baile, how inexperienced everyone was, how little they knew...and there she went again. "Is there any more whisky?"

"Maeve?" Roderick stood in the doorway. And he was wearing jeans, and what they called a T-shirt. Face impassive, he looked at the empty bottle and glasses, then at Alannah and Bronwyn. He inclined his head. "Blessed."

Bronwyn stuck two fingers in her mouth and whistled. "Rocking the jeans, Roderick."

Roderick flushed and cleared his throat. "I need to look like I belong to this time."

"Turn around." Bronwyn drew a circle in the air with her forefinger. "Let's see if you look as good leaving as you do coming."

It made Maeve giggle so much that she couldn't sit up straight.

With a hard stare at Bronwyn, Roderick sighed. "Is there a reason you're getting my Blessed drunk?"

"She did that all on her own," Bronwyn said. "And I'm drowning my sorrows."

"Hello. Love what you're doing to those jeans." Alannah giggled and waved. "We've been chatting."

Roderick picked up the bottle and read the label. "What are you chatting about?"

"Well, I'll tell you what we're not chatting about." Maeve really hated it when he made her feel like a naughty little girl. "Not the situation we find ourselves in." Raising her brow, she dared him to challenge her. Roderick was her coimhdeacht, not her father.

"I see." Roderick stared at her. "I have been speaking with Thomas."

Alannah sighed. "I like Thomas. He's funny and sweet."

"He's a philandering whoreson," Roderick said. "And death has not changed that. I would stay away from him if I were you."

"He's nice." Maeve patted Alannah's hand. "Roderick likes to keep all the witches for himself."

Roderick drew his shoulders back. "And you're the worse for drink."

"I think she's the better for drink." Bronwyn giggled.

Drawing a careful breath, Roderick said, "Quite so. I came to tell you I have an appointment outside the castle. It's why I'm dressed as I am."

"With who?" Bronwyn scowled and swayed in her chair. "You don't know anyone in this time. Other than—"

"Indeed." Roderick turned on his heel, calling over his shoulder. "Nobody is to put a toe outside Baile until I return. This won't take long."

CHAPTER NINETEEN

A lexander contemplated the night outside his kitchen and indulged in pointless musings about Bronwyn. Even as he blinked her face away, he swore he could still smell honey and sage. His connection to her ached like a phantom limb. He hadn't anticipated missing her as much as he did.

Typically Roderick, he issued a psychic summons as subtle as an eighteen-wheeler careening downhill without brakes and with a joy-riding fifteen-year-old at the wheel.

Alexander crossed his arms behind his back and stared at the star strewn sky. He could ignore Roderick stomping about, tossing off a challenge Rhiannon would definitely hear, or he could deal with the sod now.

Alexander really didn't like the idea—as in really, really, really didn't like that idea—of working with Roderick, but necessity made strange bedfellows. Instead of untangling that metaphor, he put his whisky down and opened the secret compartment behind the coat closet in his hall.

On a wood panel, rested his collection of arms, none of which he'd used in more years than he cared to remember. He selected a broadsword and closed the panel.

This would not be a midnight picnic of cake and ales. On the plus side, it had been years since he'd crossed swords with an opponent as worthy as Roderick.

He let himself out of his manor and padded into the still night. It was well past the time anyone would be up and about, and Greater Littleton slept around him as he slipped silently through the village.

Pervasive and jarring as an air raid warning, Roderick's presence drew him to the village green. Of course, Roderick would have used the tunnels to meet him there. The man wasn't stupid, and Alexander had given Roderick more than enough reasons not to trust him. The last time they'd tangled, Alexander had the entire village supporting him.

Standing in the scant moonlight near the plinth, Roderick waited for him. He was wearing jeans and a T-shirt and looked as if he'd been raised in this time. The man knew how to adapt as well, which was a good thing because those baby witches at Baile needed him up to speed.

"You look better than when last I saw you." Alexander made sure Roderick caught his approach. The warrior was too quick and deadly to risk surprising.

Roderick unsheathed his sword. "Which time was that?"

"When I woke you." Alexander palmed his sword and tested his wrist. Tonight he was dealing with Roderick at full strength, and his years in stasis looked to have done nothing to weaken him. He prodded the beast. "Of course, the time before that you weren't looking so pretty either."

"You mean when you attacked me with an entire village by your side?" Roderick circled, gaze intent, his sword at the ready. Alert and in command of himself, he was poised to strike.

Alexander remembered that day in the village differently. "The villagers may have been there, but it was me you fought." He bared his teeth in a mockery of a smile. "And lost."

"Is that what you tell yourself?" Roderick was too seasoned a warrior to let himself be angered into a precipitous attack. "Instead of arguing about it, why don't we settle it now?"

He moved so quickly Alexander barely got his sword up in time. Their blades caught on the bind, and Alexander shoved his way free. He needed to pay attention. Roderick could carve him into thousands of tiny pieces and still keep him alive. "Is that why you called me here?"

"Partly." Roderick struck again, a rapid strike, pivot and then back hand.

Steel clashed loudly in the silent night. Sparks flew from their swords. The shock of connecting steel blades jarred his arm and slammed his shoulder joint. The bastard was strong as an ox. Alexander refused to show any weakness. "What's the other part?"

"Why?" Roderick dropped back, circling, looking for an opening or a weak point to exploit. "Need to catch your breath?"

Alexander swept right to left, shifted his grip and reversed his stroke.

Grunting, Roderick caught him on the bind and kicked. "I don't like mysteries."

Alexander danced clear. "You're going to have to be more specific."

"Why did you wake us? Then shove us to safety." He came in, and all conversation died in the thrust, block, parry of sword play.

Winded, Alexander dropped back to catch his breath. Easy modern living had softened him, and every time Roderick blocked, it felt like striking solid granite. "I'm afraid you're really not going to like the answer."

"Color me amazed." Roderick came in for a fast exchange.

Alexander had no idea where Roderick had picked that saying up from but he was too busy to give it much thought. He met each blow, blocked, and waited for the volley to end.

Breathing heavily, sweat beading his face, Roderick pushed clear of him.

"Would you believe I've had a change of heart?" Alexander kept his attention locked on Roderick's chest. The blows would telegraph from there.

Roderick laughed. "No."

"Color me amazed." He had expected nothing less from Roderick. For as long as they'd known each other, and that was a long time, they'd been trying to kill each other. "But there it is."

"Eh?" Roderick's guard wavered for a second. "You expect me to believe you've had a change of heart. You! The son of that heinous bitch."

"Your skepticism is valid." For many of the years of his long life, he'd been that heinous bitch's henchman. Like a good soldier, he had fulfilled the purpose for which she had created him. All except his ultimate purpose, and it looked like that play was on the field. "But how else would you explain me waking you in time to save those lost witchlings up there in Baile? They have no idea what they're capable of or how to do what needs to happen to save the coven."

His words must have registered because Roderick lowered his sword arm slightly. "Why should I believe you?"

"You don't have to." Alexander would have been the same. "But believe this, Bronwyn is the daughter of life, and not only because she's going to have a kid who will be a game changer. Bronwyn herself is important. She's the one who needs to wake the water cardinal point."

Roderick growled. "We know that. Don't tell me our business."

"Someone has to." Alexander got his sword up in time to meet Roderick's rapid strike. Either the big man was tiring or had lost some of the intent to kill him, because the blow was marginally less anvil-like than his previous blows. "You need to keep her clear of Rhiannon. Rhiannon wants her, and she wants her badly enough to do anything to get her."

"Rhiannon can't get behind the wards." Roderick scowled, perhaps not as certain as he appeared.

"Not yet she can't," Alexander said. "But I can." He spoke slowly and clearly, lowering his sword for the next bit. Roderick needed to understand and understand well. "If she finds out what I can do, and she uses me to get her hands on Bronwyn, she's going to be unstoppable. You and I both know the prophecy will come about. Bronwyn is going to have a baby, and Rhiannon will use that baby to blow those wards wide."

"You'd have to get near enough to Bronwyn to make that baby for the prophecy to happen." Roderick tested his wrist as he circled Alexander. "I'm not about to let that happen."

"You know your Goddess." The respite had recharged Roderick, and the tenacious bastard was ready to go again. "This is her prophecy, and she will make it happen. Regardless of what you or I think of it." He stepped to the left and feinted right out of the path of a coming blow. "For the record, I have no interest in becoming anyone's father."

Roderick winced. "I don't know what your game is, but I'm going to stop you."

"You don't have to know what my game is, but you do need to take care of Bronwyn." Their talk had gone better than Alexander could have expected. "Heed my warning and watch her because Rhiannon is poised and waiting for her chance."

Roderick studied him, then sheathed his sword. "Let's end this." His fist connected with Alexander's jaw and sent him reeling. "Stay the fuck away from my witches."

Spitting blood, Alexander came in for more. Roderick was right; it was time to end it, and beating the shit out of each other sounded like a much more satisfying alternative. "Gladly."

HOLY FUCK, but Alexander really needed to be more careful about what he wished for. He'd gotten his fight with Roderick all right.

Alexander rolled to his belly and spit blood and grass from his mouth.

He ached. Like all over ached. Like it would be a waste of time cataloguing each excruciatingly painful body part. Pressing his forehead into the cool, damp grass, he hauled a ragged breath into his lungs. His ribs let him know all about how much they didn't want to do the whole inhale-exhale song and dance. They'd much rather hang in his chest like a pair of limp footballs and whimper.

A car engine growled closer, and Alexander considered crawling behind the bench and out of sight. His body would repair itself in time, and he didn't want some well-meaning soul dragging him to an emergency room.

Digging his fingers into the pliant earth, he tried to haul himself into hiding.

Ke-rist! That wasn't happening.

Breath in, breath out.

If he had to break it down to a good news / bad news scenario, the good news was that he hadn't forgotten how strong Roderick was and how hard the bastard could hit. That was pretty much the bad news as well.

The car engine grew louder and then ended in a series of bangs and wheezes.

He might have cried a bit at the thought of Roderick being in that Land Rover.

Footsteps swished through the dew on the grass. He breathed jasmine and almond in through his busted nose.

"Mags," he managed to lisp through his swollen lips.

Mags wove into view above him, backlit for a moment before she crouched beside him. "Oh dear." Her luminous green eyes took him in. "You look terrible."

"Surprisingly, I feel terrible as well." At least his sense of humor wasn't broken. His pride was a lost cause right now. Roderick may have lost their previous fight, but this one was definitely chalked up as a win under the R column.

"Here." Mags held out a bottle of water and dropped a couple of tablets into his hand. "Just a couple of aspirin, but I thought they might help."

Even the remote possibility they would help had him gulping down the tablets with a swallow of water. "Thank you."

"My pleasure." Mags beamed her big, beautiful smile at him. "I had this feeling you would need me when Roderick was done with you."

He nodded and dragged himself into a sitting position. The pain left him lightheaded, and he thought he might pass out. Again. After beating the crap out of him, Roderick had left moments before Alexander passed out. It was downright heart-warming that Roderick hadn't chopped his head off. "Roderick and I go way back."

Mags snort laughed and peeped at him from beneath her long, dark lashes. "Talk about your understatements."

Alexander was fond of all the Baile girls, but Mags had an endearing mix of innocent and worldly that brought something protective and fraternal out in him. The thought of losing her friendship and trust hurt more than his ribs. "I'm sorry, Mags. I couldn't tell you all of it."

"I probably wouldn't have believed you anyway." Mags took a seat beside him, unmindful of the damp grass. "The whole thing is doing my head in a bit."

"I can imagine." He'd had hundreds of years to get used to Rhiannon, Goddess, magic, all of it, and there were still times when he hit a reality-check moment.

They sat in silence as he sipped his water. Already, his accelerated healing ability had started knitting together muscle.

Birds in the oak trees above them twittered and chirped as

they sensed dawn drawing closer. Car lights illuminated the Landy, parked with two wheels on the pavement, and swept on.

"Despite the past." Words he'd never spoken but wanted to for so long gummed up his throat. "Everything I've done. I would never have hurt you."

Mags cocked her head and smiled. "I know that, Alexander. Can you walk yet?"

Her gentle acceptance almost unmanned him. He looked down and blinked rapidly. It must have been the pain of his injuries making his eyes water. If it killed him, he'd get to his feet.

Getting vertical very nearly did kill him, and he had to lean on Mags as the lightening green spun around him. Without her, he wouldn't have made it to the Landy. She was tall enough that her shoulder fit beneath his arm, and her willowy strength guided him into the vehicle.

She set off for his house, the Landy letting out a volley as they went.

"Thanks," he said, and it was so inadequate but all he had.

"You're important to us, Alexander." Streetlights flashed orange across her fine bone structure. "Your part in this is only beginning."

Mags was growing in her power, and he felt like a proud parent. He nodded that he'd heard her, and the rest of the drive passed in silence.

At his house, she helped him to the door and left him there with a kiss on the cheek. "Take care of yourself." Her big eyes filled with worry. "Know that what's about to happen is not the end. I promise you that."

On that ominous note, she rushed back to the Landy and accelerated out of the driveway. If she hadn't, Alexander would have shoved her out.

"Hello, Alexander." Rhiannon was waiting for him in his kitchen. She had a goblet of ruby red liquid in front of her that he was not naive enough to believe was red wine. Her gaze swept him from top to toe. "You look like shit."

"I feel like shit." And if he guessed correctly, was about to feel a whole lot shitter.

Malice pulsed from Rhiannon, thick like an overfed tick as she was with magic. "Roderick do that to you?"

"Yes." He leaned against his travertine countertop and met her gaze without flinching. She fed on fear, and he refused to give her that.

"Hmm." She clicked her black lacquered nails against her goblet. She was channeling Morticia Adams in her long, black velvet gown. "We're lucky he didn't kill you."

He didn't make the mistake of thinking she was expressing latent maternal affection. If she lost him now, she'd only have to make herself another son of death, and with the daughter of life so close, she couldn't risk it. All that remained a mystery was how much she knew.

"Why do you think he didn't kill you, my son?" She drummed her nails against the countertop. "Would you like to hazard a guess?"

"I'd rather you told me." He gripped the countertop hard enough to make the healing cuts over his knuckles open and ooze. "It would be so much more expedient."

She laughed, and on any other woman, it would have been an attractive sound. "Always so defiant." She shook her head. "I almost admire that about you."

"Thanks, Mum." He had nothing to lose now. "They should make a card with that on it."

"You woke them up." She rounded the island toward him. "It took me a day or two to work it out, but then I did. I must say, I never thought you had that much courage. Misplaced courage, but still almost admirable."

Denial was pointless, and he'd rather not. It was odd, but since the day he'd set himself on this path to stop her, he'd known this day would come. For a brief shining moment after he'd met Bronwyn, he'd found himself wishing his betrayal of Rhiannon could have another outcome. Looking at Bronwyn, he'd wanted a different future for himself, but his reality promised a grim ending, and he'd done his part to shape it.

Rhiannon stopped in front of him. Magic swelled in her, red bleeding into the whites of her eyes. The stench made him retch.

She raised her hand and rested it over his heart. "You are my greatest disappointment, darling. I bred you for two reasons, fucking and fighting. You were supposed to vanquish Roderick, but you've failed me in this."

By his tally, he and Roderick were level pegging.

"I need you for one more reason, Alexander." She pressed her nails into his chest and drew her magic into a tight channel. "And I really must insist you perform your part."

Pain, everywhere pain, stemming from her hand, breaking through his skin and penetrating the muscle and bone of his chest. Alexander screamed his throat raw, but he couldn't move, could only feel the endless agony. Bronwyn's face filled his mind, and he reached for his precious few memories of her. With Bronwyn, he'd experienced as close to happy as he was capable. As the pain engulfed him, he clung to his image of Bronwyn's smile.

Rhiannon gripped his heart in her hand and squeezed. "But first, I feel a lesson in humility is in order."

CHAPTER TWENTY

B ronwyn woke with her chest on fire, the pain almost unimaginable. Outside her window, a pale early morning sky hung low over a wind-whipped sea. She tried to breath, but it hurt too much. Then the pain stopped.

The door flew open, and Roderick ran in looking like he'd gone twelve rounds with Mike Tyson and a velociraptor. Arms braced, poised for action, he searched her chamber. "What's amiss?"

The state of him pushed her nightmare from her mind. "What happened to you?"

Roderick paced her room. "You screamed."

"This pain woke me." She placed her palm over her chest for the reassurance of her still beating heart.

He frowned and looked at her. "A pain in your chest?"

"It was intense, but it's gone now." She tried to reconstruct the dream she'd been having before the pain had ripped her out of sleep. "I was sleeping and then this pain." She clenched her T-shirt over her breastbone. "It was like I was having a heart attack or something."

"And now?" Roderick frowned down at her.

Bronwyn took a deep careful breath, but everything seemed fine. "It's gone."

"And you are well now?" He studied her.

The irony caught up with her of him standing there sporting a swollen jaw, a split lip, a bruise on his cheekbone, and that was the damage she could see. "Right back at you, big guy?"

"I had some difficulties." He drew himself up.

The tough guy routine—surprise, surprise! Their medieval meathead didn't want to acknowledge he was in pain. She threw back her covers and climbed out of bed. "Let's have a look at you."

"Blessed." He drew his shoulders back and looked down his crooked, puffy nose at her. "I—"

"Save it." She was wise to him now, and he wasn't that scary.

The stone floor was warm beneath her feet, and she pointed at it. "Did you do this?"

"The floor?" He eyed her warily.

"It's warm." She had to peer up at him. "It was cold when I first got here. You arrive, Baile wakes up, and now we have warm floors." Amongst other things that threatened to blow her mind. Rooms with enough light and no visible light source. Dust that never settled on anything. Your everyday sentient castle type stuff.

He shrugged. "It's not like Baile and I have entire conversations."

"Whatever." He was so much taller than her that getting a good look at his injuries was never going to work. "Could you conjure up a chair or a stool and sit on it?"

He cocked his head. "There is a healer's hall, you know?"

"No." She hadn't known that because there was more to learn and get comfortable with every day. "Would you be less of a pain in the ass about me checking you out if I took you there?"

"Blessed." He growled and loomed over her like a street dog caught after a fight.

"Warrior." She hadn't even attempted to pronounce coimhdeacht yet. "I'm nearly hundreds sure this is not your first brawl, and as certain it won't be your last. You know how this goes."

His cold, cold blue eyes seared her, and then they warmed a moment before the most beautiful smile split his somber face. And, holy shitballs! That smile, though. It bore repeating, so she did—holy shit balls. With Roderick marching about being all toxic masculinity and arrogant male throwback, it was easy to forget what a good-looking son of a bitch he was. There was a reason he'd manwhored his way through the coven, and she was seeing it now.

"You have large opinions for such a small woman," he said.

"And you're a huge wuss for someone built like a brick shithouse."

He shook his head. "Only half of that made sense, but come along, and I'll show you the healer's hall."

"Then I check you out," she said as she trotted along in his wake. "Where's Maeve?"

"Sleeping." He glanced over his shoulder. "It's still early and she does not sleep enough, so I did not wake her."

He might do so in an outdated manner, but Roderick did care for his witch. "How old are you anyway?"

Not breaking stride, he laughed. "A gentleman never tells."

"You know I can google this right?"

"No." He strode across the great hall and down the stairs into the kitchen. "I am fairly certain I have never googled anything in my entire life, nor will I want to."

"I wouldn't go that far." Bronwyn had to run to keep up. "You'll become a slave to the almighty goog like the rest of us."

He stopped and shook his head at her. "You are a peculiar little thing."

"Ah, no." She made a grab for his arm, missed and had to run after him through the kitchen and into the bailey. "You did not just call me that."

"Pretty sure I did," he said. His attempt at an American accent was not bad, all things considered.

"Are you mocking me?"

"Come, Blessed." He stopped at a large set of double wooden doors. Like most of the outer doors in Baile, they bristled with thick metal hardware. Roderick pushed them open and stepped aside. "Behold, the healer's hall."

Bronwyn stepped into a wide room with vaulted ceilings and stone floors. West facing windows occupied the wall opposite the door. "This is amazing."

"It used to be a kitchen when Baile was first built." Roderick stayed beside her. "Then we decided we liked hot dinners better and moved the kitchen into the main keep. This became the healer's hall."

"It's amazing." The air smelled like astringents and drying herbs. The source of the lovely smell was a bank of floor-to-ceiling wooden shelves filled with neatly labeled glass jars. Bronwyn moved closer. She wanted to touch but dared not, so she read the labels. "Valerian root. That would help Maeve sleep." Beside the valerian was vanilla, then verbena (lemon), vervain, vetiver oil, and vinegar (apple cider)—everything neat, orderly, and in its place. "I know these."

Roderick nodded. "You are a healer."

"I am." She kept reading. Self-heal for bruises, cuts and sprains, and wounds. The fresh leaves and flowers could be bruised and applied directly to a wound. Dried, it combined well with other herbs in a tea as an antibiotic, particularly good for eye infections and conjunctivitis.

She stood on her toes to read the higher labels. Comfrey, used in a salve or an ointment for the treatment of burns, skin ulcerations, abrasions and lacerations. It also worked a treat on flea and insect bites. Almost any skin irritation including eczema.

Perhaps it was only the herbs, but she felt like she belonged in that place.

A scrubbed wooden table dominated the center of the room. In its kitchen days, the table must've been used for pounding bread dough and chopping the heads off chickens, but now it was littered with jars, vials, mortars and pestles, and surgical instruments. All the tools of her trade, all spotlessly clean and looking like someone had left them not ten minutes ago. They also looked like they were waiting for her to pick them up and use them. "Do the others know this is here?"

"I'm uncertain." Roderick shrugged. "Baile is often selective with her many secrets."

Hanging above the table, were bushels of drying herbs. Near the windows, in soldierly rows, sat empty window boxes. Positioned as they were, they would catch maximum light. She could plant all kinds of medicinal plants in those boxes.

"There is more." Roderick led her to an arched stone doorway to the left of the window boxes. A short flight of stairs opened into another large room—vaulted ceilings, stone floors, lots of wood, and even more light. The windows faced east, and the sun was forcing its way through the clouds.

"This was the infirmary." Roderick looked grim. "That last time I was down here, it was full of gravely ill witches and villagers."

The sadness in him drew her. "How did they get sick?"

"Rhiannon." His jaw tightened. "She managed to spread contagion through the village. The healers, of course, had to go and heal it."

Pieces dropped into place. "Ah! When Maeve went to the village with them."

"She told you about that?" He raised an eyebrow.

"She told us she nearly got you killed."

He snorted. "She exaggerates."

"Maybe." For two people who'd been bonded such a brief time, Maeve and Roderick had shared a lot. "But there is some truth to be found at the bottom of a bottle."

Roderick laughed, and that smile...wow! "Along with a fair amount of bullshit."

"True that." She motioned him to a small wooden stool close to the windows. "Now, let's get to why we're here."

"It is no longer necessary, Blessed." Roderick's grin was more than a touch smug. "I am healed."

Bronwyn didn't intend to take his word for it, so she carried the stool over to him and stood on it.

His eyes twinkled with amusement as she got eye to eye with him. "Son of a bitch!" The bruise around his eyes had faded to a shadow, and his lip was normal. His nose had lost the swelling and knit itself back straight. "You did this on purpose, didn't you?" She glared down at him, because she could. "You distracted me by showing me this wonderful hall so I wouldn't check on your injuries."

"Blessed." He did a passable attempt at looking innocent. "That would make me duplicitous."

"Yes, it would." She fixed him with a stare. She was wise to him now, and this wouldn't happen again. "Where I come from, we'd even go so far as to call you a low down, sneaky varmint."

"What, by all that's holy, is a varmint?"

Bronwyn grim eyed him. "I'm looking at one."

"I showed you this hall, Blessed, because this is where you belong," he said, and his eyes grew serious. "You are a healer, and your place is in this hall. You are a cré-witch; your place is at Baile." His gaze bored into her. "You are called, water witch. Your Goddess needs you."

MAEVE COULDN'T BELIEVE she was awake this early after her night with Alanna and Bronwyn. She could sense Roderick in the healer's hall and guessed he would be with Bronwyn. If there was any justice in the world, Bronwyn would also be feeling the effects of their night. Unable to sleep and needing the comforting presence of the sigils, she'd slipped out of bed and come to the caverns. Roderick thought she was still sleeping. She liked Bronwyn, but she was worried. Bronwyn had yet to accept who she was and where she fit into the future of the cré-witches.

Strange that, but it was a familiar confusion to what she felt.

Keeping a tight hold on Roderick's bond, she wandered through the caverns. She stopped at the wall and laid a hand upon the nearest sigils. The sense of witches past was so faint. The place where her magic bloomed was like a tiny spark to the inferno that had once been hers to command. Her loss of magic was an empty void within her.

She refused to believe she would never walk with the spirits again. Pressing her forehead to the rock, she whispered, "I am here. I will walk with you again."

"*Sister.*"

"*Spirit walker.*"

Voices that had once sounded so clearly in her mind where now muted to almost imperceptible.

"You'll have to show me how to reach you." She raised her voice. It echoed through the caverns. "I don't know how."

A particular sigil stopped her. Maeve brushed her fingertips over it. Here, she had scribed Rose on the cavern walls. Rose, so young and such a talented healer, and the first witch carried to the sacred isles by the village contagion. It was also the first time Roderick had witnessed her scribing magic. After, as she lay exhausted and devastated by the passing of a life, he had picked her up and cradled her. For the first time when Roderick had found her and comforted her, she had shared the burden of grief that passed over her once she had scribed a life on the cavern walls.

Roderick must have perceived her emotions because he quested for her through the bond.

Maeve reassured him and walked into the central cavern. The pool was a milky opalescent this morning. She approached the rock outcrop at the far end of the cavern, behind Goddess Pool. Her mind veered from the last time she had taken the secret tunnel to the village. Thomas had rushed them all into the tunnel, thinking he was hurrying them to safety. He had given his life to ensure they got to the village.

In the end, it had all been for nothing, because Rhiannon had been waiting for them on the other side.

A cold draft stroked her nape, and Thomas wove into view. He looked so corporeal, as if she could reach out and touch him.

"Go ahead and try." Hands held out to his sides, Thomas grinned roguishly, and it was heartbreakingly familiar.

Heart in her throat, Maeve tried to keep it light. "You can read my mind now?"

"A small perk." He shrugged. "And not entirely how this works. I'm more connected to Roderick somehow, and he can read your mind, so I can catch echoes of that."

"Ah." One man plundering her thoughts was enough. She hardly needed another.

"I did it willingly." Thomas sounded serious, and she looked at him. "My death," he said. "I don't regret it, even if matters didn't transpire as any of us would have chosen."

"We had no idea her poison ran so deep through the coven." Maeve relived those last days of the coven more than she would have liked. Roderick chastised her that it was purposeless, but she couldn't stop herself. Questions circled her mind constantly. Why had they not seen what Rhiannon was up to? Why had they waited to accuse Fiona?

Thomas folded his arms and shook his head. "It serves no

purpose, Maeve, it really does not. Hindsight is always so exact. It was hard to believe so many of our own could turn against us."

She nodded because he expected it, but the guilt lingered. If they'd acted faster, they might have prevented all those deaths.

"I need to show you something." Thomas moved closer. His legs went through the walking motions, but his feet made no contact with the ground. It was disconcerting. "Roderick should come with us. We're going to the village."

"In the daylight?" Maeve had never risked discovery like that.

Thomas shrugged. "It is still early and there is nobody about. What I need you to see can only be glimpsed in the morning light."

Last time she'd gone to the village without Roderick was one time enough, and she nodded. "Roderick is with Bronwyn."

"She is the one?" Thomas tilted his head. "The daughter of life?"

"We believe so." She sent a surge through the bond for Roderick to hurry. "Alexander appears to believe so as well."

Thomas grew thoughtful. "That one has changed much, but he has to hide it from Rhiannon."

That name made her shiver. "He killed witches."

"No." Thomas shook his head. "Mainly he fought coimhdeacht, and he did not use magic."

"Shall we give him a medal?" Maeve couldn't keep the anger out her voice. "Because I remember clearly how he tried to have the village drown me."

"I have thought on that." Thomas stroked his chin. "He had to have known Roderick would get there before you were drowned."

Maeve snorted, because she was certain of no such thing.

Roderick strode into the caverns. "What is this about?"

"Hi." Bronwyn was almost running to keep up with him. "I came along for the ride."

Maeve didn't bother to ask. When Bronwyn made statements like coming along for a ride, it sounded nonsensical at first, and then the meaning became clear in context.

"Brother." Thomas greeted him with a raised hand. "Maeve is needed on the green."

"No." Roderick folded his arms.

"Way to go on the seeking consensus thing, big guy." Bronwyn slapped Roderick on the shoulder.

Bronwyn wasn't interested in Roderick that way. Maeve reminded herself one more time for luck and let it sink in. Also, Roderick may be her coimhdeacht, but she did not own him mind, body, heart and soul.

With a chuckle, Roderick glanced at her. "Near enough you do."

Blast! She really needed to master the masking her thoughts thing better. She turned to Thomas. "Why do you need me to go to the green?"

"It matters not." Roderick thrust his chin out and scowled at Thomas. "She is not leaving Baile's wards, and most especially not when it is light outside."

Thomas thrust his chin out and scowled back. "Rhiannon is not there. I would know if she were."

"I care not." Roderick glared. "Last time Rhiannon was not supposed to be there either."

"She can't go near the part of the green where I want Maeve to go," Thomas said. "When you were cast into stasis, it extended Baile's wards to that point."

"Still no."

Bronwyn was studying Thomas. "Not to be rude, but how are you even here?"

"Magic." He widened his eyes at her and then chuckled.

"Roderick." He jerked his chin. "He is the original coimhdeacht, and he will call more to him."

"More ghosts?" Bronwyn made a face. "Yay."

Thomas laughed, his hazel eyes crinkling at the corners. "Not all of them will be ghosts."

"Are you a seer now?" Roderick raised an eyebrow at him.

"Perhaps." Thomas shrugged. "Brother, you know I would not ask her to go to the green, and at this time, if it wasn't important."

Roderick frowned and mulled this over. "What is there that is so important?"

"You need to see it." Thomas looked serious. "Maeve needs to see this."

Shaking his head, Roderick said, "The passage may not be safe."

"What passage?" Bronwyn looked from Roderick to Thomas, her eyes alight with interest.

"It's safe, as you already know because you came that way on first waking," Thomas said.

Bronwyn gasped. "No! Are you guys talking about a secret passage?"

"Not as secret as I would like." Roderick gave her a repressive stare.

Clearly Bronwyn had recovered from her awe of him because she grinned back. "That is so cool."

"A secret passage impresses you?" Thomas smirked. "Goddess Pool, the sigils, the magic, Baile being sentient, even me—these things you take in your stride. But a secret passage makes you smile like a delighted child."

Shrugging, Bronwyn grinned wider. "This is very Hogwarts."

CHAPTER TWENTY-ONE

B ronwyn used her cellphone to light the way. The gloomy passage was tall enough for Roderick not to have to bend, but narrow. It smelled stale, but there were no signs of damp, and thankfully, no spiders. Her imagination kept leaping to *Indiana Jones and the Temple of Doom*. The scene where he follows a secret passage infested with bugs. And really, what had Spielberg been thinking? Actually, her last two weeks could very well be part of a Spielberg movie.

Flitting along ahead of them and not needing any light, Thomas led the way. He hadn't said anything since he'd muttered some sort of spell, and a hole in the rock wall had opened. It was taking more and more to shock her since her arrival in England. Secret passages appearing in walls—no problem!

They followed the passage through a number of twists and turns until it ended in more rock. Again, Thomas muttered his spell and fetid air flooded in.

Bronwyn keep her breathing shallow as she stepped into a space even darker than the passage. It smelled of rot and mildew. Things with claws that scrabbled along the floor retreated as they advanced. She for damn sure wasn't going to investigate.

"These are the crypts beneath the church," Thomas said. "In the nineteen sixties they tried to turn this into a restaurant and gift shop, but I persuaded them not to."

"What did you do?" For all his charm and easy smiles, Thomas had a steel core running through him that might make him a formidable enemy.

His smile was feral. "I made them run away."

"You went full ghost, didn't you?" Bronwyn could only imagine how wicked he could be.

Thomas's grin widened. "There are few enough advantages to this state of being."

"It stinks in here, and it never used to," Maeve said, scrutinizing where she put her feet.

Bronwyn didn't blame her. The floor was suspiciously slippery and squishy underfoot.

"With Baile being silent for so long, the crypts have suffered from her loss." Thomas led them to a small door at one end of the crypt. Being underground messed with Bronwyn's sense of direction, but she suspected they were on the western side of the church.

Roderick stepped in front of the door and motioned her and Maeve back. "I go first."

"Fine with me." If he wanted to charge around being brave, she wasn't planning to stop him. He made a far better hero than her anyway.

Opening the door, Roderick paused and drew his sword.

Light flooded into the dark space.

Bronwyn had no idea where the sword had come from. It looked like he'd produced the sword from thin air.

Winking at her, Thomas whispered, "It's a kind of magic."

She made a face at him. Apparently ghosts could watch movies.

Roderick stepped into the stairwell beyond the door and looked around. He stood a moment, poised and alert, and then glanced at them. "Come."

He took Maeve's elbow and pointed. "The stairs are slippery; be careful."

Even though Maeve and Roderick weren't lovers, what they had was what others craved, the intimacy of knowing each other so well, the deep caring and sense of connection. And may her feminist heart forgive her, but the way Roderick looked after Maeve and protected her made Bronwyn long to be that important to someone.

"It's a grand thing." Thomas smiled at her, his face wistful. "I didn't understand until Lavina bonded me how it would enrich my life."

"You must miss her."

Thomas lost his habitual cocky expression. "Like a piece of my soul."

Roderick reached the top of the stairs and peered into the churchyard.

Over the morning chirp and chatter of birds, Bronwyn strained to hear if anything or anyone else was about.

"Come." Roderick motioned them up and into the churchyard.

Strengthening sunlight striped across the gravestones littering the small churchyard. Some gravestones still stood proud and tall, others leaned like drunken frat boys, and the older ones were worn by time into stubs. Thick grass grew up and around the stones, the last of the daffodil stalks almost bent over double amidst the grass.

The tense silence was getting to Bronwyn. "Sneaking around a graveyard in broad daylight, what could go wrong?"

Thomas chuckled. "I like you, Blessed."

"I bet you say that to all the girls."

Roderick glared at them over his shoulder.

Maeve stopped and looked at Roderick.

Standing statue still, Roderick stood beside his former plinth and studied the silent churchyard.

"Why are we stopping?" Bronwyn sidled closer to Thomas.

"The wards." Thomas pointed to a spot in front of the empty plinth. "That's where they end. Once we step beyond them, we no longer have Baile's protection."

"Oh." She had felt that strange feathers-sliding-over-skin sensation of the wards when she'd approached the caverns alone from the beach, and again the day she and Niamh had snuck out to Tesco.

The green was still empty, and nobody was moving about its perimeter, but the villagers would be stirring and ready to be out and about. Still, they waited, all gazes locked on Roderick and waiting for his okay. The longer they hesitated, the more chance someone would come along.

Finally, with Bronwyn toeing the edge of screaming point, Roderick nodded, and he and Maeve moved forward.

Thomas stopped at the wards and shrugged. "I can go no further. I'm tethered to Baile."

"Why are we here?" Roderick looked tense and unhappy.

"Wait." Thomas's voice grew raspy. "The sun strikes the green just right and they'll come for the spirit walker."

Bronwyn looked around them. "Who?"

"Lavina." The way Thomas said her name was loaded with pain so longstanding and deep that, like wood, it had petrified.

Maeve frowned and tilted her head, as if listening to something.

"What is it?" Roderick drew closer to her. "Maeve?"

A strangled gasp came out of Maeve, and her spine snapped straight. "No." She covered her mouth with both hands. "Oh, no, no, no."

"Maeve?" Roderick reached for her.

She pushed his hands away. "No-o-o!" She crumpled from within, hugging her torso. "They're still here."

Anguish creasing his features, Thomas watched Maeve.

Roderick glanced from Maeve to Thomas and looked like he wanted to kill whatever was hurting Maeve but had no idea what that was.

At first, Bronwyn thought she was imaging the shapes flitting around Maeve. They didn't look like much of anything, just disembodied body parts that appeared as they crossed the slanting sunbeams and disappeared again as they passed beyond.

Maeve turned to Thomas, her eyes like bruises in her face. "They are trapped here."

"Yes." Thomas stared at the shapes around Maeve. "The blood magic they performed to put you in stasis severed them from Goddess."

"The final casting?" Roderick looked at Thomas. "Those witches are trapped here?"

"Yes." Maeve walked further into the green, following the flitting shapes. Tears streamed down her face. "Roderick, they're trapped, and they're hurting. They can't move on, and they can't leave this plane. Their souls are cut from the cycle of birth and rebirth."

Striding forward, Roderick took her by the shoulders. "This is not your fault, Maeve. You didn't choose this for yourself. When they cast that spell, they knew what they were doing."

"No, they didn't." Thomas's anger was all the more potent for its unexpectedness. If he could have crossed the wards, he might have attacked Roderick. "How can you stand there and say that as if anything about that sodding day was thought out?" He gripped his nape. "Everything was insane, a total panic, and Lavina and Colleen did what the spirits of the first three told them to do. They did as they were bid, but they wouldn't have wanted this."

"Blessed." Roderick followed Maeve across the green. "You stray from the wards."

"They need me, and I cannot fail them." Maeve stared at the ghostly witches. "That day they gave their all for me. They gave their very souls."

There was a lot about that day Bronwyn still didn't understand, but now was not the time to ask. She moved to Maeve's side and put her arm about her shoulders. "You'll help them, Maeve. We'll find a way."

Growing more agitated, the wispy shapes around Maeve flitted this way and that.

"They severed themselves from Goddess so we could live and reach this time." Maeve reached for the trapped witches. "They are begging me to free them."

"You will free them." Bronwyn didn't know how, but she refused to believe these women who had made the ultimate sacrifice deserved this fate.

"You have to free them," Thomas said. "I can still feel echoes of Lavina's pain, and no soul should be allowed to exist like that for eternity." He looked at Bronwyn. "That is the true meaning of hell, having your soul forever cut off from the source of life, trapped in the moment of your death for eternity."

The healer in Bronwyn rose to the surface as she turned to Maeve. "You can do it. I bet nobody had survived all those hundreds of years as a statue before either. Compared to that, anything looks possible."

"I want that to be true more than I can say." Maeve shook her head, then drew in a deep breath and said, "But you are right this is a new time with new rules and new possibilities. Once I have my power again, if there is a way I can release them and return them to Goddess, I will do it."

Bronwyn gave Maeve a squeeze. "They did the blood magic to save the cré-witches? That has to count for something, right?"

Roderick shook his head. "Not necessarily. Cré-witches are forbidden from using their magic to take life or harm, even to protect themselves. For this reason, the coimhdeacht were called. Even when her life is in danger, a witch may not use her magic for harm." He grimaced. "And they used blood magic, the magic of death, to send Maeve and me into stasis. They took their own lives, and it matters not why they did it; it matters only that they did it."

"I will free them." Her face fierce in her determination, Maeve turned to Thomas. "I will free Lavina."

Thomas bowed his head to her. "My thanks, spirit walker. My Blessed has need of you."

A weird smell made Bronwyn shudder. Coppery and dark, it smelled like rotting corpses. "What stinks like that?"

Roderick tensed. "Get behind the wards."

A knockout blonde stepped out from behind a tree. "Oops." She giggled. "I guess hiding has become pointless."

"Edana." Maeve gasped.

Roderick lunged for Maeve.

"Hello, Roderick." Edana smiled at him, coy as a girl on her first date. "You are looking as fine as ever."

Grabbing Maeve by the waist, Roderick propelled her across the wards, turned and ran for Bronwyn.

She had no idea what this was about, but she trusted Roderick. Bronwyn ran toward him, only to be stopped short as something grabbed her hair and yanked her back.

"Where do you think you're going?" A woman spoke from behind her. She tightened her grip on Bronwyn's hair making her roots scream in protest. "We've gone to a lot of trouble to get our hands on you, sweeting."

"Fiona." Roderick snarled and raised his sword. "Get away from her."

"I would." Fiona laughed and pressed something cold and

hard against Bronwyn's temple. "But she really is too important, and we can't let you have her."

"Roderick!" Thomas thrust out his hand. "Stop! That's a gun."

A gun! Someone had a gun to her head. Bronwyn fought the rising tide of panic. Someone had a fucking gun to her head.

Roderick hesitated and glanced at Thomas.

"The gun can kill her before you can reach her." Thomas shook his head. "Your sword is useless against it."

Edana put her hands on her hips and giggled. "Poor darling. You really are quite out of date, aren't you?" The look she gave Roderick was pure carnal lust. "I see you have made some concessions to this time."

"Edana. How are you alive?" Maeve glared at Edana with more venom than Bronwyn would have thought she possessed. "My one comfort was knowing you'd died."

"Sorry." Edana shrugged and indicated Fiona. "But Fiona and I made a deal with our lady, and here we are."

"Fiona?" Her brain was slow in getting there, but Bronwyn put the pieces together. "As in the old coven leader."

"One and the same, sweet cheeks." The gun pressed into her temple. "And Rhiannon is most eager to see you."

Face intent and deadly, Roderick stepped closer.

Fiona yanked Bronwyn's head back. The cold click of the hammer cocking seemed impossibly loud. "I will kill her. Rhiannon would prefer her alive, but between dead and hiding in Baile, she'll take dead."

His face hard as steel, Roderick said, "You're lying. Bronwyn is no use to her dead."

"Perhaps you're right." Fiona laughed. "But are you going to risk it?"

"Roderick." Maeve grabbed his arm. "You can't let them take her."

"He can't stop us." Fiona dragged her back.

Bronwyn's scalp burned from the tension on her hair.

Roderick moved in a blur of motion, coming for Fiona.

Edana pulled out a gun and shot.

The bullet slammed into Roderick and stopped his forward momentum. Blood bloomed across his chest.

Maeve screamed.

Roderick surged forward again.

"Jesus, Edana, it's the fucking morning," Fiona yelled.

Stepping in front of Roderick, Edana fired again. And again. And again.

Roderick jerked as bullet after bullet slammed into him.

"Shit." Fiona increased their pace as she dragged her back. "She'll have the entire sodding village up and around our ears."

Bronwyn tried to fight free of Fiona, but the woman was unbelievably strong.

She stopped and yanked Bronwyn to a halt. "Get her in the car."

Hands reached for her, grabbed her and shoved her into a car.

On the green, Roderick staggered to his feet, his entire shirt red with blood.

Stepping up to him, Edana fired one more bullet and he dropped.

CHAPTER TWENTY-TWO

The car was moving, buildings blurring past the windows, and someone was screaming.

"Shut her the fuck up," Fiona snarled from the passenger seat.

A sharp slap whipped Bronwyn's head to the side. It was her; she was screaming. The person beside her hit her again. Her face went numb.

The final image of Roderick, blood soaked and collapsed on the grass was seared on her brain. "You killed him."

"Roderick?" Edana's voice came from the driver's seat. "I should be so fucking lucky. That bastard is as strong as an ox. As much as I'd like to believe you, I won't believe he's dead until the day I dance on his corpse."

"You just had to do it, didn't you?" Fiona sneered at Edana. "You'll never get over him choosing Maeve over you."

"He didn't choose her. He was called to bond her, and that's not the same thing as choosing her over me." Edana sniffed. "Besides, that has nothing to do with it. I bought us time to get away."

"By firing a gun in broad daylight?" Fiona shook her head

and stared out the window. "You're going to explain to our lady why you let your obsession with Roderick almost screw up this entire thing."

He had looked dead to Bronwyn. Nothing short of death would stop Roderick. She might not have known him long, but she knew that about him. Oh God, Maeve. She would be broken without him.

"Don't." Fiona jabbed a finger at her. "If you start screaming again, I'll make you wish you were dead."

Panic almost got the best of her anyway. The stench of copper and rot in the confined space of the car made her gag. Buildings and trees flashed past her window, and then they were on the highway.

A man sat on either side of her, both staring straight ahead.

"What do you want from me?" she asked the car in general.

After a pause, Edana answered, "You're one of those American witches, right?"

"Yes." That seemed a safe enough piece of information to reveal, and it wasn't like her accent gave her any choice.

Edana turned to Fiona. "How did she get to England? I thought we managed to kill them while they were still over there and clueless."

"Does it matter?" Fiona shrugged. Her profile was strong and clearly etched against the windshield. She had long red hair caught in a ponytail. "She's here now and Maeve is awake."

"Huh?" Edana glanced at her.

"The cardinal points?" Fiona scowled at Edana. "The one she's supposed to reactivate?"

"Oh." Edana giggled. "I didn't think of that."

Fiona shook her head and stared out the windshield. "Right, because you were always such a deep thinker."

"You're a bitch," Edana said, in a tone that suggested it was neither a new thought nor a new sentiment. "I just thought we wanted her because of the prophecy."

"We do." Fiona breathed deep.

"But—"

"Just drive!"

Bronwyn put her head back against the headrest to try to steady her thoughts. These bitches might have been part of killing her family, killing her mother and then Dee. They would pay for that. She would make sure of it by surviving this and making them pay.

In the cars they passed, people went about their morning with no idea of what was happening to her, but Maeve knew and Thomas. And Roderick.

Roderick couldn't be dead. *Please, Goddess, don't let him be dead.* To have survived the coven massacre and existed in that living death for all those hundreds of years, just to get shot and killed. It didn't make any sense.

Please. Bronwyn reached for a deity she wasn't even sure could hear her. *Goddess, please, take care of your own.*

"Better rest up." Fiona grinned at her over her shoulder. "You're going to need it."

A year ago, Bronwyn had buried Deidre. At the time, she'd thought that was the worst thing that could happen to her. With Deidre's death, she'd lost the only person she had in the world. Then she'd taken her inheritance and come here, chasing some dream of finding her roots and the answers to the curse plaguing her family.

Welp! She'd discovered the curse hounding her family. These bitches, in the car with her now, they were part of the curse and the death that had decimated her life. She shared that bond with Maeve, and hopefully, still Roderick. As she calmed, she refused to believe him dead. Such a force of nature didn't end with a whimper.

"You realize Roderick will come for me?" They didn't need to know she was unsure.

Edana glanced at Fiona. "Will he?"

"Of course he will." Fiona shrugged. "But he's bonded to Maeve, and he cannot override the compulsion to look after her first." She looked over her shoulder at Bronwyn. "That's assuming the cunt is still alive."

Wow! They were breaking out the c-word now. "So, you two sell your entire coven to Rhiannon and get eternal life out of it?"

"Close enough." Fiona shrugged. "You're an infant witch, not even bonded yet. You have no idea the power we hold at our fingertips."

"We?" Bronwyn couldn't stop the laugh. "You say that as if we have something in common. I'm nothing like you."

Fiona turned in her seat, her eyes glittering. "I'm sure it's a comfort to you to think that. One of us is the bad guy." She pointed to herself. "And the other is the hero." She chuckled. "God, I love your American oversimplification of life. Shall we all have a Disney moment and end up friends?" Her expression turned brutal. "That's not going to happen, princess. You're a pawn in a game so much bigger than you. You have bugger all value in and of yourself. You're not even a proper witch."

"Ooh burn!" It was so childish, but it felt so good. "Next you'll tell me I can't sit with you."

Edana glanced at Fiona. "Why can't she sit with us?"

"Jesus." Fiona rolled her eyes and glared at Edana. "I'm conflicted between admiring and resenting how stupid you are."

"Shut up, you minger bitch."

"No, you shut up."

They were drifting into *Hocus Pocus* territory now. If she wasn't so shit scared, she'd be laughing.

―――

EDANA DROVE through the day without stopping. Places blurred past the windows and Bronwyn tried to catch a village or city name from the road signs they passed. When they passed the sign for Stoke Mandeville for the third time, she realized Edana was driving them in circles.

"I need to stop," she said. It wasn't lie. "I need to use the bathroom."

Fiona glanced back and shrugged. "Don't really give a shit."

"Settle down, princess." Edana's toffee-dark eyes met hers in the rearview mirror. "In case you're not getting this, nobody cares what you want or what you need. You're nothing but a vessel."

"Vessel?" It was a peculiarly specific word to use. "You're talking about that stupid prophecy, aren't you?"

"Christ! You really are a dumb bitch, you know that?" Fiona glared at Edana. "If you open your mouth and piss Rhiannon off, you're on your own. I'm not running interference for you."

Edana scowled at Fiona. "I don't see what difference it makes if she knows or not."

"Yeah, you really don't see." Fiona shook her head. "Drive and try not to speak. Even better, try not to think either. You really suck at it."

"Fuck you." Edana went with a tried and true, if not original, response.

The argument devolved from there into a verbal bitch fight but produced no more useful information.

Another two hours by the dashboard clock later, the bright, beautiful day seemed a mockery as Edana pulled the vehicle into a service station. She hopped out.

Fiona glanced at the silent goons on either side of Bronwyn. "Don't let her move. Even if she threatens to pee on you, keep her there."

A Mercedes-Benz sedan with tinted windows glided up beside them. Alexander climbed from the passenger side.

Bronwyn's gaze locked on him with starved desperation. A brief, bright flare of hope coursed through her.

He walked to the back of the vehicle she was in and opened the trunk.

She called his name, "Alexander."

Without looking at her, he hauled two bags out and carried them over to the trunk of the Mercedes and tossed them in.

It hurt so much it robbed her of breath. Roderick had been right about him all along. Alexander had only been acting on behalf of Rhiannon. She breathed deeply, refusing to cry in front of these assholes. When Roderick came for her and took her back to Baile, then she could cry.

Edana approached Alexander and slid her arms around his neck. She pressed her body against his.

Jealousy ripped through Bronwyn, followed by a sense of betrayal. Alexander had lied to her from the beginning. There would be time later for the tears locked tight in her chest.

She couldn't hear what Edana was saying to him, but Alexander's arms stayed by his side and his face remained blank. It was not the sort of expression she'd seen on his face before. His expression was completely devoid of animation. Peering past her goon bookend, she studied him closer. There was something seriously off with him.

Fiona stopped beside Alexander and Edana and spoke to them. She snapped her fingers and Alexander grimaced. A trickle of blood drifted over his lip, and Edana wiped it away and licked the blood off her finger.

Shuddering, Fiona gave her a look of disgust and strode for the car Bronwyn was in. She yanked open the door and jerked her head. "Get her out." She smirked at Bronwyn. "Pucker up, princess. Your date is here."

Right side goon clambered out and dragged her out by her upper arm. His grip was hard, not bruising, but there was also no chance she could break it.

Other than them, the service station was empty of people.

"Edana." Rhiannon climbed out of the back of the Mercedes. "He's not for you. Never was."

With a grumble, Edana stepped away from Alexander.

"Alexander." Rhiannon stared at Bronwyn. With her glittering dark eyes and flushed cheeks, she was quite beautiful, but in the way of a deadly, sharp blade.

Blade made her think of Roderick, and her heart ached. With everything she had, she prayed he was still alive.

At the sound of his name, Alexander jerked and strode toward Bronwyn. "You need to come," he said, his voice flat like his expression. His gaze fixed over her left shoulder.

With Rhiannon in such proximity, the shared genetics between them was clear. Except in her skinny jeans and close-fitting button-up shirt, Rhiannon looked like she could be his younger sister.

Staring up into his beautiful face, Bronwyn found it hard to believe nothing that had happened between them had been real. He had been lying the entire time.

His dark, dark gaze shifted to her, and there was nothing there. No recognition, no connection. A chill swept through Bronwyn. Some tiny part of her must have been holding out hope that Alexander being there meant help.

"Come." He put his hand on her arm. His gaze stuck on where right-hand goon still had hold of her bicep. Alexander stilled, his focus on the point where goon touched her. "Take your hand off her."

Goon dropped her arm like it was radioactive. "Yes, my lord."

"Very good, darling." Rhiannon spoke to Alexander like he was a favored dog. "This will go so much easier if you actually like the girl." She glanced at Fiona and laughed. "I never thought him getting fond of her would be a good thing, but you see how it is."

"Yes, Rhiannon." Fiona lost any trace of attitude and inclined her head deferentially. "A fortunate side benefit of their spending time together."

"Alexander?" Bronwyn spoke his name quietly. Something was not right with him, and she went with her gut.

"Come." He tugged her across the parking lot to the Mercedes and opened the door for her.

Rhiannon's sky-high heels clicked over the concrete as she sashayed closer. "Get in, dear. Be a good girl, and things will go much easier for you."

"What do you want from me?" Under the gentle pressure of Alexander's hand on her shoulder, she eased into the back of the Mercedes. She cast one more desperate look around the service station, hoping for something, someone, to see what was happening. A pigeon cooed from the trees bordering the lot.

She stared in the direction of the sound. It was a tiny connection with Niamh and Baile. She reached for the pigeon, honey and sage filled the air.

"Ah, no." Rhiannon waved a hand and Bronwyn's gut clenched as if she'd been punched in it. She struggled to draw her next breath. "There will be no magic, dear girl." She leaned into the car and tangled her hand in Bronwyn's hair and brought her head up. "I can make you hurt so bad you would wish for death." The way she said it, almost pleasantly, was the most chilling part of the statement. "But I won't kill you, I'll keep you alive and aware enough to feel every moment of suffering."

The pigeon cooed again, and this time, it made her feel even more alone as she thought of Roz and Niamh and all the others at Baile. They would have no idea how to find her. If they were even looking. Maybe she was wrong, and Roderick had died, and they were mourning him.

Alexander shut her car door, sealing her in the warm interior that smelled of new leather and the underlying stench she was beginning to associate with blood magic. God, and how she wished she'd never encountered blood magic, let alone enough of it to identify its smell.

The other rear door opened, and Rhiannon slid in beside her.

Alexander climbed into the front passenger seat, and the car glided into the road.

Rhiannon turned sideways and stared at her. "You're not what I expected."

That made two of them, but Bronwyn refused to reply and stared out the window.

"The old cré-witches were much more impressive." Rhiannon chuckled. "But then, it's not your magic we all want, is it?"

Bronwyn kept her mouth shut. She didn't know what Rhiannon was capable of, but Roderick had said to never underestimate her, and Bronwyn didn't intend to. If she played this smart, she might make it out alive. Like Maeve had told them she did with the Roderick bond, Bronwyn built barriers in her mind and shut herself behind them. If Rhiannon could read minds, Bronwyn intended to show her nothing but a blank wall.

She kept her attention on the landscape sliding past the window. With Edana's driving in circles, they could be anywhere in England, but the directional indicator in the rearview mirror told her they were now heading north.

The smooth, comfortable ride of the car and the barely discernible engine purr lulled her into a kind of trance. Nothing beyond the windows looked at all familiar. Time blurred, and she lost all sense of it. She came alert when the car stopped, and the engine was turned off.

"Finally." Rhiannon nudged her. "We're here."

"Where are we?" Bleary eyed, Bronwyn peered out the window.

Rhiannon chuckled. "Somewhere nobody knows about but me and my disciples."

Disciples? Talk about delusional. Then again, Rhiannon had managed to get her kidnapped and taken to God alone knew where. They could have traveled as far north as Scotland, and Bronwyn would have no idea.

A roof poked up from behind thick, dark green foliage, and they appeared to have stopped in a driveway. The longer shadows of late afternoon crept around the car.

Alexander was already out and taking bags from the trunk.

"Come." Rhiannon slid out the car and motioned her to join her.

Bronwyn eyed the driveway. She could make a run for it.

"Don't be tedious." Rhiannon clicked her fingers, and Bronwyn couldn't move. Her feet felt like they were nailed to the floor. A crushing sensation in her chest robbed her of breath.

"Yes, dear." Rhiannon smirked. "That is me doing that. I warned you earlier, but you clearly required a demonstration."

She turned and led the way up the stone path. They walked through a gap in the obscuring shrubs to a small, thatched cottage, which Bronwyn might have found charming if it wasn't about to be her prison.

Opening the door, Alexander motioned her inside. Sunlight slanted through mullioned windowpanes in a mellow golden glow that bounced off rows of copper pans hanging from the ceiling. A wooden table gleamed with polish in the center of a charming kitchen. An old range burped out low lingering heat.

Bronwyn wandered into a living room furnished with two huge, squishy sofas covered in floppy pink and red cabbage roses.

"You're through here." Alexander opened one of the three doors leading off a central corridor beyond the living room.

Her bedroom fit the rest of the cottage, complete with a beckoning fourposter bed covered in a welcoming barrage of pillows.

Alexander put the bags in the room, and said in that strange wooden voice, "Are you hungry?"

"No." She pointed at the bags. "Who's are those."

"Yours," he said and left.

Bronwyn stared at the bags but didn't dare go any closer. She had no idea what was in there, but it looked like enough stuff for an extended stay.

"Ah!" Rhiannon walked into the room and gave it a thorough once-over. She smiled at Alexander. "Well done. I had to trust one of my disciples to set this up, but it will do nicely."

For what? But Bronwyn didn't voice the question. She had the distinct sense Rhiannon wouldn't answer her anyway.

Rhiannon pressed the bed like people did to establish if it was as comfortable as it looked. She beamed at Bronwyn. "It's almost romantic."

"If you consider abduction romantic." Bronwyn couldn't stop herself. "Personally, I don't. But that's just me."

Rhiannon eyed her speculatively. "You have spirit. Unfortunately for you, I'm not an admirer."

Alexander moved to stand between them and stared down at her. "You need to eat."

"And I will. When I'm hungry." Bronwyn tried to read the strange dynamic in the room.

Alexander stood and stared at her like he was planted on the pretty Aubusson rug.

Glancing between them, Rhiannon cocked her head and tapped her forefinger on her chin. "If you have any notions of leaving here, forget them now," she said and walked up to Alexander and smirked. She looked over her shoulder at Bronwyn. "You're mine now, and I've spent more years than you can imagine waiting for you, preparing for you."

Alexander cleared his throat. "You know where the kitchen is if you change your mind."

"Be quiet, Alexander." Rhiannon placed her hand on his

chest, over this heart, but she spoke to Bronwyn. "You have no idea what has gone into having you here, mine to command."

"I'm not yours to command." Bronwyn would die before she let that happen. She very well may die, but not before someone paid for what they'd taken from her.

"You have so much to learn, little healer." Rhiannon's eye whites went pink and then red. The rot and copper scent of blood magic punched Bronwyn in the solar plexus. "Perhaps a lesson would make my point so much clearer."

Alexander flinched.

"Nobody will save you here." The stench grew, and her eyes went glassy. "And having come this far, I intend to make sure nothing stops me now."

With a grunt of pain, Alexander crumpled to his knees. Blood seeped from his nose and ears.

"What are you doing to him?" Bronwyn dropped to the carpet beside him.

He jerked like a live wire and his back bowed. A low keen of agony seeped through his clenched teeth.

"He is my creature, and I can do whatever I want with him," Rhiannon said, calmly as if she was explaining the weather. "I created him, and I can destroy him. He thought to save you, poor deluded boy, and I had to show him how that would never happen."

Rhiannon pulled more magic. Like metal filings, it scraped along Bronwyn's nerves. The magic seemed to drain Rhiannon from within, but she didn't stop.

"For reasons that will soon become clear, I may have to make sure you stay healthy." Rhiannon smiled. "But know this, he will pay, and pay dearly, for each one of your transgressions."

Alexander fell to his side and jacked his legs to his chest. He coughed and blood and saliva dribbled down his chin.

"Stop it!" Bronwyn didn't know what to do. She wanted to touch him, comfort him, stop his pain, but she didn't know how.

Alexander opened his mouth and roared, a sound of pure animal pain and impotence.

"You see." Rhiannon took her hand from his chest and stepped back. "He is mine to do with as I want. Remember that. I can and will kill him when he ceases to be of use to me." She leaned down and got in Bronwyn's face. She was paler, and her eyes bloodshot, but she was even more frightening like this. "This is the only warning you'll get."

The door slammed behind her, and Alexander whimpered and went still.

Bronwyn turned his head to her and tapped his cheek. "Alexander! Can you speak to me?" She pressed her ear to his mouth and with relief caught the jagged inhale and exhale of his breathing.

She tried to move to check the rest of him, but his hand fastened on her nape and held her ear close to his mouth. His breath hissed in her ear. "Little witch."

It was so soft Bronwyn didn't know if she'd heard him properly.

His eyes were open again and he was looking at her, staring into her as if trying to tell her something. He was a mess with blood in his hair and streaked over his face and chest, but his eyes were like the Alexander she knew. In there somewhere, was the man she'd been so drawn to, the man who had kissed her and made her world stop.

Confusion clouded her brain. Everything she'd heard of him, and now knew of him, warned her not to trust him. He was Rhiannon's son, and he did her bidding. But her heart didn't give a shit. His pain was her pain.

"Let's get you cleaned up." She crouched behind him and hooked her arms beneath his armpits. There was water in the bathroom, and it called to her.

He tried to help her, but his legs kept giving way beneath

him. Weaving like Saturday night bar crawlers, they staggered and stumbled into the attached bathroom.

Bronwyn turned on the shower, and without waiting for it to heat, she hauled them both inside and sat on the shower floor.

His body limp, Alexander pressed his face into her neck. His arms slid around her waist and he clung to her.

Water fell like a benediction on her head and down her back. It covered them in a bubble and Bronwyn reached into it for power.

"Careful," Alexander whispered. "She's weakened herself by showing off for you, but she can sense you using magic."

His voice sounded stronger and like the man she knew.

Bronwyn put her arms around him and called up her healing power. Amplified by the water, it slid into him.

Alexander whispered, "She has placed a magic tether to my heart. She can crush it with one thought."

"No." Bronwyn wanted to weep for him, for both of them. She had known something was wrong. "Why am I here?"

"Shhh!" He tucked her closer to him. Vitality crept back into his body as she kept her healing hands on his bare skin. "Need to get to Baile."

"We will."

"Not me." He coughed and winced. "You."

"Both of us." No fucking way she was leaving him with his bitch mother. She grabbed his cheeks and made him look at her. "We get out of this together. Hear me?"

Alexander's smile was sad and sweet, but he laid his head back against her shoulder. Exhausted, he slumped against her, but she welcomed the solid, strength of him. He was still with her, breathing and alive. There was still hope.

Water rained down on them, growing warmer, and she took as much strength as she dared from it.

Movement drew her eyes, and a rat poked its head out from under the vanity.

"*See me.*" She willed the small creature to hear her mental shout. "*See me and tell Niamh.*"

The rat's whiskers quivered, and it disappeared beneath the vanity again.

God, she'd lost her mind. She was trying to communicate with a rat, sitting on the floor of a shower with a man whose mother wanted both of them dead. Despair rose and threatened to engulf her. She tried to beat it back, but the tears came anyway.

"My little witch." Alexander's arms tightened around her. "I will get you out of here."

With a huge indrawn breath, she got her tears under control, but her voice wobbled as she said, "We'll both get out of here."

CHAPTER TWENTY-THREE

CRÉ-WITCH CHRONICLES

Maeve took a deep breath before she entered the barracks with something Mags called ibuprofen. In the five days it had taken him to heal, they'd all agreed—behind his back instead of risking poking the bear—that Roderick was not a good patient. He wasn't even a halfway decent patient. He was a bloody nightmare to care for.

He was chafing at how long his bullet wounds were taking to heal. They all understood his impatience. Out there, fates alone knew where, Rhiannon had Bronwyn. As the only living corporeal coimhdeacht, Roderick had taken it as a personal affront and was desperate to find her.

Mags appeared in the corridor ahead of her, brow furrowed. "We're in fighting fettle this morning."

"Oh, marvelous." Despite Roderick's attempts to shield her from a full assault of his pain and guilt through their bond, it nagged at her like a toothache. He had taken it as a failure that he hadn't reached Bronwyn in time to stop Fiona. "Is he still abed?"

"Ah, no." Mags looked disconsolate. "He insisted on trying his sword arm this morning. Nothing I said could stop him."

"Bloody hell." Maeve hurried along. If she had been by his side last night, this would never have happened. She'd been sharing his bedchamber since they'd dragged him back to Baile pouring blood from five bullet wounds. In those early hours, she'd stayed with him and then through the next three nights. Last night, Mags had finally persuaded her to sleep in her own chamber and let somebody else stay with Roderick.

Unfortunately, the other witches were still partially in awe of him—except Sinead, who'd been busy with Alannah—and let him bully and bluster them into seeing matters his way. She found Roderick in the practice hall, blood already seeping through his shirt. He raised his sword, grimaced and cursed.

"Roderick." Maeve needed to put a stop to his nonsense, and she was the only one who could.

He turned and scowled at her. Then he picked up his sword and went through a careful range of motions. "I don't have time for this now."

"Then make time." She stepped close enough to him that if he swung that sword, he would hit her.

With a curse, he stopped his sword arc short. "Bugger it, Maeve. She's out there, and I'm the only one who can get her."

"I know that." Through their bond, his impotent fury pulsed, and she put a hand on his chest, trying to settle him with the contact. "But you need to heal before you go after her."

"Has Mags found her?"

Mags stepped into the practice chamber. "I'm trying, Roderick, really I am." She shrugged. "But I can't...my gifts have never worked that way. I can't will my seeing."

Mags should be able to see through time whenever she wanted, and also to scry someone who needed finding. For the hundredth time, Maeve wished for a seer from her old coven. Even an apprentice seer would be able to do what Mags could not. She tamped down on her impatience. Mags was hardly to blame for her stunted abilities. Without becoming a conduit to

Goddess power, their gifts were like sparks to the powerful conflagration of a true cré-witch. Their two pitiful attempts to bond Goddess to the new witches had fizzled and died without elemental magic to draw on. And without waking the cardinal points, there was only a flutter of elemental magic available to them.

"We will find her." Maeve patted his chest. "And then you can kill that bitch once and for all."

Fierce determination flared in Roderick's eyes. "I'm going to end her, Maeve. For all that she's done to all of us."

"And I'll help you do it." She slid an arm around his waist and turned him toward his bedchamber. "But you need to get strong first. We need you to be strong."

He grunted but let her lead him off the sand and into his bedchamber. "I need to learn about guns."

"What about them?" Such deadly weapons, these modern guns, that the thought of them made Maeve shudder.

Roderick's arm tightened about her shoulder. "I need to know my enemy, Maeve. I am useless if I cannot fight them with their weapons."

"You will learn." She eased him to sit on the side of his bed and gently tugged his shirt over his head. "We are both adapting to this time."

"Like your jeans?" He managed a ghost of a smile.

Maeve laughed. "You have taken to them as well."

"Rhiannon is already so far ahead of us in this time. We need to catch up, and we have no time to do so."

"We will do it. She didn't beat us before, and we won't let her win now either." She handed him the ibuprofen and a glass of water. "Take these."

"What are they?"

"I don't know, but Mags says to take them."

Roderick shrugged, popped the pills into his mouth and took a swallow of water. "We were right, Maeve. Bronwyn must be the daughter of life. Rhiannon went to a lot of trouble to take her alive. It would have been much simpler to just kill her."

Rhiannon's soul was stained scarlet with all the witch blood she had shed. "Then they'll keep her alive until she can bear this child."

"Yes." Roderick looked grim. "But she needs to be impregnated before that can happen."

Neither of them could bear to utter the word that would entail. "Do you think Alexander will do it?"

"Before we found ourselves in this time I would have said without a doubt." Roderick shrugged. "But this new version of Alexander...I am uncertain."

Uncertain was still too near to Alexander obeying his mother for Maeve's taste. They were all anxious about Bronwyn.

Mags came in with a basin of water and some cloths. "Let's see how much damage you did."

Grumbling, Roderick allowed her to examine his wounds. Fortunately his stitches were holding, and already the wounds were closing.

Mags wiped away the blood seeping from his wounds. "You really do heal super fast."

Which was fortunate for them all because his wounds would have killed a normal man.

"Mags!" Niamh's bellow preceded her. Of all of them, Niamh was the most desperate to find Bronwyn. She'd been trying to connect with animals and find out if they'd seen anything. "Where are you?"

"Here!" Mags yelled back,

Roderick winced and shot Maeve an amused glance. No, these new witches were nothing like the old ones, and that wasn't always a bad thing.

"Anything?" Niamh and her pack streamed through the door. Today a rabbit, three foxes, two dogs and a weasel made up her menagerie. As she tried to connect with animals, her existing furry friends surrounded her more than usual. "Did you scry?"

"I tried." Mags smeared ointment on Roderick's wounds. "Nothing."

"Bugger it." Niamh peered over her shoulder and grimaced. "Ouch!" She patted Roderick's shoulder. "You're one tough motherfucker, Hot Rod."

Roderick looked confused, frowned, and then slid Maeve a sideways glance. He mouthed Hot Rod and she nearly giggled. Nagging worry about Bronwyn cast a pall over Baile, but it felt good to laugh.

Niamh plopped on the bed beside Roderick. "What we need is more like you."

CHAPTER TWENTY-FOUR

Living in a coven with ninety witches from childhood, Maeve had seen more than her share of strange behaviors and people. Witches ran the gamut from buttoned down to eccentric, and their gifts could create even more havoc. She had not, however, experienced anything like Roz.

Coming to the kitchen for breakfast the following morning, Maeve was greeted by Roz, the oddest of the lot, squatting on the kitchen table, doing that sickening head turning thing and shrieking loud enough to wake the dead.

"What the bloody hell is she doing?" Sinead stood behind Maeve, as if this was something she should handle. "It is too bloody early for this."

Whipping her head around, Roz fixed her with a strangely lucid light in her green eyes as if trying to convey something.

"I don't understand." Maeve threw up her hands.

Roz screeched, sharp enough to curl her toenails.

"Holy fuck!" Sinead clapped her hands over her ears. "Whatever she wants, can someone please give it to her. Now."

Alannah stood beside the stove with a pot of oatmeal forgotten in one hand. "We should get Niamh."

"Niamh is already here," Niamh said as she streamed into the kitchen amidst a stoat, two cats and a small raptor perched on her shoulder. The raptor bobbed taller and flapped its wings.

Roz stared at the raptor, puffed up her chest, flapped her arms and screeched.

Sinead yelled, "Get that falcon out of here."

"Kestrel," Niamh said and stroked the bird's cream and black dappled chest. The kestrel calmed down and tucked her wings into her body. "And Roz is trying to tell us something."

"Whatever it is, can you make her do it without that godawful noise?" Sinead stomped over to the range and snatched up the large copper kettle. "We're all going to need tea if this carries on."

Niamh approached Roz slowly. "I'm not sure how to understand her."

Bobbing her head up and down, Roz seemed to be encouraging Niamh to come closer.

The kestrel chirped and fluted as if offering encouragement.

Niamh looked to Maeve. "Any ideas?"

"Um..." She ventured closer, ever cautious of upsetting Roz and punishing all their ears. "Thomas!" The idea popped into her head. "He bonded Lavina, and she was a guardian. He might be able to tell us how she did it."

"Let's get him here." Sinead filled the kettle and plunked it back on the range. She looked at Maeve. "How does one summon a ghost?"

"You ask." Alannah smiled sweetly, and without raising her voice, simply said, "Thomas?"

"Sweetheart." Thomas strolled into the kitchen like he was a living, breathing man. "You called?" He glanced at Roz, and then snapped his gaze back again. "Why is someone sitting on the kitchen table?"

"That's Roz," Niamh said. "And she believes she's an owl."

"Indeed?" Thomas looked at Maeve and raised an eyebrow.

Maeve was hard pressed not to giggle. "She's a guardian, and as best I can understand has her awareness trapped in an owl's."

Thomas raised his brow. "She did not take her pact with Goddess?"

"What does that have to do with it?" Niamh turned to stare at him.

Thomas approached Roz, and she cocked her head and watched him. "It's something Lavina used to warn all acolytes and apprentices about when they used their gifts before their pact. It's a danger guardians face when Goddess is not present in their magic, tethering it to her."

"That could happen to Niamh?" Alannah paled.

"It does not always happen." Thomas ducked his head until he was eye to eye with Roz. "Some witches are more susceptible than others."

"How would I know if that might happen to me?" Niamh stared at Roz with trepidation.

"When you become like Roz," Thomas said. He looked to Alannah. "Is that why you summoned me?"

"Er...no." Alannah glanced at Maeve to take over.

Nobody in her old coven had looked to her for anything, let alone as if she had some authority. Maeve wasn't entirely sure she liked it. "Niamh thinks Roz is trying to tell her something, and we thought you might know how guardians manage to do what they do." Maeve didn't have the right words to describe guardian magic. All she'd ever done was transpose the story of their lives and magic on the cavern walls.

"Hmm." Thomas studied Roz. He clicked, remarkably like an owl.

Roz fluttered her arms and clicked back at him.

"Niamh is right," he said. "She is trying to tell you something, and for her to be here and communicating directly has to mean it's of vital importance."

The kestrel bobbed and whistled from Niamh's shoulder.

Thomas held up his hand and the kestrel flew to him and perched on his fingers.

"Such a pretty girl," he crooned, stroking her downy breast. He looked up and saw them all watching. "What? You think I could have bonded a guardian if I didn't have a natural affinity for animals."

"It's not that." Alannah cleared her throat. "She's sitting on your hand as if you're corporeal."

Thomas blinked at her and then looked at the kestrel. "Bugger me!"

"Never mind that." Sinead jerked her thumb at Roz. "Can we get her off the table."

Roz shrieked and this time Sinead shrieked back.

"Dear Sainted Mother." Thomas looked ill. "By all means let's get her off the table. How can I help?"

Niamh motioned Roz. "How did they do it? The guardians. How did they get inside an animal's mind?"

"I only ever observed it through Lavina." Thomas stroked the kestrel. "And it seemed less of a getting into the animal's mind and more a surrender to that animal."

"Oh-kay." Niamh took a breath.

"Wait!" Maeve held up her hand. Someone needed to be the voice of reason. "We cannot risk Niamh ending up like Roz. We have few enough witches as it is."

"Yeah." Niamh bit her lip and eyed Roz. "I'm not so keen on ending up like that either."

"Tether yourself to your element," Thomas said. "Use it as an anchor to find your way back again." He came to stand beside her. "Lavina would spread her mind wide, like a fog and the animals would be in the fog."

Maeve rummaged in the dresser and found some candles. She lit them with a flick of her fingers. "Here." She put the candles close to Niamh. "Use these as your starting point and know you must always return here."

"Your magic grows stronger," Thomas said. "Goddess wakes."

Alannah looked at the kestrel. "Do you think that's why—"

"Middle-age woman sitting on the kitchen table and scream-ing," Sinead said. "Can we deal with that first?"

"Good idea." Alannah shot Thomas a secretive smile.

Maeve knew that sort of smile, and it gave her pause. Thomas had been too charming as a man, and he'd lost none of his appeal as a ghost, but that's what he was, a ghost, and it would do Alannah no good to develop feelings for him.

But that was not their current problem. "Thomas, do you think you can track her as she works?"

"I can try." Thomas shrugged. "But she's not my witch, so I can only be of limited use."

NIAMH BREATHED deep and stared at the four candles, their flames flickering.

Thomas said to spread her awareness like a mist.

She tried, but thoughts popped into her head. Her worry for Bronwyn, the awareness of the entire kitchen watching her, feeling inadequate and silly for even trying it.

"Pull the flame." Thomas spoke from right beside her. "Reach for it and pull the power it offers."

The earthy tang of basil twined with the sweet of strawber-ries rose around her.

"That's it," Thomas said. "Your magic is there, waiting for you."

She focused on the candle flame nearest her. It jumped and flared. Spreading her magic further she encompassed all four candles. They flared high and stayed steady and strong.

"Yes," Maeve whispered. "Exactly like that."

Niamh's gift swelled within her, a bubble rising from a dark, unexplored center within her. That was what Maeve was talking about? She locked her attention on the mysterious unplumbed depths of her gift. There was so much latent power there that she had never suspected.

Maeve gripped her hand. "Stay on the surface, Niamh. You can't go there yet."

Every part of her being strained to get closer to that untapped well. Then she caught the flicker of something in her web. It was the kestrel, it's eyesight disconcertingly sharp. She touched on it and the cats, the stoat and finally an awareness that felt human but other.

Reality lurched in a sickening spin, and she was looking at a service station. The scene was mostly monochromatic, but the detail was startlingly clear. She was seeing this through bird's eyes. The realization amazed her so much she almost lost the connection.

Roz whistled and clicked.

Niamh drew on the candles and surrendered to her connection with Roz. Details became clearer and she saw a small redhead being bustled out of an SUV and into a sedan. "It's Bronwyn," she said. "She's alive." The scene played out in front of her. "She's with those two women and Rhiannon is there. Alexander too."

"Good," Thomas said. "Now use the bird to look around."

Niamh frowned. "I can't. It won't let me."

"That's because you're seeing a memory," Thomas said. "This isn't happening now."

"How is this happening at all?" Maeve asked. "Roz did not fly off and watch this happen."

"I don't know," Thomas said. "I've never known this to happen before, but it's information we didn't have two minutes ago, so I'll take it."

Something brushed against Niamh's awareness, like the lightest touch on her skin. She pulled more fire and tracked it.

The scene skewed into a distorted view. A large dark shape

loomed in front of her, and she tested the air—with her whiskers. Somehow she was in a different animal's perception now. Niamh widened the connection and opened her senses. She sampled the air. Scent broke into its myriad components: wood, wood polish, dust, fabric, sacking, feathers—it all came at her in a rush, and she nearly panicked.

"Breathe," Thomas whispered. "It's disorientating the first time because animals perceive things differently. They notice different things. Tell me what you see."

"It's blurry." The image moved and she was looking at more gray objects. A large rectangular shape hung above her and to her left a vertical cylindrical object that smelled of wood and metal and polish, and so many other scents she had no name for.

She clung to the calm of Thomas's voice as he spoke. "Are you bigger or smaller than the objects around you?"

"Smaller, much smaller." That cylindrical thing was a furniture leg, and the thing above her was the underside of a piece of furniture. "I'm under the furniture."

"Good," Thomas said. "You're probably sharing headspace with a rodent of some kind."

That fit, so Niamh nodded. Her legs were limber and supple. Claws extended from all four of her feet and her whiskers moved constantly, sifting sensory information. She almost laughed as she realized what she was. "I'm a rat."

"Lavina always liked rats," Thomas said. "She said they were a lot brighter than most animals and easy to guide."

"Guide?" Niamh's heartbeat sped up with her host as he tested the air in front of them. He poked his head out to another battery of new scents and more light.

Thomas grunted. "This is the tricky part. If you push, the animal will frighten and shove you out of his mind, but if you don't try to manage what it sees, you won't get the information you need."

"What does this rat want to show me?" Niamh spoke the question aloud, but the rat looked about as if responding to her request. She sent a questioning pulse to the small beast.

"It must be trying to tell her something Niamh really wants to know." Maeve's voice sounded closer. "Is it possible Roz or one of Niamh's other friends sent a request through to other animals, and they are responding?"

"That's ridiculous," Sinead's voice. "Niamh is not Dr. Dolittle."

Not far off though, and Niamh motioned them to silence. She kept a tight hold on the power, not wanting to startle her host.

Opening to her invasion, the rat let her take over his senses. No fight for supremacy or instinctive panic. The rat seemed to want to help her. Niamh loved all animals, but this was giving her a greater appreciation for rats.

They were under a wardrobe, peering out from beneath it. The wood smelled old, petrified. She bet with time she'd be able to smell the difference between types of wood, but this wood smelled old, so they were probably in an old building.

The wrong almost made her gag. It smelled like decay and blood, and Rat's instinct was to flee. Niamh tightened her hold on the animal and kept it beneath the wardrobe.

Keeping them still, she let the rat assess for possible danger. Their heartbeat slowed, and their breathing returned to normal. Their whiskers absorbed more information. The room was warm with a trace of damp.

Her hearing was so much sharper, and the steady breathing of a living creature nearby sounded unnaturally loud.

Rat's peripheral thoughts flit through her. He was hungry and had more hunting to do before the night was over. He'd been drawn into this room by the strong smell of food and...something else.

Tingles danced down her spine. She coaxed the something

into the forefront of Rat's mind. Magic and the right kind. Her kind of magic.

"Bronwyn," she whispered.

Thomas's voice was in her ear. "Find her, Guardian. You can do this."

His words gave her the confidence she needed.

The rest of the kitchen occupants' intense waiting energy pushed at her awareness. She sensed a change in the kitchen's power as Roderick walked in. His energy was ascendant and powerful, an apex predator.

Niamh dropped deeper into Rat. His incredible sense of smell battered her at first, until she retuned her mind to accept the sensory overload. The food smell came from deeper in the room.

Cheese. She almost laughed. Go figure! Bread. Ham. Mustard. Butter. A sandwich.

There. On one of those 70's TV trays sat a plate with half of what her nose identified as a cheese and ham sandwich. A pack of unopened crisps lay beside it, and a glass of milk.

She couldn't see farther into the room, but the tingle of Bronwyn lit her up like fireworks.

Obligingly, Rat sniffed for danger, then pattered out of their hiding place. He hesitated at a piece of cheese on the floor. It only seemed polite to let her host eat it before they went on.

They scampered over wide wooden planks that were scent laden. She let Rat sniff for danger again. He'd survived this long on his instincts, and they would probably keep her alive as well.

A bed leg came into view, half concealed by a frilly white bed skirt. The sort one expected to find in a teenager's room. Rat moved her to a good vantage point.

Bronwyn lay on the bed, eyes closed but her limbs too tense for sleep.

Beside her lay Alexander. He didn't look well, and Rat's nose confirmed the truth. The wrong pulsed inside him like a living thing, but it was a parasite, draining the life from him. Rat identified blood, dried now, but shed within the last few days.

"Alexander."

"I knew that whoreson would be neck deep in this," Roderick said. His predatory energy washed over her and she shut it down before it could panic Rat. "Is she hurt?"

"No." It was disconcerting operating in two realities at once. The room swirled around her, and for a sickening moment, she couldn't tell it if was the kitchen or the room the rat was in.

"The flame." Maeve gripped her hand and squeezed. "Find the flame again, Niamh." Speaking to someone else, she said, "She shouldn't stay there much longer."

Running out of time, Niamh leaned into Rat's thoughts. It took some exerting of her will to get Rat to climb the bed skirt to the bed.

Bronwyn's eyes snapped open. She opened her mouth to scream.

Rat froze.

Alexander opened his eyes and touched Bronwyn's arm. He peered at Rat and shook his head. "It's Niamh."

"Niamh?" Bronwyn stared at Rat.

Rat wanted to flee. It went against every instinct to be this close to a human. Not wanting to terrorize him by forcing him closer, Niamh let him remain in an alert crouch. She moved his gaze about the room. They were in a bedroom, on a beautiful canopied bed. The old wardrobe they'd been hiding beneath was to the left of a large, mullion-paned window. Through the aged wavy glass, dawn limned a church spire.

Yes! A point of reference.

"Is that you?" Bronwyn shifted closer.

Rat nearly bolted then.

Bronwyn eased back. "Okay, I won't come any closer." She closed her eyes. "Goddess, I'm talking to a rat. I damn well hope it's you, Niamh, otherwise I'm going to never stop screaming."

Alexander chuckled. "I don't know how she's doing it, but Rhiannon will know."

Reacting to her fear, Rat scented the air. There were other scent markers close to them. Several people had been in this room. Without a prior reference, Rat couldn't produce an image to go with the scent. But there were three distinct scents other than Bronwyn.

"I'm not sure where I am," Bronwyn pulled a face. "But Alexander is with me, and he's hurt."

"Bronwyn hasn't been hurt, but Alexander has." Niamh spoke aloud for the benefit of those in Baile's kitchen.

Roderick grunted. "Best news I've had today."

Rat tensed.

Bronwyn looked alarmed. "He—"

Pain speared through Niamh's head. Everything went dark. Absolute nothing. No sound, smell or sight. The only thing here was pain pounding into her brain.

She needed to get out of the nothing. Panic turned to acid in her throat.

"Very good, Niamh." A woman's voice raked through her brain like claws. "So quiet I nearly didn't pick you up."

Niamh reached for the flame.

An oily backlash gripped her and flung her away. She may have screamed and screamed, but the nothing absorbed everything in it and around it.

"Say goodbye to your friend." The woman's voice pounded in her head.

Another sharp spike of pain and she knew Rat was dead. The voice would die. She wanted to smash her beneath her heel like she had Rat.

"That's not very nice, Niamh."

The voice saw every thought she had.

"Yes, I do," Rhiannon said. "Everything."

Niamh hunted for some point of reference in the nothing.

Something she could hang on to. The flame. Maeve had told her to stay anchored to the flame. She reached for it but there was nothing there. Blank. Not even a shift in the darkness. "Say goodbye, Niamh."

Her imminent death swelled through Rhiannon's voice, and Niamh knew she would die. Like Rat.

Goddess, Rat deserved better than such an awful end. The rage gave her a grip.

A dog howled in the terrible dark, and she used the sound as an anchor.

The nothing grew more intense as it chewed through her connection with life. She was cold, freezing, her teeth chattering in the absolute silence. This death would be more than physical. Cut off from all sources of life, her soul would drift into nothing and never be reborn again. The power to do such a thing was terrible.

Niamh refused to go out like that. She could flee or fight. Instead of trying to escape the nothing, she threw herself into it. Sharp edges sprang out of her, points that she drove into the nothing.

A tiny shift of two darks beside each other gave her an opening.

She grabbed for the candle flame, reaching out blindly. Fire flared as a tiny spark. Not enough. Throwing her power out further, she seized all four candles and heaved. Fire swelled through her. Not much, but enough that she shaped it into a javelin and plunged into the subtle shading between the two darks.

It tossed her back.

Niamh dragged more fire, gathered and thrust.

A crack appeared in the nothing.

Fire in the kitchen range responded to her call and gave her more power.

Pain ricocheted through her head with each beat of her

heart. Life waited for her on the other side of that crack.

Niamh split her power into hundreds of needles and drove them against the crack. A wedge opened. Gray poured through, tasting bitter and burning acrid in her nostrils.

"Niamh!" Maeve's voice, but so far away she didn't think she had the strength to reach it. Already the nothing coalesced back into shape again and closed the wedge.

Heat touched her skin as she drew all her power into one word, sucked a breath, and drew more and more and more again. It swelled in her.

The nothing kept coming.

She poured all that power into one word and came to screaming, "Baile!"

Sights, sounds, smell, touch, taste all rushed at her at once, and she whimpered under the excruciating barrage.

"I've got you." Even whispered, Maeve's voice dug into her sore head.

Her hand rasped like sandpaper against Niamh's spine, but she needed that connection to life.

Stoat brushed her bruised consciousness lighter than thistle-down, letting her know they were there.

Her cats kneaded her thighs, purring loudly.

"Maeve." Her throat hurt like she'd been screaming. It came out as a croak, and she swallowed and tried again. "Maeve?"

"We're all here"

"She had me. She wouldn't let me go."

A glass appeared at her lips. "Drink it," Alannah said.

Niamh took a careful swallow. Apple juice.

"So strong." Niamh shuddered. It would be a long time before she forgot the sheer helplessness and how effortlessly Rhiannon had held her there. "She could have done anything she wanted with me."

"You did well." Thomas crouched in front of her, and Roderick stood behind him. "Could you see where Bronwyn is?"

"Jesus." Thomas scowled over his shoulder. "Did you miss the part where Rhiannon nearly fucking killed her?"

"Sorry." Roderick gave her an apologetic grimace. "But my duty here is clear. I have to get to Bronwyn."

She'd almost died. It took a second for the panic to subside.

Niamh's nose itched, and she wiped it. Her hand came away covered in blood.

Alannah hovered in front of her and passed her a damp cloth. "You're bleeding from the nose and ears."

Niamh touched her neck where it itched. Russet stains under her fingernails confirmed blood. "I must look a mess."

"Going to be honest with you, girl." Sinead leaned into her field of vision. "You remember the time you spent a weekend with that rugby team?"

Snarled hair, stinking to high heaven and covered in stale beer. "Yes."

"This is worse."

CHAPTER TWENTY-FIVE

A lexander was so much bigger than her physically that Bronwyn couldn't wrap herself around enough of him to be of any use to him. He'd retreated into that cold-eyed automaton again, and she couldn't reach him.

Truth was, she was scared to try in case Rhiannon came back in and took her anger out on him. So she obeyed her instinct and wrapped herself around him like a big spoon, her cheek pressed between his shoulder blades, and listened to the steady beat of his heart.

Six days locked in this room together, and there were moments she could pretend they weren't prisoners. Times spent lying side by side and talking, talking about everything and nothing, clinging to each other for sanity. Alexander stayed away from the huge, looming questions between them, and she let him, because she couldn't deal with his possible answers yet.

Fuck, but she'd thought Rhiannon had killed him with her last attack. After stomping the rat into a bloody smear, she'd turned her anger on Alexander. Rhiannon had kept at him for so long that Bronwyn had screamed for mercy, but Rhiannon had only stopped when Alexander was passed out in a pool of his own blood on the floor.

Bronwyn had done her best to wipe away the dried blood around his eyes, ears, nose and mouth and had struggled with his dead weight until she got him on the bed.

Before Rhiannon had left them alone, she'd warned Bronwyn that any contact with Baile would result in swift retribution. Not to her, no because Rhiannon had all these plans for her, but Alexander. The crazy fucking bitch must have some plan to get her pregnant and keep her here until she had the baby, some next level *Handmaid's Tale* shit that Bronwyn veered away from thinking too long and hard about.

By the steady, slow draw of Alexander's breath, she guessed he was sleeping. Sleeping was good. Sleep healed.

She pressed her ear to his back. His heartbeat, slow but steady *bwa-dum, bwa-dum, bwa-dum* became the measure of time. She clung to the soft suck and blow of his lungs moving air in and out, in and out, as her ward against her fear.

If she'd done as Maeve had suggested and taken her pact with Goddess, she might have been able to help him. To take her magic and slip it beneath his skin and find the source of pain. She could even try to break the manacles Rhiannon has fastened about his heart. Fear had kept her passive, but now a greater fear might cost Alexander's life.

No closer to understanding the insane connection between them, and not wanting to name the tight bundle of feelings she kept tucked deep inside, she took and gave what physical comfort she could.

The light beneath their door blinked out, and the deep black of night shrouded them.

Bwa-dum, inhale, bwa-dum, exhale—the soundtrack to her life, proof that he was alive, proof that she was alive and not alone. She and Alexander were fundamentally intertwined, and she would not, could not, let him die.

His breath hitched on a soft sound, and she froze and waited.

"Little witch?" So soft she barely heard him.

She gently tightened her hold around his middle. "I'm here."

"I'm glad."

A door slammed in the cottage, and he tensed. Footsteps moved away from them, and the door slammed again. More footsteps approached the window from the outside, clip-clopping on the paving stones, and then a car started up and drove off.

Tension drained from Alexander. "She's gone."

"Are you sure?" Bronwyn kept her whisper as soft as she could. Six days since Rhiannon had brought them there, and she'd never left once. Sometimes Edana brought their meals, and at others Fiona, but they could always sense Rhiannon like a dark, stinking cloud in the cottage.

"I can feel her moving away." Alexander lifted her hand from around his middle and pressed it to his chest. "The tether she placed on me is like the bond Roderick and Maeve share, but her twisted version of that."

Maeve and Roderick could think and feel like one person. "Does she know when you speak to me?"

"She can sense my attention on you." His breath caught as he shifted position. "But that's what she wants, so it doesn't bother her. Right now, she's not concentrating on me."

"Good." Bronwyn pressed closer to his back, using the most elemental of human comfort. "Are you okay?"

"Fine."

But she knew he was lying.

"We need to talk," he said. "And we might not have this chance again." His muscles eased, and some of the tension drained out of him. There was so much about being here like this with Alexander that made sense to her. It sounded corny saying it to herself, but it was like they were meant to be.

"*Dee.*" She reached deep inside for her connection to her grandmother. "*I think maybe I love him.*"

Tree branches tapped against the window, and for a moment, she swore Deidre's whisper rode the wind. *Trust your instinct.*

"Bronwyn." Alexander raised her hand and kissed it. "I'm sorry."

"For?"

"All of it." He interlaced their fingers. "For being who I am, for not being honest with you upfront." He took a deep breath. "And mostly because whatever there is between us will always be tainted by what is happening around us."

"Yeah." She couldn't know if she loved him or not because of that stupid prophecy, and she didn't know if she could trust him because of stuff that had happened hundreds of years before her birth.

He tensed and then stilled.

Bronwyn froze.

The faint stink of blood magic seeped out of him. After a few minutes he relaxed again. "She checked in with me."

"And?"

"Saw my blank mind."

Maybe a wiser woman would get as far away from him as the room allowed, but his heart beating in time with hers comforted her. "How does she do that thing where she hurts you."

"The tether." His grip on her hands tightened. "She tightens it around my heart."

"Is there a way to get it off you."

He shrugged. "Don't think about that. Let's concentrate on getting you out of here."

But she did think about it and would continue to think about it until she had an answer. "Do you know how long she'll be away?"

"No."

From a distance, perhaps Rhiannon wasn't as aware of magic being done. Bronwyn spread her hands over his torso and reached for the healing warmth.

He covered her hands with his. "Be careful. She can still sense the magic being used."

"Then you let me know when she tunes in and I'll stop." Painfully slowly, she let the healing warmth spread through his chest. "Any better?"

"Thank you. Don't spend your strength on me." He sighed. "I've been alive a long time, Bronwyn, and for most of those years I've done things I can't bear to even think about. I'm reaping as I sowed."

"Bullshit!" She'd take a lot from him, but that kind of defeatist crap wasn't going to happen. "We're getting out of here."

"Little witch." He half turned his head to look over his shoulder at her. "She'll know the minute I leave here. It's why she doesn't care about leaving us alone. And she has people watching."

"All we need is one lapse." She sat up. This conversation was too vital to have lying down.

"She's not big on lapses." He rolled to his back, stilled and raised his hand. He relaxed.

Bronwyn wrinkled her nose at the faint smell of blood magic. "She checked in again?"

He nodded.

"But she does make mistakes." Bronwyn would be damned before she gave up and withered. "Putting us together, that's a mistake. Thinking this connection between us is only about that prophecy, another mistake."

He rolled over and stared into her eyes. "Is it about more than the prophecy?"

"I think so." In this room, there was no room for saving

pride. Here they were both stripped raw. "I'm not sure. All I know is I feel it all the time, and I can't be without you."

"Sweetheart." He touched her cheek. "You must leave here without me. I can't leave with you."

"Yes, you can."

"Bronwyn." His expression softened. "I need you to be safe. If I can accomplish only that in my long and misbegotten life, I can be at peace." He kissed her forehead. "My little witch. You are so much more important than that fucking prophecy."

"I'm not leaving without you." Talking about it made it feel too real, and she was barely hanging on to her sanity as it was.

Alexander struggled into a seated position and took her hand. "Don't be naive, Bronwyn. Neither of us can afford that. Since the day the coven chucked her out, she's been obsessed with defeating it and taking over from Goddess. You're her ticket to wonderland."

"I know that." The walls crept closer, and the air grew thinner. "She locked us in together for a reason."

He cleared his throat and looked pained. "She wants you pregnant with my baby, and all the options for getting you that way scare the crap out of me. And they should scare the crap out of you."

"I can't think about this or I'll lose it." Not able to stay still, Bronwyn stood and paced the room.

Alexander watched her. "You need to think about how she plans to get her way, because she will get her way. The only reason she had a son was because of that prophecy. That prophecy is her one shot at the power she's been craving for thousands of years."

"So she created you for me to fall for?" As evil plans went, and if she were into the hatching of them, this one wasn't bad. Except for a few pertinent details. "Did she have a contingency in case I didn't even like you?"

A trace of his charming self crossed his face in a grin. "We didn't think that likely."

Despite everything, it felt really good to laugh. "Is that why you never..." Her face heated. "Why you never took things further with me?"

"Not for lack of wanting, but I couldn't risk you falling pregnant." He chuckled and then grimaced in pain. "I would never do that to any woman without her knowing the risk." His expression gentled. "Least of all you."

To get a woman pregnant without her knowledge or consent was too horrible to contemplate. "So, what happens now that the first part of her plan has failed?"

"You're living it." He gestured the room.

"And this is supposed to make me get it on with you?" She couldn't afford not to think about the scary parts of being imprisoned with Alexander. Maybe due to circumstance, but the implications of what he was telling her were slow to sink in. "And if I don't lie down like a good girl and allow myself to be impregnated?"

Alexander winced. "Now you know why you have to leave me here." He took another Rhiannon check in break before leaning forward and taking Bronwyn's hand. "This." He indicated his chest. "Is partly to punish me for waking Maeve and Roderick and getting them to Baile." He pulled a face. "But also so she has absolute control of me." Turning her hand over, he pressed her palm to his cheek. "I'm a danger to you, sweetheart. She can make me do things I would never want to do." His dark gaze held the burden of worlds. "That can't happen."

"When she has you under her control, it's like the real you disappears and this robot takes over." Cold, dark terror crept up her spine.

"Her robot." Alexander nodded. "She can make me do anything she wants me to do, and I won't even be aware of what I'm doing until it's too late."

They were silent for a long time. Bronwyn stared out the window. Like the last time she'd checked, the window was still barred and locked. The door was as well.

She couldn't process the ramifications of all Alexander had told her, so she concentrated on the other part of what he'd said. "You said I'm more important than that."

Hand raised, he let Rhiannon check in before he spoke again. "When you get out of here, I can cover for you for a while. But I can't tell how long, and you need to get to Baile as soon as you can. You need to call a coven sister and let them send Roderick to meet you. He'll get you there or die trying."

In Alexander's version of how the future looked, a lot of people would be dying to see her safe. "I'm only one witch. I can't be that important."

"Over and above the prophecy, you're a water witch," he said. "Which is why you're here. You need to take your vow and activate the water cardinal point. Roderick and Maeve know that's what has to happen, and I'm guessing we're giving you time to get used to the idea. Free will is big with Goddess." He gave a wry smile. "Free will is nonexistent with Rhiannon.

"I'm getting that loud and clear." Regret piled on. "Maeve really wanted me to take my vow. I should have taken it"

"Yes, you should have."

That was all very well to say now. "I wish I had." But for more reasons than he believed. The idea of waking the water point paled in comparison to her need to get them both safely to Baile. If she'd taken her vow, she would have had access to so much more power now. Enough power to heal Alexander, maybe even enough power to destroy the tether Rhiannon had placed around his heart. Damn, but talk about your problem mothers. Alexander didn't look open to the discussion, so she settled for saying, "I'm not leaving here alone. You're coming with me, and we're both getting to Baile."

He gave her an enigmatic smile. "We'll see."

There he sat, looking all Yoda-like and thinking he was as stubborn as her and would get his own way. Show always worked better than tell in any case, so she said, "Yes, we fucking will."

CHAPTER TWENTY-SIX

Before Bronwyn opened her eyes, she sensed she was being watched, and with the nauseating smell of blood magic strong in her nose, it wasn't too hard to guess who was watching her.

Bronwyn didn't know why Rhiannon was in the room, but that she was, and Alexander not warning of her approach couldn't be good.

She opened her eyes to a new morning with Rhiannon leaning over the bed and watching her and Alexander. Not one line, wrinkle, blemish or even freckle marred the eggshell perfection of Rhiannon's skin. Her dark eyes were ringed with thick, dark lashes, and her eyebrows were on point enough to make a YouTube beauty influencer weep with envy.

"Clever wench." Rhiannon smiled at her, perfect teeth within the pillowy fullness of her red lips. "You have used his feelings for you well."

Bronwyn sat up, not wanting to show her underbelly to this freak. "I thought that was your thing."

"And so spirited." Rhiannon laughed. "It makes this so much more interesting."

"You're sick." It oozed out of Rhiannon's every pore. "You're a sick, evil woman."

Rhiannon shrugged and cocked her head. She stroked the side of Alexander's face. "He is so beautiful, isn't he? I made him this way. The perfect breeding machine."

She didn't see her son as any part of her, but merely a tool to get what she wanted. And what Rhiannon wanted was Bronwyn pregnant by Alexander.

Bronwyn's stomach lurched, and she dug her nails into her palms to keep the fear off her face. Rhiannon would love to know how frightened she was. There was only one way Alexander was getting her pregnant, and her mind veered away from the horror of that happening to her. The double horror of it being this man, a man whom, despite everything, she had feelings for, almost drove her into panic. "Alexander won't hurt me."

"You say that as if he has a choice." Rhiannon tapped his cheek. "Wake."

Alexander's eyes shot open, so dark it was impossible to distinguish his pupils. He stared straight ahead.

Rhiannon leaned closer to her and sniffed the air. She stood with a smirk. "You are ready. It is the right time."

"What?" Bronwyn scooted away from Alexander. He hadn't so much as blinked since Rhiannon had woken him. "Alexander?"

"By all means, try and reach him." Rhiannon laughed. "I shall enjoy watching you try and fail."

Bronwyn shook his shoulder. "Alexander, it's me, Bronwyn."

"Some misguided sense of fair play persuaded me to see if he could get the job done without my insistence." Heels tapping on the wooden floor, she strolled away, and sank into a large armchair by the empty hearth. "But I had underestimated your influence on him. He has become disappointingly sentimental." She examined her nails with a frown. "I chose his sire so carefully for being duty first and sentiment later." She sighed. "The strongest and the best, or so I thought."

"Alexander." Bronwyn shook his shoulder harder. Somewhere in there was the man who had made her laugh, teased her, kissed her, made her feel like she was finally alive. "I know you're in there. I know it."

She reached for water.

"Uh-uh." Rhiannon chided and wagged her finger.

A backlash of putrid blood magic slammed into her and shot through her like putting her finger in an electric socket.

Bronwyn didn't care. She couldn't let this happen. Her hands on his chest warmed with her healing magic, the smell of honey and sage surrounded them.

"I said no." Rhiannon flickered her fingers, and more blood magic scoured Bronwyn from the inside out. The heat in her hands vanished and she was left doubled over and retching. "Do you know how long I have waited for the right witch, the one in the prophecy?"

"That's not me." Bronwyn dragged in air, trying to push herself up again. "I didn't even know about the prophecy."

"Oh, it's you." Rhiannon smiled at her. "That bitch Goddess stirs for the first time in hundreds of years. Roderick and Maeve have been woken to protect you. And he knows." She pointed at Alexander. "From the moment he caught sight of you, he's been like a dog with a bitch in heat."

Alexander liked her for who she was, not because of some insane prophecy. She knew he did. The tenuous, fragile connection between them had to be real. She wished she had as much conviction as she put into her voice when she said, "You can't know that."

Rhiannon laughed. "You have no idea what I can and cannot know. Clueless as to what I can and cannot do." She shrugged, the red silk of her blouse catching the light. "It matters not. On the small chance you're not the one, then we'll know as soon as your child is born. Either way, you will have served your purpose."

Bronwyn slammed her hands on Alexander's chest.

He lay there staring at nothing.

"Wake up," she yelled. "You hear me. I know that somewhere in there you hear me."

"As distasteful as this will be, I can take no chances." Rhiannon grimaced. "I will stay here and make sure the job is done properly. You're in your fertile time; this shouldn't need to happen more than once."

"He won't do it. He couldn't." But despite her words, Bronwyn scooted off the bed. She didn't know where she was running to, but she had to get away.

Rhiannon clapped her hands.

Alexander blinked.

"Take her," Rhiannon said. "She is yours."

Alexander moved with lethal speed. Here was the warrior Roderick had warned her about.

She ran for the door.

He caught her around the waist and hauled her back.

"Alexander," she screamed, clawing at the arm around her waist.

His free hand fastened around her throat, forcing her head back. A thin trickle of blood escaped his nostril. He was trying to fight Rhiannon.

"Fight her, Alexander. Come on." She kicked and writhed against him, but he was impossibly strong. "Please, baby, fight her. For us."

And Rhiannon watched with those awful dark eyes that didn't move from them.

"Please." Bronwyn's voice rushed out on a sob. She stared into the lifeless black of his eyes. No trace of her Alexander was in there, only that thin red smear beneath his nose to give her hope. "Please, Alexander, you don't want to do this. Please."

He threw her on the bed.

Bronwyn rolled and lunged for the far side.

Like iron, his hand fastened on her shoulder and yanked her back. Pain shot through her deltoid as she tried to resist, but he slammed her back down on the mattress.

His face was an impassive mask above her as he pinned her wrists together and yanked them over her head.

He was going to rape her, while Rhiannon watched, and there was nothing she could do about it.

The bedside lamp was out of her reach. There was nothing she could do.

Rough fingers yanked at her jeans button.

She was sobbing and begging, pleading with him to see her, know her.

And Rhiannon watched, sitting in her chair with her legs crossed.

A large man appeared behind her.

Bronwyn stilled and blinked him into focus.

Roderick.

Raising a huge metal war hammer Roderick slammed it into Rhiannon's head.

She slumped forward, blood spattering her chair, her silk blouse, the wall behind her and Roderick.

Roderick hit her again with a nauseating squelch.

Alexander collapsed on her, his dead weight pinning her down.

Alexander's weight made it hard to draw a deep breath. "Roderick?"

"Bronwyn." Roderick's voice came closer, and then she was free of Alexander's body. Roderick reached her for. "Blessed."

Bronwyn opened her mouth, but inarticulate sounds came out, and she couldn't shape them into words. She scrambled for Roderick. He was real and he was there, and he would save her.

"Come, Blessed." He lifted her in his arms, his voice gruff. "I have you."

"How?" She gripped his neck and held. She was never letting go. "What?"

"Later." Roderick carried her past the bloody mess that was Rhiannon.

"Is she dead?"

"Not likely." He kicked the door open. "But you are my first concern."

Alexander lay on the bed like a broken rag doll, and she couldn't leave him. "Alexander."

"Once you are safe, he dies. They both die this night." The awful finality in Roderick's voice broke through her terror.

"No." She wriggled in his hold. "He's under her control." Just like she had been. As much a victim as she had been. "Roderick."

He growled as he ran with her in his arms through the cottage. "Do not ask that of me."

"Please." She couldn't leave Alexander like that. "You need to bring him too."

"No." He kicked open the front door and cool, moist air enveloped her.

Suddenly there were other arms and familiar faces. Niamh looking concerned, Maeve was crying and holding out her arms. And the Land Rover sat idling outside the cottage with Sinead at the wheel.

"Get in." Sinead slammed her palm against the side.

Bronwyn dug her heels in. Every part of her wanted in that Landy and away, but she couldn't leave Alexander. Rhiannon had been right about that. For better or worse, she and Alexander were linked. She looked at Roderick. "Please."

"Fucking, sodding shit, hellfire and damn!" Roderick deposited her in the Land Rover and motioned Maeve and Niamh. "Get in that car and don't fucking move."

Bronwyn scrambled into the back, and Maeve and Niamh

bracketed her.

With a loaded look at Roderick, Maeve nodded. "Bring him but finish it. It ends this night."

Roderick nodded and disappeared inside the cottage.

"I've got you." Niamh wrapped her arms around Bronwyn and held her. A large retriever popped up from where he'd been lying and put his head on Bronwyn's lap. The fear and the horror of the last few days unraveled faster and faster and her tears melted into loud, wracking sobs as Niamh held her tight and rocked her.

The back door to the Landy opened, and Roderick tossed Alexander at their feet like a bag of bones. The thunk of Alexander's head on the Landy floor made Bronwyn wince. Even though she knew it wasn't him that had tried to rape her, Bronwyn recoiled.

Roderick and his bloody hammer headed back to the cottage.

Rubber squealed against asphalt as three cars screeched to a halt. Doors opened and bodies leaped out, converging on the Landy.

"We're out of time." Sinead revved the engine. "Get in here, big guy because I don't fancy fighting that lot."

Another car lurched to a halt and more bodies ran for them. Three, five, ten, more than she could count as they ran for Roderick and the Landy.

"Roderick," Maeve yelled. "We must be safe first."

For a moment, it looked like he hadn't heard. He stood there, legs braced, war hammer clutched in both fists as the first person reached him. He swung and hit something with a sickening wet smack followed by a crack of bone and an agonized scream. Roderick spun and connected more flesh. The converging attackers slowed, but kept coming.

Roderick spun and ran.

Sinead had the vehicle moving as he jerked open the

passenger door and threw himself in. He tossed his bloody war hammer on the dashboard. Revolting bits of skin, hair and globs of flesh spackled the head. "Gave her an extra crack for good measure when I went back to get him."

Sinead patted his shoulder. "Good job." Then she punched the gas and Bronwyn lurched into Niamh.

"Get out the bloody way," Sinead yelled as she barreled the Landy straight for the knot of people.

Closing her eyes, Bronwyn braced for impact.

With a few more expletives and some quick jerks left, right and right again, the Landy surged forward down the road.

Clutching the dashboard, Roderick glanced behind them. "They do not pursue."

"Probably checking on Rhiannon." Sinead glanced in the rearview mirror, took a traffic light at a rolling stop and plunged them through a roundabout and onto the highway.

"Blessed." Roderick trained his pale blue eyes on her, his face gentle. "You are not harmed?"

"Not too much." Bronwyn mopped her face with a tissue Niamh had handed her. "More frightened than anything else." She had been so surprised to see him standing behind Rhiannon with that war hammer. "Thank you for saving me."

"Of course." He shrugged. "You are Blessed, and I am coimhdeacht."

Niamh toed Alexander with her foot. "What's the story with him?"

"He tried to rape me—"

"Motherfucker." Sinead jerked the Landy to the side of the highway.

A truck roared past them with a blast of its horn.

"Sweet Goddess, preserve us." Maeve looked pale enough to pass for paper.

"Get him out." Sinead jabbed a finger at Alexander.

"He didn't mean it." Bronwyn couldn't quite touch him yet.

"Rhiannon has some sort of hold on him. She could make him do things. He said she had some kind of magic tether around his heart."

Roderick and Sinead looked at each other. With a grunt, Roderick shook his head. "Drive. I can always kill him later." He shrugged. "It would be more satisfying if he was awake in any case."

"Good thinking." Sinead eased back onto the highway.

"Was it the prophecy?" Maeve frowned, her eyes filled with concern.

Bronwyn nodded. She didn't want to talk about that stupid prophecy ever again.

"We couldn't be sure." Biting her lip, Maeve sighed. "There is so much we don't know and need to discover. We can be certain of very little."

"We can be certain that I missed a golden opportunity to separate Rhiannon's head from her neck," Roderick said.

"That's a bitter pill for you to swallow, big guy." Sinead squeezed Roderick's shoulder. "But you'll get her next time."

Roderick nodded. "That is another certainty. There will be a next time."

"And next time bring a sword." Sinead stared at the road. "Take her head right off, that will."

"I prefer the hammer." Roderick picked up his hammer and cleaned it with a cloth he found in the seat well. "And I shall learn to use a gun."

Tense silence filled the vehicle. There was so much to discuss and come to terms with, but none of them seemed inclined to break the silence. For now, they had survived, and Bronwyn was with her coven sisters heading for Baile.

One thing was sure, she couldn't relax until Baile's ancient stone walls surrounded her. "How far are we from home?"

"Two hours, three max," Sinead said and looked at her through the rearview mirror. "Try to get some rest."

CHAPTER TWENTY-SEVEN

The steady rock and hum of the Land Rover soothed Bronwyn and her tears dried. The retriever kept his head on her lap, big brown eyes assuring her he was there, and she was fine. Maeve and Niamh, pressed against either side of her, provided back up comfort.

"How did you find me?" She almost hadn't believed her own eyes when Roderick had appeared behind Rhiannon.

"Ratty." Niamh looked sad. "Before that bitch killed him, I was able to get enough details from his mind to guide us."

"And Edana and Fiona weren't that good at hiding their tracks." Maeve snorted and scowled at the back of Roderick's head. "That Edana was always trouble. I don't know how she managed to convince people she wasn't."

Roderick shifted and cleared his throat.

"Some people." Maeve raised her voice. "Thought rather too much of her."

Roderick glanced over his shoulder. "Give it a rest, Maeve. I can't undo the past."

Maeve snorted and rolled her eyes.

Eyes alight, Niamh looked from Roderick to Maeve, and then winked at Bronwyn. "What—"

Alexander groaned and opened his eyes. He blinked at the Landy's roof before his eyes tracked left and found her. "Bronwyn?"

"Yes." The terrible blank look had gone from his eyes, but the memory of how strong he was, how effortlessly he'd overpowered her might take time to fade.

He groaned and flopped to his back. "Where am I?"

"At my mercy." Roderick scowled down at him. "And I'd like nothing more than to end your suffering."

"Roderick?" Alexander blinked at him and then at Niamh and Maeve. He looked at the retriever and said, "I don't think we're in Kansas anymore, Toto."

"He's clearly addled." Roderick looked at Sinead. "I should end him."

"I feel your pain, big guy." Sinead gave him a sympathetic grimace. "But ending people is not really our thing, right?"

Roderick grunted and scowled at Alexander. "This is the only warning you get."

"We were rescued," Bronwyn said. "Rhiannon—" The words to tell him what had happened dried on her tongue, and she stared down at the retriever.

Niamh curled her lip up at Alexander. "You tried to rape Bronwyn."

Paling, Alexander's gaze flew to Bronwyn. "Please tell me that's not true."

"You tried, but you didn't..." She shook her head. Tears threatened beneath her eyelids.

The retriever whined and pressed closer to her legs.

Bronwyn sank her face into the dog's nape. Musty dog smell gave her an anchor.

"Bronwyn, sweetheart." Alexander sounded pained. "Please look at me."

"Are you making demands?" Roderick's voice had gone deadly soft. "You don't speak to her, and you don't look at her. You don't even fucking breathe in her direction."

Alexander shifted. "Understood."

Bronwyn could feel his gaze on her, but she couldn't meet it. Since the moment she'd met him, she'd pinged from one emotion to the other. She couldn't deal right now. All she wanted was her bed in Baile and space and time to make sense of all that had happened.

"Rhiannon made him do it," she said.

"Sweetheart." Alexander's voice was unbearably gentle. "You don't need to make excuses for me. Roderick knows only too well the depth and breadth of my sins."

Surrounding traffic provided a bass hum to the silent vehicle interior. The wheels of the Landy swished over the damp road.

Bronwyn sat up and leaned her head against the side of the Landy. "Can you sense her?"

"No." Alexander eased up and leaned his back against the front seats. "But she's still alive."

Roderick grunted.

"You should have left me there," Alexander said. "She'll come after me."

Grunting, Roderick said, "Finally something on which we agree."

"She wants both of us." Bronwyn braved looking at him.

He didn't look so threatening now. Pale, with dark rings beneath his eyes, he looked exhausted. His elbows rested on his raised knees and an air of defeat hung around him.

"And in this you're as much a victim as I am."

"Only a healer could think that." He gave a humorless huff of laughter.

They rode in silence, and Bronwyn let the motion of the vehicle lull her. She had lost track of time when Sinead glanced over her shoulder. "We're almost at Baile."

"What should we do with him?" Roderick looked at her.

She didn't know. Alexander didn't belong in Baile but leaving him outside the castle was like handing him to Rhiannon on a platter.

"Bronw—" Alexander's back bowed, and his face contorted in agony.

"It's the wards." Maeve dropped to her knees beside Alexander. "He can't cross them."

"He says he can." Roderick leaned over the seat and grabbed his shoulders. "But we're not crossing the wards now."

"It's her." Bronwyn scrambled into the well beside Alexander. "Is it her?"

Face a rictus of pain, Alexander nodded. He clawed at his chest, gasping for breath.

"She's killing him." Bronwyn had never felt more helpless. Her pathetic healing hands were almost useless, but she put them on him anyway.

Beneath her palm, his chest labored, and his heart beat erratically.

"Hurry!" Maeve shouted. "Get him into Baile. Rhiannon's magic cannot reach him there."

Blood bubbled out of Alexander's mouth. He coughed, and fresh blood poured down his chin.

"What should I do?" Desperately, Bronwyn turned to Roderick and then Maeve. "I'm a healer. I can help him."

Roderick frowned and glanced at Maeve. "Goddess Pool."

Maeve gasped. "That might kill him."

"It's all he has." Roderick looked grim. "It might not. Either way we'll know for sure what's in his heart."

Convulsing, Alexander jacked his knees to his chest, his mouth open in a silent scream of pain it was unbearable not to hear.

"Go faster." Roderick urged Sinead. "Get behind the wards."

The Landy's engine screamed as they hurtled around

corners. Bronwyn slammed into the side. Niamh wrapped her arms around the dog and held on to him.

Dust and sand sprayed as the tires hit the side of the road. The Landy rocked on its axle and recovered.

And then it all stopped as the wards brushed Bronwyn's skin.

Alexander slumped on the floor.

She scrambled to his side. He had no heartbeat. Her ear next to his mouth gave her no breath sounds.

"No." She refused to give up. She had lost so many people in her life, too many. If she was this powerful healer, then it had to count for something now when she needed it most.

Roderick was out before the Landy had fully stopped. He hauled Alexander's limp body over his shoulder.

Bronwyn stayed right behind them, taking the stairs to the caverns three at a time.

Alexander's head lolled from side to side over Roderick's back, but there was no time for gentleness.

Goddess Pool was pale, milky lavender.

Crashing into it, Roderick dropped Alexander in the water.

Sloshing in after them, Bronwyn reached for Alexander and held him suspended in the water. "How do I do this?" She looked at Roderick. He had to have the answer. "How do I heal him?"

"I don't know." Roderick shrugged and touched his fore and middle fingers to her breastbone. "Listen to what your power tells you."

"*Trust your instinct,*" Deidre whispered.

How long had Alexander been without air? He didn't have time for her to work this out. "Goddess!" Her voice rang through the caverns. "Wherever you are. If you're even there. I need you."

Roderick's harsh breathing, or maybe it was hers broke the silence.

Niamh and Maeve stood by the side of the pool, arms around each other. Mags ran in with Sinead and Alannah behind her.

"Your magic," Maeve shouted. "Reach for it."

Bronwyn yanked for her magic. Honey and sage filled the air. "Please, Goddess. I need to save him."

Alexander's hair floated like seaweed around his head.

"*Child.*" So soft she nearly missed it

"Mother." Bronwyn reached for the voice. Words she had never known popped into her head. "Mother, in water I come to you, in water I serve you, in water bind me to you."

Light flared beneath the pool, lavender darkening into purple and finally changing into cobalt blue so pure it almost hurt to look at it. *"Blessed, you are mine. You are of me and I am of you."*

Blue light surrounded her, sliding through her and around her, holding her in its nascent power. It burst through her pores razor sharp and pure, and Bronwyn screamed. Blue light surged out from the pool in blinding glory, swallowing Roderick and then Maeve and Niamh. It reached Mags, and she smiled as it enveloped her and went on to surround Alannah and Sinead.

"In water are you born, child, and water is born through you."

A chime rang through the caverns, so clear it hurt the ears.

Honey and sage swelled to her command and Bronwyn gathered it and pushed it into Alexander. It surged through his veins to his still and broken heart. Bronwyn pulled water and the power galloped through her, almost too strong to control.

"Hold it." Roderick's voice reached her as if from down a long tunnel. "The power of water is yours to control and channel, don't let it take you over."

It was hers. It responded to her touch. Bronwyn ripped the dark, roiling manacles away from Alexander's heart. They surged into her and through her and shriveled and died as she shoved them into Goddess Pool.

Then she eased up and used gentle, precision arrows of her gift to knit the broken flesh together, to repair the torn arteries and clear the spilled blood from Alexander's heart chambers.

His heart contracted and grew dark red with fresh, healing blood.

Alexander's heart beat. Once, twice, and then fell into a rhythm. His lungs filled with air and he took a breath.

"Let it go." Roderick cupped her elbow.

Bronwyn's knees buckled as she let the power rush away from her.

Roderick supported her as she almost collapsed and sank beneath the sparkling blue water.

"Look." Maeve stared at the cavern walls in wonder. "Water lives."

All around the caverns, blue crystals flickered into life and glowed. There were large dark areas on the cavern walls where crystals still lay dormant but for today, they could celebrate the waking of water. One of the four elements was alive.

Along with Rhiannon's son.

Alexander had dragged himself to the side of the pool and lay on his back looking at the crystals. He turned to look at her and smiled. "Little water witch. You did it." He wheezed a chuckle. "Mummy dearest is going to be so pissed off."

CHAPTER TWENTY-EIGHT

B ronwyn opened the door to the healer's hall and walked inside. The astringent smell of herbs comforted her. What fun she and Deidre would have had in there. She trailed her fingers over the worn wooden surface of the big central table.

Her power rested like a slumbering dragon within her. In the two days following her waking water and bonding herself to Goddess, she had only begun to explore her gift.

Piled up in the center of the table was the stack of books Roderick had carried in for her. Some of them ancient with their covers embossed in precious gems. She was almost afraid to open them, but she would open them and discover all the knowledge of her craft. So many healers had come before her and written their knowledge in these books. Her family had died not knowing anything about Baile, or the cré-witches or their blessing as healers. She owed it to them to be the healer they hadn't been able to be.

Maeve had told her the healers had been fascinated by all aspects of healing and had been as interested in making cures as they had in using their abilities. These books would only open for another healer.

She reached for water—its response was instantaneous and sweet—and touched her hand to the top book. The clasp released on a soft click, and Bronwyn opened the book.

A Study of the Persistent Problem of Warts.

"Hey." Alexander stood in the doorway.

She'd left him in the kitchen, trying to weigh in on the raging argument about which element they woke next.

Roderick's assertion that Goddess would decide had done nothing to quell the argument. Maeve and Niamh were fighting for fire to be activated, Sinead and Alannah going for earth. Mags sat in the middle smiling mistily into a mug of tea, like she knew what came next, which she probably did.

"Hi." She felt awkward around Alexander. So much had happened between them that she was confused, pulled in so many different directions.

Strolling in, he looked around him. "So this is the healer's hall. I heard about this place."

"Really?"

He nodded. "It used to make Rhiannon froth at the mouth. The first healer, Deidre, and Rhiannon never got on well."

Her Deidre would have gotten a kick out of her name being the same as the first healer. Bronwyn kept her tone light. Rhiannon squatted like a steaming pile of offal between them. "Who would have thought anyone could disagree with your mother's winning personality?"

He winced. "It's been a long time since I've thought of her as my mother."

"Sorry." She did understand, but she couldn't pretend the connection between him and Rhiannon didn't exist. "Will you stay in Baile?"

"If I want to keep breathing, I don't have much choice for now." He shrugged. "Baile is the only place I'm safe from her." He looked so melancholy, staring out the large window to the sea.

"Is that what you want?"

"I want many things, little witch." He looked at her, his eyes holding the wisdom of his hundreds of years of life. "For the first time in longer than I can remember, I want something badly enough to wait for it."

The truth of their feelings for each other sat unacknowledged between them. "Even if you can't be sure you'll ever get that thing?"

"I have time." His swaggering smirk appeared, and he cocked his head. "And I've been assured I am an extremely persuasive and patient man."

MAEVE FOUND Roderick standing in the central cavern, examining the sigils. He sensed her there through the bond.

"Water is awake." She stood beside him and shared his appreciation for the gentle blue glow of the water crystals. "Any change to Goddess or Baile."

"Alexander tells me Goddess will strengthen as our witches use more magic." He grimaced. "I cannot credit that I just spoke thus of Alexander."

His disgruntled expression drew a laugh out of her. "Hard to believe, isn't it?"

"I would have said impossible." Turning, he looked down at her, his gaze warm. "Baile feels more alive each day."

"Good." The look in his eyes disconcerted her and made her shy. She could peer into his heart through the bond, but that felt intrusive and wrong. "What happens next?"

Raising her hand, he kissed it. "Take a stroll with me, Blessed?"

"Why?" Had she missed something important that he needed to tell her? Her hand still tingled from the imprint of his mouth.

Laughing, he placed her hand on his arm. "Because the day is beautiful and balmy, and I want to take a stroll in the sunshine with a lovely woman."

"Oh." When he put it like that, it made perfect sense, and there was nothing more she'd rather do.

Arm in arm they left the caverns and took the stairs down to the beach. With the tide out, the sliver of sand, golden in the warm sun, invited them to join it.

The sea was languid and the air still. Gulls swooped and dived from the boulders, arguing noisily with each other. Beneath her feet, the sand was warm and the sun gentle on her head.

Where the tide reached its highest point, Roderick stopped and tugged her in front of him. Wrapping her in his arms, he pressed her back against his chest.

Matching her breathing to his, Maeve let the welcome warmth and comfort of him surround her.

In the day's beauty and peace, it was almost possible to forget the still looming threat. "What happens now?"

"Now we enjoy the sunshine." Roderick's voice rumbled through her. "When we return to the castle, we will have to find the cardinal point for fire and discover how to wake it."

She nodded but stayed where she was. "Fire as the next point makes sense. I need to spirit walk, find what answers and help I can amongst the witches past."

Waves frothed closer to their feet, and a playful breeze tugged at her hair.

"I regret Edana," Roderick said. "But I cannot change the past."

"I know." She sighed because she hadn't been fair to him about that. When he and Edana had been bedfellows, none of what they now knew had yet revealed itself.

"You were not my first witch." Roderick's deep voice blended with the whisper of the waves. "But you will be my last, Maeve."

"How can you know that?" Her heart beat erratically as he came closer to acknowledging what lay between them.

Roderick chuckled. "You know how I know that Maeve, because you can see into the deepest part of me." He rested his cheek atop her head. "But for now, let us be a man and a woman together on this beautiful day. Nothing more."

"Just a man and a woman on the beach," she said. "Nothing more."

Roderick tightened his arms about her. "For now."

CHAPTER TWENTY-NINE

Bronwyn padded through the great hall with only moonlight to guide her. She pushed open the barrack's door and entered.

"Blessed." Thomas materialized in front of her. "You are well?"

"I'm well." Her magic coursed inside her, ever present, a living part of her that she couldn't imagine now being without.

Thomas smiled. "You are strong in your power, Healer. I feel we will have more need of you before we are done."

She nodded, because as much as she didn't want to acknowledge it, she knew he was right. "We need more Rodericks."

"Anything is possible." Thomas smirked and drifted away.

Roderick's door was open, but he wasn't in his room, and his bed was still made. He didn't admit it, but the big guy was no fonder of sleeping than Maeve was, and the two of them often spent their nights together.

Light glowed from the doorway beside Roderick's, and that's where she was headed. There was so little certainly around them, and it really left her with no good options but to follow

Dee's advice. Her gut had kept her alive this long, and she would need to trust it more and more in the days to come.

Alexander stood with his back to the door, staring into the night. "You should be sleeping."

"So should you." She joined him by the window.

Twinkling village lights ended in the dark mass of the sea.

They'd never spoken about what had happened in that cottage, and it poisoned the air between them. Alexander's guilt writhed like living flame. It had taken her a few days to process it, but making her pact with Goddess had helped heal her pain.

Bronwyn put her hand between his shoulder blades. Her magic quested for his heart, swirling around his previous injury, searching for residual damage.

A soft smile tilted his mouth as he looked down at her. "I'm fine."

"I know." She smiled back. The low light from a bedside lamp loved on the clean, aquiline lines of his beautiful face. Rhiannon had succeeded in making a nearly irresistible man. "We should talk."

"Three words no man relishes." He shoved his hands in his pockets and stared at the view.

Bronwyn took that as a sign he was listening. "I don't blame you," she said. "For what happened, for what she forced you to do."

"Really?" He scoffed. "Because you should."

"Really?" She'd let him explain why she should.

"You know you should." He hunched his shoulders. "I knew what was happening, and you didn't. You were mine to protect, and I failed you."

"That doesn't make you responsible for me." Yeah, this medieval man thing had its drawbacks. "I belong to me, and I am responsible for my safety."

"Indeed." He didn't believe a word of what she'd said, and

they needed to work on that. "It might have been better had Roderick left me there."

Pain pierced her chest and robbed her of breath. "No."

"For as long as I am alive, you are not safe." He finally turned to look at her. In his eyes, she read a torment so long and soul-felt it made her want to cry.

She did the next best thing and put her arms around him. "Don't say that. Your dying is no longer an option."

"Little witch." He cradled her face. "You and I can't be together. You must know that."

She was so tired of people telling her what she could do, and what she couldn't. This beautiful man had appeared in her life like a blessing, and then it had all turned nasty. She hadn't even had the chance to enjoy him before everything went to crap.

Strangely, all the players in this drama agreed one thing: Alexander was hers, and she was his. But she was also tired of everyone—including some ridiculous prophecy—telling her what life looked like and what she should and should not do.

"I'll tell you what I know." She covered his hands with hers. "I know you had ample opportunity to get into my bed. I wanted you there, and you could have had me at any point, yet you didn't." Rising to her toes, she looped her arms around his neck. "I know that you almost died trying to protect me from her and trying to fight her." She pressed her face to his warm, smooth neck and inhaled the unique scent of him. "And I know I've never felt anything close to this with anyone else, and I don't believe I ever will."

"That could be the prophecy talking." His expression gentled, and his gaze warmed.

"It could be." Bronwyn brought her body flush with his. "It could be a lot of things, but putting labels on things seems truly counterproductive right now."

His hands gripped her hips and his voice sounded rougher as

he said, "We cannot take chances with the prophecy. If you and I lie together, we will create a child."

"About that." She gave in to temptation and kissed the underside of his jaw. "I know something the prophecy couldn't possibly predict."

He groaned and pressed her closer to him. "What's that?"

"Durex." She positioned her mouth over his. "Birth control."

Heat flared in his eyes, and a flicker of hope. "It may not work. I've seen stranger things happen."

"I'm also on the pill." She touched her lips to his. "Got any more thoughts you want to discuss?"

He lifted her off her feet and headed for the bed. "Not at this precise moment."

Lowering her to the bed, he came down beside her. Gently, he brushed the hair from her face. "You are so lovely."

"You're biased." She was pretty enough, but with him looking at her like she was the center of the world, she felt beautiful. Tugging his head down to hers, she kissed him.

Unlike their other kisses, this one was tentative and unsure, as if they were both waiting for something.

His tongue touched her bottom lip and she opened for him.

Still, he was hesitant as he explored her mouth. Beneath her hands, his muscle was taut with controlled tension. He was holding back, because of her.

She broke the kiss and slid her hands into the silky hair at his nape. "I want this."

"I don't want to frighten you." His eyes were dark with concern.

"I know." Bronwyn shifted and rolled them over. "I'm not frightened."

Taking control of the kiss, she let her reaction to him catch fire and burn. She kissed him like she had wanted to from the first moment she had seen him.

Alexander groaned and caught her buttocks in his hands. "Bronwyn, be sure?"

"I'm sure." She pressed against his growing erection. "I'm more sure than I've been of anything in my life."

He slid his hands beneath her boy shorts and stroked her ass. "No going back now, little witch."

"Not even if you beg me." She sat up and whipped her shirt over her head.

His eyes darkened as he looked at her, lingering on her breasts and then down her stomach. Sliding his hands up her sides, he stopped with them resting frustratingly close to her breasts.

"Touch me." She put his hands on her breasts.

Sensation shot through her, and she arched into his caress. All the pent-up emotions he'd stirred in her since meeting him surged to the forefront and swept her along with them. Being with him was more right than anything in her life, and she didn't care why. The connection between them flared into brilliant, hot life and demanded fulfillment. They belonged together. It was visceral, it was powerful, it was inevitable.

He plumped her breasts in his hands, then sat up and fastened his mouth around her nipple.

Wet heat of his mouth made her cry out. Her body was on fire for him. Heat pulsed between her thighs, and she ground down on his cock.

She grabbed his shoulders, needing to anchor herself before she got swept away. His T-shirt pissed her off, and she tugged at it. She was desperate for his skin against hers.

He released her nipple to tug his shirt over his head, and then he moved back to her breasts.

Bronwyn stroked his shoulders, his chest, his biceps, any part of his hot, silken skin she could touch.

"Lift up." He gripped her hips and lifted her off him.

Bronwyn whimpered at the loss of him against where she ached.

Alexander tugged off her shorts and then slid off his jeans and boxers.

Naked, he pressed her back into the bed.

Friction of his chest against her breasts was almost too much, but not nearly enough and she writhed beneath him.

"Little witch." He pressed hot sucking kisses to her chest, and to her stomach. "My everything." He trailed his mouth over her hipbone and settled between her thighs. "I've dreamed of you like this."

Raising her leg, he placed it over his shoulder, opening her to his gaze and then his mouth.

A sob broke out of her as he worked his tongue over her, taking his time and learning what she liked. His mouth drove her close to release and then backed off. She was almost screaming her frustration as he drove her higher and higher but denied her the pinnacle.

"Please," she sobbed, her voice hoarse with need.

Alexander sat up and reached for the condom. "I want you to come with me inside you," he said as he slid the condom over his cock. "I've waited a lifetime for this."

Hard and thick, he pressed into her.

Her wet slick flesh made space for him and took all of him. When he was seated fully inside her, Bronwyn gripped him tight with her arms and her thighs. She'd never felt anything like it. The connection was complete, perfect, and she surrendered.

Alexander moved inside, deep and hard.

Tension coiled in her belly and spread through her. She grabbed his ass and dug her nails in. He was exactly where she needed him most.

Heat built quickly, flaring out of control. His thrusts grew deeper, less controlled.

Face taut with concentration, he locked his dark gaze on hers and held her captive.

Reaching down, he used his fingers as he continued to thrust in and out.

Their gazes stayed locked as Bronwyn's climax overtook her.

She watched as he joined her, the connection almost too intimate to hold.

Tears gathered and seeped down her face.

Wiping them away, his face gentle, he said, "You are mine now, little witch."

Her smile felt like it came from the deepest part of her. "And you are mine." Her tears of joy eased into laughter. "And I'm not giving you back."

ALEXANDER LEFT Bronwyn curled up in his bed, one hand tucked beneath the pillows, her hair spilling over her shoulders. Fierce primal emotions warred in his chest. She was his, his to protect, his to love and his to keep. Goddess help the person who thought to change that.

And it seemed the prophecy had not taken modern prophylactics into account. No broken condoms to worry about. Perhaps his little witch was right about that after all.

Perhaps not, and either way, he would be happy. He didn't deserve her or the joy she brought but he would cling to the gift like a starved mongrel.

His bare feet slapped against the stone floors as he made his way through the silent barracks.

"I'll be watching you." Roderick emerged from the gloom of the practice yards. "I'd love you to prove me right not to trust you."

Some things never changed, and Alexander grinned at him. "Aren't you sweet?"

Roderick folded his arms and watched him.

Alexander went through the dim castle and let himself into the bailey. He opened the door and took the stairs to the caverns. She was in there, Goddess, and they needed to chat.

Goddess was an almost tangible presence now that the water cardinal point was awake and functioning. She would have to grow a lot stronger to face Rhiannon. And the confrontation was looking inevitable.

In the central cavern, Goddess Pool glowed azure.

Alexander checked behind him to make sure nobody was watching. He had no idea what to make of his secret, and he wanted to understand it. He took his hand from his pocket and called his power. Delicate lines of red, green, yellow and blue played between his fingertips before twining into one thin white line that shot out of his hand and flared into a bright white light.

It looked like magic, even felt like magic, but that was impossible because there had never been a male witch.

Ripples broke over Goddess Pool.

Alexander glanced at it and smiled. "You seem to have left me with a somewhat confusing gift."

A woman's mellifluous laughter rolled gently through the caverns. *"Blessed."*

EPILOGUE

W arren Masters didn't believe in hunches, gut instincts or inklings. He believed in the power of his fist, the steadiness of his aim, and the thoroughness of his training. Regardless, this thing wringing him from the inside out demanded he do something, and it wouldn't leave him alone.

It had started about a week ago, a woman's voice in his dreams, calling him to come to her. At first, he'd dismissed it, but the same dream every night had shaken him. The dream got stronger each time he had it, and the gut sense that he needed to do whatever this voice wanted grew with it.

He pressed his hot face against the cool glass of his grime-smeared window.

"What?" Warren whispered into his dingy room, "What do you want?"

Outside, a gaggle of kids made their way to school, back-packs sagging as they yelled at each other.

The nagging tug at his consciousness crept around the decrepit furniture and the stench of antiseptic to fill his room. It hounded him with the searing certainty that he was in the wrong place. This morning it rampaged through him, tightening his lungs and increasing his heart rate. Sweat covered his torso and soaked into his sweatpants waistband.

"What do you want from me?"

Warren was a logical man, a soldier. Surrendering to the compulsion, he flipped on the desk light. A map he'd bought yesterday concealed the desk's scarred and stained surface. As he leaned over the map, the desk rocked under his hands.

"Where?" Jesus, if his neighbors heard him talking to himself, they'd think he'd gone around the fucking twist. They already went out of their way to avoid him, taking the next lift rather than being in one with him, walking as far away from him as the narrow hallways would allow.

With the escalating demand tying him in knots and growing stronger with each passing day, he might have lost his mind. If insanity lurked, then let it come.

His breath rasped, his heart pounded and the knot in his belly tightened around his breakfast of sausage, egg and chips.

He pinpointed his current location on the map, east and a little south of Manchester. Jabbing his finger on the spot, he waited. He breathed. In and out.

South. Staffordshire, Warwickshire, Wiltshire and still his index finger slid down the map to where the yellow of the land abutted the blue sea. A tiny black dot along the coastline drew him.

Air rushed into his lungs, and he took his first proper breath in hours. Peering at where his finger had stopped, he read the name. "Greater Littleton."

Yes. His pounding heart stilled. Deep peace flooded him. Greater Littleton, a village he'd never heard of but knew without a doubt he had to reach.

Clear as the kids shouting at each other on the street below his window, a woman's voice spoke. "*Coimhdeacht. You are called.*"

And the story continues in Purged In Fire,
#2 Cré-Witch Chronicles

THE QUEST FOR FIRE.

The witches of Baile are back, and the battle to save cré-magic intensifies.

Guardian witch, Niamh, surrounded by her animals and loved by all, deep down still harbors the secret ache of being alone amidst a crowd. When newly summoned warrior guardian, Warren Masters, arrives to accept the challenge of standing between her and danger, she feels an unbreakable connection. However, Warren isn't as trusting of the feeling and must fight to overcome his disbelief and any reservations he's worthy of his new calling to be the protector she needs.

Danger closes in as Warren and Niamh race to activate the fire cardinal point before the evil blood witch, Rhiannon can destroy it. Cré-magic, once again, must fight to stay alive.

And for avid Chroniclers, your coven favorites are also back.

An ancient prophecy presents a daunting challenge for predestined couple, Alexander and Bronwyn. While Roderick and Maeve struggle to find their footing in a world five hundred years from when they began.

Order Purged In Fire

Chapter 1

NIAMH'S FUR ruffled in a freshening breeze, and beneath her paws, the earth pressed cool and damp. She raised her face to the cold full moon, distant and so achingly beautiful. The moon called to her, reaching silvery remote rays within Niamh and illuminating the dark barren center of her.

Persistent danger pressed, and she scented for the source. Air quickened across her nostrils and brought the night's olfactory bouquet—brine, tree sap, humus, bark, a vole, older rabbit droppings, and the lingering scent markings of a deer. That last made her heart pump thick with the thrill of the hunt, but she wasn't hungry.

Life, abundant and busy, was happening all about her, yet she stood alone beneath the temptress moon. She had no litter; she had no pack; she had no mate. Surrounded by all creatures irrevocably drawn to her magic, she stood. Alone.

From within her, solitude pressed out, stretching her skin as if it could no longer be contained. Niamh threw back her head and howled. She howled to the moon who had forsaken her. She howled the ache of her loneliness.

From the west, the wind brought a faint answering howl.

He comes.

For first dibs on news, deals, and giveaways, and so much more, join the @Home Collective

Or if Facebook is more your thing, join the Sarah Hegger Collective

Anything and everything you need to know on my website http://sarahhegger.com

ABOUT THE AUTHOR

Born British and raised in South Africa, Sarah Hegger suffers from an incurable case of wanderlust. Her match? A hot Canadian engineer, whose marriage proposal she accepted six short weeks after they first met. Together they've made homes in seven different cities across three different continents (and back again once or twice). If only it made her multilingual, but the best she can manage is idiosyncratic English, fluent Afrikaans, conversant Russian, pigeon Portuguese, even worse Zulu and enough French to get herself into trouble. Mimicking her globe trotting adventures, Sarah's career path began as a gainfully employed actress, drifted into public relations, settled a moment in advertising, and eventually took root in the fertile soil of her first love, writing. She also moonlights as a wife and mother. She currently lives in Ottawa, Canada, filling her empty nest with fur babies. Part footloose buccaneer, part quixotic observer of life, Sarah's restless heart is most content when reading or writing books.

f

Drove All Night

"The classic romance plot is elevated to a modern-day, wholly accessible real-life fairy tale with an excellent mix of romantic elements and spicy sensuality." Booklife Prize, Critic's Report

Positively Pippa

"This is the type of romance that makes readers fall in love not just with characters, but with authors as well." Kirkus Review (Starred Review)

"What begins as a simple second-chance romance quickly transforms into a beautiful, frank examination of love, family dynamics, and following one's dreams. Hegger's unflinching, candid portrayal of interpersonal and generational communication elevates the story to the sublime. Shunning clichés and contrived circumstances, she uses realistic, relatable situations to create a world that readers will want to visit time and again."
Publisher's Weekly, Starred Review

"Hegger's utterly delightful first Ghost Falls contemporary is what other romance novels want to grow up to be." – Publisher's Weekly, Best Books of 2017

"The very talented Hegger kicks off an enjoyable new series set in the small Utah town of Ghost Falls. This charming and fun-filled book has everything from passion and humor to betrayal and revenge." – Jill M Smith, RT Books Reviews 2017 – Contemporary Love and Laughter Nominee

Becoming Bella
"Hegger excels at depicting familial relationships and friendships of all kinds, including purely platonic friendships between women and men. Tears, laughter, and a dollop of suspense make a memorable story that readers will want to revisit time and again." Publisher's Weekly, Starred Review

"…you have a terrific new romance that Hegger fans are going to love. Don't miss out!" Jill M. Smith – RT Book Reviews

Blatantly Blythe
"Ms. Hegger has delivered another captivating read for this series in this book that was packed with emotion…" Bec, Bookmagic Review, Harlequin Junkie, HJ Recommends.

Nobody's Fool
"Hegger offers a breath of fresh air in the romance genre." – Terri Dukes, RT Book Reviews

Nobody's Princess
"Hegger continues to live up to her rapidly growing reputation for breathing fresh air into the romance genre." – Terri Dukes, RT Book Reviews

"I have read the entire Willow Park Series. I have loved each of the books … Nobody's Princess is my favorite of all time." Harlequin Junkie, Top Pick

ALSO BY SARAH HEGGER

Urban Fantasy

The Cré-Witch Chronicles

Prequel: Cast In Stone

Vol l: Born In Water

Vol ll: Purged In Fire

Sports Romance

Ottawa Titans Series

Roughing

Contemporary Romance

Passing Through Series

Drove All Night

Ticket To Ride

Walk On By

Ghost Falls Series

Positively Pippa

Becoming Bella

Blatantly Blythe

Loving Laura

Willow Park Romances

Nobody's Angel

Nobody's Fool

Nobody's Princess

Medieval Romance

Sir Arthur's Legacy Series

Sweet Bea

My Lady Faye

Conquering William

Roger's Bride

Releasing Henry

Love & War Series

The Marriage Parley

The Betrothal Melee

Western Historical Romance

The Soiled Dove Series

Sugar Ellie

Standalone

The Bride Gift

Bad Wolfe On The Rise

Wild Honey

Printed in Great Britain
by Amazon

80667050R00176